Death of a Prof

The Nursery School Murders: II

Death of a Prof
The Nursery School Murders: II

Jake Fuchs

CREATIVE ARTS BOOK COMPANY
Berkeley • California

For information contact:
Creative Arts Book Company
833 Bancroft Way
Berkeley, California 94710

Library of Congress Cataloging-in Publication Data
Fuchs, Jake.
     Death of a prof / Jake Fuchs.
          p. cm. -- (The nursery school murders ; 2)
     ISBN 0-88739-335-7 (pbk. : alk. paper)
     1. Berkeley (Calif.) --Fiction. 2. Preschool teachers--Fiction. 3.
English teachers--fiction.   I. Title.
     PS3556.U3133 D44 2001
     813' .54--dc21

                                                                    2001028150

Printed in the United States of America

Death of a Prof

The Nursery School Murders: II

Prelude

Berkeley, California
1970s

A fat man about forty was sitting at his desk in a university building. He laughed, but he didn't sound happy. The young student he spoke to was very short, but very determined.

"Leave my office, please," said the fat man. "I've tried to clear this up for you, but you don't seem willing to listen. Now, go. I have a class to prepare for."

"No. Not until you tell me what you will do. No, Professor."

"Nothing. I'll do nothing. You can't...get out! Get out this instant, or I'll call campus security."

"Go ahead. Call them. You'll find they're all in the Plaza for the Fuck Dick demo, Professor."

"Is there something wrong with the word? My title. The way you sneer it. You little, accusing...asshole!"

"You don't deserve your title. Your title! Do you know what your title *should* be?"

"Prove it. You can't, because it's nonsense! And you admitted you have no copy of the purported paper. You little, malevolent...darky!"

"I read it to the seminar, Professor. Someone will come forward."

"No, they won't. Tell me, are you here on a passport, a green card, what?"

"Sorry, Professor. I'm naturalized. Here to stay."

"Not here!"

He stabbed his index finger into the phone, the appropriate dial

1

hole. He called. Soon someone came. The campus cops had reinforcements from the Berkeley and Oakland departments for the day, for Fuck Dick Day. He made the student leave. The professor wanted him arrested, but the cop refused.

The professor thought, I'll get that little runt. I'll fix him. Then he laughed. He was cheerful by nature. And lazy.

Prologue

Berkeley, California
1990s

A bad weekend behind them, featuring Aaron's bizarre behavior both in bed and out in their street. Now Monday was starting bizarrely, with odd visitors she hadn't expected. And, before her eyes, the passage of a small herd of deer.

There they were, when she stepped out of her front door, trotting down the sidewalk in single file. Four of them, no antlers but big, and they seemed not at all concerned about being caught out on the north Berkeley flats well after sunrise, while people were going to work. Deer often roamed from their preserve—in essence, if not in any legal sense—in Tilden Park and walked about the Berkeley hills neighborhoods at night, grazing, but never here, never this far down.

Of course she watched them go, until they disappeared, turning either on Beverly Street or up someone's driveway into a back yard. Maren realized she needed to breathe, which she did, then turned around to ask Aaron if he'd seen them.

"Son of a bitch," Aaron said. "Pair of idiots!" And he slammed the heel of his hand into the door, which he must have just closed. "They'd *better* be gone."

So she didn't tell him about the deer.

Up at the nursery school a few hours later, Maren had one of the kids, Boris, in the bathrooom, cleaning him up. Standing, just standing by himself, he'd managed to fall down on top of their corn meal table, which bore a collection of legos, rather than corn meal, and had cut his lip. Not badly. He'd cried. His frantic, grouchy mother would be even more than usually upset, if she was the one coming. Anthony, Boris's father, had brought him that day. Both parents were difficult.

"Look! On the slide!"

Holly, the third teacher. The kids all ran over to the window, to look at the slide out on the deck. Maren heard them all say, "Ohh," but it was an "oh" of disappointment.

"He was," said Holly. "He *was*!"

When Maren emerged from the bathroom with a scrubbed Boris, who immediately sought and received a hug from little Deirdre Blake (that was nice, those two quiet ones becoming friends), Holly told her what she saw. Lion, their big, immensely fluffy angora rabbit, had slid down their slide. He couldn't have made it up the steps; he must have scrambled up the slide itself, which was broad and not very steep. Probably he had then simply decided to scramble down again. But Holly declared that he had been lying on his back, while waving his feet in the air! "He liked it," she said. Though Holly sometimes failed to grasp certain things, such as why other cars honked at her when she was going forty on the freeway, she had a very keen eye for child and animal behavior. He must have done it.

Maren told Holly and Judy, the head teacher, about the four deer. It was a strange day for animals, they all agreed. It got stranger.

When Maren was taking the garbage down, just a few minutes before pick-up time, she saw a cougar, hot orange in color, standing in the street below. She dropped the bag, strewing the remnants of seventeen kids' lunches over most of the seventeen steps that descended from Hillside School to Culloden Drive. A cat, it must be a cat. But it was the size of a dog, a medium-sized dog, and it had a long, loopy tail of a kind possessed by no cat. It was wild, it was bad! She was afraid the thing would yowl at her. Recently people had spotted cougars in Tilden Park—the rangers hoped it was just the same one each time—and heard them. Their scream was supposed to be piercing, paralyzing.

Maren screamed first: "Get out! Get out, you!" Noticing Cloelia Ginsberg-Coffin's uneaten apple on the step below her, she stooped for it, then hurled the apple down the steps. It hit and broke a few feet away from the cougar, who slouched over and nosed the pieces.

"Go! Go!" The parents would be coming any minute.

Finally the cougar got going. "All right, all right," it seemed to say, with its slow, reluctant slink, its drooping tail. And went around the curve in the road. Maren waited a bit, then picked up the trash, walked it down the steps and dumped it. Walking back up again, she felt a bit…chilled, not frightened exactly.

"What were you yelling at, a dog getting into the cans? I put a bungee on that one."

"Judy, I saw a cougar."

"Oh, shit. Now? At pick-up time? My God, put Lion in his hutch!"

Other people thought they might have glimpsed one on other streets that were, like theirs, near the park. But late, when night was falling, not in the full light of afternoon. Judy didn't doubt her, though, didn't say, "Probably just a big cat." Strange day.

Did the parents wonder? Why was Judy standing by in the street when the Volvos rolled up, holding her softball bat? The best hitter in the women's league, she happened to have left the bat, a shiny metal item, in her office when the season ended. So she stood there, bulking as well as she could. When you see a cougar, make yourself look big! That's what the signs said on the trails in Tilden Park.

Driving home, down through the hills, Maren kept her eyes open. No cougar, no deer either. Was there something else she should be looking for? She felt distinctly odd. First the mess in her house with the unexpected visitors, then this business with the animals—all non-threatening, of course. Even the cougar. Just strolling, as if this posh Berkeley street was where he belonged, was his—like the deer on her own, far humbler, flatland street. The rabbit on the slide.

No white 4X4 in front of her house. They'd gone. Good. Parking her aged VW Bug, she noticed through its window that her front door was slightly open. Not good. She bounced the car's tiny tires off the curb. Probably Cedric just forgot to close it. But people, even those as silly as Cedric, don't forget things like that. She pushed the door all the way open, listened. It was too quiet. Then Maren realized that, in fact, she could hear the usual background noise, her fridge humming, a loud ticking from the kitchen wall clock, other sounds she recognized without knowing exactly what made them; the difference was that an unusual smell, sweet and hot, was coming out of the house. It was muffling all the sounds.

Maren felt stuck. With part of her mind she remembered being stuck there yesterday—no, Friday—but then the door was closed, and she couldn't open it because she'd left her keys in the car and didn't want to go back until Derek had driven off. Derek Blake and Deirdre. And was this, somehow, the third Blake, Diane?

No, it wasn't. When she looked at the body, at first she didn't even recognize it. All she could think for a moment was that she must have been wrong about the cougar. She couldn't hear a thing.

Chapter One

Seated in a canvas-backed director's chair, Maren was reading the *Chronicle* in a rather unusual venue, the sunny deck of her school. It wasn't her own paper, which she hadn't had a chance to read at home that morning. She remembered Aaron glancing at it and seeing something that interested him; then the paper was gone. He must have taken it along on BART for his commute to San Francisco. The *Chron* she was glancing at now had been abandoned on the deck by some parent, waiting for his or her time to confer with Judy, the head teacher at Hillside Nursery School, and either Holly or Maren, the underlings. It was nice to relax, finally. Thursday was always tough. It was parent conference day and they'd had two such meetings, during which the single teacher not attending had to manage all the kids. Once it had been Maren, once Holly. But that wasn't all that had happened.

Scrawny, picky Derek Blake, the one who always wore a little hat, had thrown a fit. He was a parent, not a kid. Usually he, not Diane, the wife, came to pick up little Deirdre, a job he appeared to loathe. He never spoke to the teachers, just snapped a "let's go" at Deirdre and hustled her off. Today, however, he'd had quite a lot to say.

"I don't see that Deirdre's learned anything," he opined. "She can't do anything she didn't do before. She hasn't improved, and I'm getting pissed off!"

He happened to be holding Deirdre by the hand while saying

7

these things, just as other parents and au pairs, mostly the latter, were starting to arrive for pick-up, always scheduled for 1:30. It wasn't quite that. At least he'd come a bit early, limiting the size of the audience for his fuss-fuss, for Deirdre's embarrassment. Perhaps she was too young to be embarrassed, really. But still, what a jerk he was! No reasonable person could expect a detectable difference after only the first month of school. What did he expect the child to be able to "do"? Go home by herself? Quite possibly he did.

But he wasn't really mad at the school anyway. The real source of his frustration was the senior female Blake, Diane, the wife.

"She," he said, meaning Diane, "was supposed to get her"—he yanked poor Deirdre's arm straight up—"today, for once, but no! So I have to do it, as usual, which means I have to miss an important meeting with Reptiles R Us! As if you cared."

He was yapping at Maren, who concentrated on smiling at Deirdre. Why should she care? She wasn't his wife, thank God! Derek was merely cold to Judy and Holly, but positively rude to her. Where was Judy? Judy could get rid of this oaf, but she was in the school building, still engaged in her second conference. Reptiles R Us? Ah, yes. Derek was interested in animal rights, for all animals, she thought, not just snakes and lizards. That was nice. He didn't have to work. There was family money, a frozen fish business back east. The Blakes were new to Berkeley. Diane was a graduate student in English at U.C.

"But she took off. She just took off."

Now he sounded sad. Too bad. Maren could well believe it. Diane appeared to be quite unlike her husband. While he was skinny-ugly and dour, she was cute and bright, proficient at batting her eyes, which were large, deep, and very dark. Derek had large eyes too, but watery blue and oddly flat. Yes, they seemed quite different, but Maren suspected that Diane, too, was a jerk.

The male jerk had decided to leave. He snapped his customary command: "Let's go!"

He tugged Deirdre's arm again, and made her spin around. She had eyes like her mother's, but was blond, like Derek. Her eyes widened a little when he spun her and then yanked her toward the steps. This was a child who didn't say much. She was quiet and observant. You could lose sight of a little person like Deirdre, pretty as she was.

Her mother, also pretty, was another story, with those bright smiles and eye-bats visible at thirty yards. At first she seemed nice, but the teachers had soon noticed that everything Diane said was about Diane. When she showed up at school, which wasn't often, she didn't ask about Deirdre, didn't listen when they told her things. She told them about herself. She still sent her kid to school with soup—soup!—even after being requested three times to cease.

"Bye, Deirdre," Maren now said. On the third step, Deirdre suddenly stopped, causing her father to stop as well and to look down at her, doubtless with irritation. "Bye, Maren," the child was going to say, but at that moment Irina Pownall, rapidly ascending, swept past Deirdre and her father. Perhaps she bumped him. Maren was struck by the ugly, irritated noise he made; an aggrieved donkey might produce such a noise.

Then, of course, she had to contend with Irina Pownall, mother of poor Boris. Although she had no appointment and had arrived at pick-up time, 1:30, when it was important for all the kids to make a quick, smooth transition from their day at Hillside School, she was fussing even more loudly than Derek had. All puffed up and angry, she was demanding to speak to Judy then and there. Maren could only tell her to please wait. Eventually Judy appeared, and, at first, held firm.

"No," she said, "that won't work. Not today, Irina. I'm sorry."

"No? No! Yes! I think you will see me now! Boris, go. Go there, darling. Go!'"

She pushed three-year old Boris, dazed by his mother's eruption into the school, toward the climbing structure on the deck. After he got his feet going and began to wander near it, Irina took several stout strides and planted herself before Judy. Two big women, Judy mostly muscle, Irina fat and sloppy in her white lab coat. Her face was as white as her coat, so that she always looked as if she were wearing a mask. She was Russian, a scientist, married to Anthony Pownall, a Brit, also scientific. They both had

grants for a year's research at Cal or perhaps at some private insti-
tution with U.C. Berkeley connections. They were vague on what
they did, although Anthony found frequent occasion to hint at its
importance. It paid well, certainly. They had the money to rent a
large house in the Berkeley Hills near Hillside Nursery School,
for which the tuition was not slight.

"Look, is it the lunch again? Maybe the note was too, well,
terse. But I thought you understood."

Poor Boris! Every part of him was slim or slight, except his
rather bulbous, indeed bulging, head, so that he really needed to
eat. But his Thomas the Tank Engine lunch box contained nothing he wanted, or that anyone would want. Just plastic bags of
whatever the Pownalls had had for dinner the preceding night:
bits of chicken, slimy vegetables (lima beans, usually), things that
seemed to be clots of cooked grain. She and Holly had to spoon-
feed him this trash, slowly. Even so, he didn't like it and often
tucked large wads into his cheeks for spitting out later. Judy had
let the Pownalls know, at least twice, that this would not do.

"Your attitude on the lunch is incomprehensible, especially the
kasha, but that is not what I'm about here. Is worse!"

"Really? Well, then, I suppose we could speak now, briefly.
After pick-up's finished. Bye, Uzma. Oh, Melody had a *great*
day!"

Uzma, the bracelet-laden au pair from the Middle East—no one
knew the exact country—clanked away with her charge, well-fed
little Melody O'Bannion-Bernath. All the au pairs had come by
now, natives of Mexico, El Salvador, Ghana, Sweden, all paid not
much to care for the children of Berkeley's wealthier moms and
dads. A few parents were there too. They didn't all have money.
Pick-up time. Oh, Melody had a great day. And Justin. No, Helga,
today Marcus did not vomit. This was one of their busiest times,
not a good time for Irina—they wished *she* had an au pair!—to
cause a scene. So she got her way, as the pushiest parents always
did.

The Volvo wagons roared off in several directions, to other hills
addresses in most cases. Down below on the street, from which
visitors had ascended to Hillside by the flight of splintery wood-

en steps, angry neighbor Camilla Faucett still stood wrathfully before her house. One of the Volvos had been parked there, for all of five minutes. Old Faucett had been complaining lately about the parkers and scowling at them; some day soon she might get out her hose, with which she had, upon occasion, squirted, or shovel, with which threatened. Judy was good at calming her down, and now would have been a good time. But here was Irina, this nasty, fat woman, a peasant despite her Ph.D. in something, standing before them—Judy, Holly, herself—glaring, muttering, appearing quite daft.

Holly was wearing her green Oakland A's hat, which signified independent-mindedness and a strong desire to have no truck with such as Irina Pownall, whom she presently ignored.

"I have to go," she told Judy. "Kyle has soccer practice, and I have no idea where I parked my car."

"Sure, you can go," said Judy, herself ignoring Irina, who surprised them by keeping her mouth shut for the moment, and waddling over to the climbing structure. At its base lay Boris, sprawled upon a rubber mat, feigning either sleep or death.

"Not fair!" screamed old Faucett. "Not right!" The teachers ignored her.

"You know," Maren said, "I think your car's on Keith Lane. I saw it this morning behind that pretty blue Jag."

"Oh, good! But where's that? I don't know that one. And what's a Jag?"

"Holly! My God, it's a block away! You drive up it every morning!"

"Not this morning, Judy! I would remember it if I had. The diggers."

Yes, they were digging. The city of Berkeley was always digging up the posh hill neighborhoods, possibly because the work crews, who all lived much lower down, as did the Hillside School faculty, were engaging in class warfare. But this morning they had been digging up on Preston Pans Way, not Keith Lane. Although a veteran of ten years teaching at the school, Holly had never learned anything about the local streets, which did run about in complicated ways. She couldn't help it, as Judy well knew. It was

Irina Pownall she wanted to yell at.

"I could walk you down there," Maren said, "but that'll delay the conference."

Irina was listening. "No," she called, her wide rump draped over one of the lower bars in the structure. "No, you go. Judy's the one I want to talk to. Maren, go!"

Maren stepped lively, before Irina could arise and shove her down the stairs. Fat Russian! She walked Holly to her battered Tercel, then reminded her to drive downhill until she got into territory she recognized. When Maren came back, she appointed herself Boris's overseer, so that Judy could take his mom, though this big, angry creature was hardly momlike, inside for a private chat.

She was stuck for a while, until Judy got rid of Irina. So what? It wasn't unpleasant. Looking up from the *Chronicle*, she watched Boris Pownall pluck reflectively at his penis. He probably knew both the Russian and English words for penis, being extremely bright. If he had an au pair from Mexico or Ghana, he would undoubtedly be able to converse in Spanish or Twi. Some of the other kids knew hardly any English, which showed how much time their parents gave them. On balance these children were probably ahead of the game, the au pairs being generally more civil than the parents. Boris would be much better off with some nice Consuelo or Fatima. His mom, grim-faced, vigorously intent on hauling him away at the end of the day, scared off kids who might have become his friends. Possibly. He was not good at making friends. He had nice black curls, and, Maren had to admit, his parents dressed him well, rather too formally sometimes. Today was okay, plain blue overalls. Like her husband's on the days he taped his cable show, although this outfit gave Aaron, a large, urban adult, a rather oafish look and must have attracted stares on the public transportation systems he favored. Though not exactly cute, Boris looked all right most of the time, but he needed to be more receptive, more lively.

Deirdre, too. In fact, Maren realized, Deirdre's situation was quite a bit like his. She also had a scary, grumbling parent. Neither child appeared to have the knack of playing with other children, as opposed to just playing alongside others. And Deirdre rarely said anything, although when spoken to by a teacher, she showed herself perfectly articulate for a three year-old. Boris, no doubt, had a vocabulary suitable for a college student, but the kids didn't listen to him, and he didn't listen to them.

So he was in the habit of doing things by himself, such as unlacing his shoes. He liked that. He was doing it now, as Maren watched. The Doctors Pownall did not comply with the school's desire, made clear to the parents at the opening day picnic, that the children wear shoes with velcro fasteners. And as soon as he had one shoe unlaced, he would try to run, would tread on a lace, fall down, and blubber. An endearing behavioral pattern of his. "Boris, no!" she called. "No, *nyet!*"

"Nyet," he echoed, as if to correct her pronunciation. Maren smiled at him, knowing she would eventually find something in him to like. He was terribly smart and a terrible klutz, so she felt very sorry for him, which was a start. And that mother! His father was also a jerk. Fussy little Englishman, annoying. But Boris never caused the slightest trouble. She should take more time with him.

Maren declared this intention to herself, then looked down at the paper in her lap. Her gaze swept on further, along her smoothly muscled legs to her sandaled feet, which were propped on the edge of the sandbox. She still had her summer tan, and there were a few weeks of sun left before the Bay started generating the fall fog that meant jeans and tennies instead of shorts and sandals. In which, though her forty-second year had recently come and then gone, she could still turn a head or two. Aaron's head had rust in its swivel, due to the stuff he had to take. He was better off, of course. They were both better off, all things considered.

She stopped looking at herself, sat straight up, and lifted the paper out of her lap. Mayor Willie Brown, his Williness, wanted to build some kind of palace or shrine for himself on Treasure Island in the Bay, but the city supervisors didn't want that. They wanted better bus service. Aaron wouldn't have taken the paper to read about this stuff. He taught in San Francisco, but its politics meant nothing to him. He had never complained about the buses and had never gotten in trouble on them, as he once had on BART for struggling with a man who said that Aaron was hogging a seat. There wasn't much basketball news as yet. Maybe a football story, his second-favorite sport.

Ah! A missing English professor. This was it. This interested even Maren. Aaron knew the guy, slightly; they were both experts on Edith Wharton, who had written *The House of Mirth* and other old and famous American novels that Maren could never remember. Of course, U.C. Berkeley's much-published Cedric McAulay mattered far more, she presumed, to the nation's legion of Whartonians than did SF State's Aaron Matthews. Aaron had authored only one book, printed by a minor university press in nearly microscopic type.

Once, at a party, she had met the senior scholar, a plump, bald gink, and thought he was funny, a jerk, but funny. He was condescending to Aaron, although his manner didn't seem deliberate. Aaron was curt in return, verging on snappish, but McAulay didn't notice. His attention was reserved for Maren from the moment they were introduced, at which point he had kissed her on the cheek. After that, in laborious tribute to her youthful appearance, he asked her at least three times if she were sure she wasn't a grad student. When it was time to leave, he tried to kiss her on the mouth; she head-faked, and he got her on the ear instead. It was wet, and she wanted to shiver, but since he mattered in Aaron's little world, she made herself join him in a fit of the giggles. Aaron watched them, but said nothing then or later.

Three days ago, McAulay had left his house, presumably headed for the U.C. campus, but hadn't arrived there. He had a wife. Maren hadn't actually met her at the party, which was drunken and disorganized, but remembered a dim, sad woman who seemed to follow in his wake. This wife, then, reported to the police and also to the *Chron* that lately he had been telling her of threats. People phoned him, said nasty things, and hung up. The most frequent caller seemed to have an Australian accent, but maybe it was something else. The professor had also received some anonymous e-mails, several of which were reproduced in the story.

These were ridiculous slogans that might have been dreamed up by someone making mock of Berkeley's radical past: "Fascist termite! The People's Party will have VENGEANCE!"

McAulay was also called newer names, such as "essentialist." Maren didn't know what that meant. At all such imprecations, reported his wife, he laughed. He printed the e-mails out and taped them to the door of his office. He was a sexist. That was obvious. But he didn't seem to realize that he was pissing people off. When someone called up to tell him he was, say, an "unregenerate masculinist," he would refer to the constantly pursued object of his scholarly attention. "Is Edith Wharton a man?" he would say. The paper spelled it "Warton." And then he would laugh. McAulay was an addicted laugher, it would seem. Mrs. McAulay seemed rather amused herself. Certainly not concerned.

Plop! Little Boris Pownall suddenly appeared before her, supine. He lay at Maren's feet, next to the climbing structure on which he had mounted, from which he had just now fallen, while she was reading about that fool, McAulay. Boris's eyes were tightly shut, his mouth gasping open. She threw herself to her knees, grasped his shoulders.

"Boris, breathe!"

An obedient child, Boris breathed. He sucked in a remarkable volume of air, so that she wondered when he would stop, and then howled so loudly that he hurt Maren's ears. What language? None, probably.

"My baby! What have you done to him?"

Irina all but fell on Boris, thrusting Maren away from him with one meaty paw. The little boy was shrieking something that sounded like a word, "Bog! Bog!" It occurred to Maren, suddenly seated upon the deck on her shorts-clad rear end, that he was probably fine. If they yell, they're fine, as a rule. And he couldn't have fallen very far. She had never seen him climb more than a foot up into the structure. But she should have been watching. How could she not have been watching?

"I'm sorry, Irina. He did it so fast!" That was a lie, she knew; he never did anything fast. She wanted to correct the lie, but Irina wasn't listening. Holding Boris by the ankles, she was briskly shaking him. He made loud, scary, gulping noises.

"Don't do that," Maren said. "Oh, please!"

"My baby! Boris! All this happens to you!"

"Hey!"

Judy was rushing across the deck. In an instant she had deftly snatched Boris, now pale and silent, from his mother's grasp.

"My God!" she said, to Maren. "What did he swallow?"

"Nothing! He fell off the climbing structure. One foot at most! He's fine."

"Come down!" wailed old Faucett from below. "I gotta bone to pick with you!"

"Not now," Judy shouted back. "Not now. I'll talk to the parents, I promise!"

"Bah!" exclaimed Irina, belatedly responding to Maren's explanation. And right upon that, echoing faintly up the steps from Faucett, "Bullshit!" She had never said that before. They heard her door slam.

All was silence up above. Maren arose from the deck. She observed that she had cut her knee, probably upon a nailhead, when Irina had tumbled her down. Judy placed Boris on his feet. He bent over and fussed with his laces. Then he looked at Maren. "Nyet," he said, softly. And then, with little explosions of air, "Bah! Bullshit!"

"You see?" said his mother, speaking to Judy. "He is ignored by your staff. They let anything happen to him."

Whatever happened to him before?, Maren thought. Nothing. Nothing much. He just keeps falling down.

"Are they leftists, too?" Suddenly she addressed Maren. "I know about *you*, Blondie!"

Maren, examining her knee, had no idea what Irina knew. She waited for Judy, who always had the answers.

"I don't think," said the head teacher, "that politics matter much in a nursery school. Even if the parents cared, the children wouldn't know. And I don't think anyone cares anymore, not really. This isn't the sixties, Irina, as I've been trying to explain."

Irina shook her head vigorously. Her dull black hair flopped about. "Bah!"

"Bullshit," her son said.

"Boris. Shut up with that filth." When she tried to pick him up again, he scuttled away. He crawled inside the climbing structure. Irina turned back to Maren.

"Your husband is an English professor, yes? The worst! Always attacking this 'patriarchy' that does not exist and finding capitalist oppression of everyone in harmless stories. Always the politics. I grew up in a communist country! I *know* what they are only playing with. Your husband is a fool!"

Then she stopped. Maren was supposed to say something. She waited for Judy, but Judy kept silent and suddenly looked tired, as she rarely did. Irina was crazy. Crazy parents will do that to you, drain you.

Finally Maren asked Irina, "Do you know Aaron?"

Maren knew what the patriarchy was but couldn't imagine Aaron attacking it, or, for that matter, doing anything unpleasant to a harmless story. Still, she wondered. Had they met? Aaron wasn't really a fool, but sometimes he acted like one. He insulted people who had disappointed him in some way, and he got mad easily. That is, he used to do these things. Now he was okay.

"No, I don't know him," Irina said. And then she huffed, "But they are all the same!"

"He's never cared about politics. If that's what's on your mind."

"Oh, don't act the innocent! It's women like you—"

"Irina," said Judy, loudly. "Irina, that's about enough. It's time for us to go. Boris seems fine. If you're unhappy, though, you and Anthony, you should…you should consider quitting the school."

That shocked Maren. They never wanted a child to leave, no matter how awful the parents were. And she really didn't want to lose Boris, she instantly decided, not now.

"Vot!" Irina also seemed shocked.

"It's your decision," Judy told her. "Yours and Anthony's. I'll tell you this, though: the politics of the parents, whatever they are, don't affect the kids. That's not an issue, really. And we certainly want Boris to stay. We think this is a good school for him. But if you really can't stand it here, do what you have to do. Do you understand?"

"Oh, all right."

"Which means?"

Irina shook her big head. "Where else could I go?"

"There are other nursery schools," said Judy, dryly. "But we're glad, because we really like Boris. But I have to request something of you. Please don't accuse the staff again of practicing some kind of politics you don't like. That's just, just..."

"Bullshit."

"Thank you, Boris."

For a moment Irina was quiet. She beheld her son, who lay on his back, on the safety mat within the cage of bars. From there, as if from a judicial bench, he had delivered his pithy judgment.

"I'm sorry," his mother said, shocking both Maren and Judy. "Maybe I overdo. It's not just here. In the lab. There's such tension. I don't know if what we do there is proper. But I say too much, I think. Come, Boris, come out. We must go home."

He came out, promptly. Without another word, she took his hand, led him to the steps and down. Judy plopped herself into the director's chair and sat there while Maren hunted around the deck for loose *Chronicle* pages. It had come apart during their struggle, or whatever it was. She went into the school and threw the reassembled paper into the trash. Missing professor. Fascist termite. Stupid. Maybe that was the kind of thing that had Irina so upset. She didn't know that it meant nothing.

Judy came in behind her. Together they got their purses and sweatshirts. Then out again, the steps. It was over, the day was over. There was always something. A plumber, urgently needed, who became lost in the hills. Head lice upon the treasured dome of a child whose parents would simply refuse to believe their little Geoffrey or Noah or Connor (a girl) could ever become infested. Today a crazy Russian scientist. What was she going on about? As they descended to the street, Judy told her.

Irina thought the other kids were ignoring Boris, "shunning," she called it. And they did this because their radical People's Republic of Berkeley parents had prejudiced them against a little boy from the new Russia, from the new, capitalist Russia.

"That's crap," Maren said.

"I know."

"That's utter bull—. Forget it. These parents are all rich, most of them. I mean, maybe they don't vote Republican, but they're all lawyers and software engineers and therapists. Or they don't work at all, like the Blakes. They're just rich! They all drive Volvo wagons! New ones. They eat at Chez Panisse!"

"Well, I know that. We know that. But outside of Berkeley people still think it's the sixties here. Some of the parents even, the ones who just moved into town, the Cagans, and the ones you just mentioned, Derek and Diane."

"The Blakes? They believe that?"

"I think. I know he wanted to come here because it's a good place for his animal liberation work. Lots of organizations, he told me. And she does some kind of radical literary criticism. Some kind of feminist thing. Post-post."

"Post-post? Post-post-what? Feminist? I can't believe that. Not the way she's always mincing around. She thinks she's a little sex-pot! She's absurd!"

By this time they were walking toward their cars, which were parked near each other, around the curve a bit.

"That's right," Judy said. "You don't like Diane, do you? I've noticed."

"Who says that? I have nothing against her. There's nothing to dislike. She just seems so silly."

"Does she? You know, some people think that she's a lot like you. Even looks like you, except for your being blond. Eh, Blondie?"

Maren couldn't not laugh. Nobody had ever called her Blondie before today. That made Aaron Dagwood.

"Seriously," Judy went on. "She *is* like you. Holly thinks so, too. You're the same, somehow."

"We are *not* the—"

Suddenly they were assailed by a stream of water. Faucett and her hose!

"Next one in front of my house gets…this!"

"Mrs. Faucett," Judy said. "Mrs. Faucett, we're going to talk, right now!" And she strode across the street. She was hardly wet, but Maren was soaked. In her car Maren got her T-shirt off and the sweatshirt on. Not easy making the change in a cramped, old-model VW Bug, but better than going back up the steps again. She'd had enough of Hillside School and its fusses for the day. Without even looking at Judy, engaged in yet another fuss, she started up and drove directly—as directly as one could go when traversing the Berkeley hills—to Monterey Market. Aaron was running low on fruit.

When she came home, a little red car, sporty, parked in front of their neighbor's, took off in a hurry. She had seen it before a few times, disappearing with much noise just as she pulled up or, once, as she was getting into her Bug to go someplace. It wasn't local: in this part of Berkeley, Honda Civics represented the ultimate in sportiness. She went into the house with her sack from Monterey.

No letter from Brooke, their daughter. Maren had spoken to her on the phone just last night; still, she wanted to call. But why would Brooke be in her dorm room, at U.C. San Diego, in the middle of the afternoon? There was nothing for Maren to do, it seemed, except put away the fruit. Figs for Aaron, and large, orange stalks of dried mango. He ate the most unbelievable crap, with cries of boyish excitement. She wished she could talk to somebody, but there was no one she could just call without a reason. Talking just to talk—she never did that.

Maren went for a walk, just walked out the door and turned right. Thus she found herself headed toward the playing field of King Jr. Junior High School, from which she could soon hear the shouts of girl soccer players. That meant that the Berkeley High team (King had no teams) was either having a scrimmage or, more likely, given the maenad-like vigor of the cries she was hearing, playing a league game. Soccer had been Brooke's sport at the high school, and Maren had gone to all the games. Probably she knew some of the parents who would be there now. They weren't her friends, but she could say hello. They would talk to her.

"Jerk!" Maren called herself that, out loud. Why was she doing this? Like some sad character who can't stand to be alone and always goes for coffee with her stupid friends. But she passed through the gate in the wire fence and then across the gravel running track. The last time she had walked by the field, Derek Blake had been running around the track; he held himself very erect, as if he were a skinny, frozen fish. Now, there was a jerk.

The first half of the game had just ended, she figured. The kids were sitting around eating oranges. The Berkeley team looked mightily depressed. No wonder, since they were up against Carondolet, a suburban powerhouse in girls' sports. Maren recognized the uniforms. Evidently all the squealing had been coming from Carondolet. Some of the Berkeley High parents—that is to say, mothers, for only mothers had turned out on that Thursday afternoon—were complaining to one another that all the Carondolet players were white. So were all the Berkeley High players, however, or so it seemed to Maren. She scanned the mothers and saw two she knew, but they were busy arguing about the cringing dog that one of them had on a leash.

"You have no right! This field is posted. No Dogs! No Dogs!"

"I'll come back to clean, if that's what you want. But I will not leave. At least I walked here. *You* drove. You polluted!"

The dog, a little scrawn of a thing, flattened itself against the earth.

Another mother was shouting at her orange-slice sucking daughter: "Megan, I want you to kick that big girl's ass!"

The mother, whom Maren had never seen before, had a fancy Eastern accent. "Ahs," she said, which sounded ridiculous.

No one noticed Maren. Which was all right, really. When she was almost back at the gate, she noticed a strayed soccer ball and booted it in the direction of the field. It went at least thirty yards in the air, thumping to earth right next to the disputed-over dog, who cringed even more. Maren was small, had been called cute all her life, and had particularly cute feet, small and high-arched; nonetheless, she had very strong legs and could kick like a mule even when barefoot, as she virtually was now, except for sandal straps. When Brooke played, Maren had appointed herself the finder and kicker-back of lost balls, and one of the moms must have recognized her style, for she waved and smiled. But what was there to say?

Back home, she felt like sitting on her front lawn and waiting for Aaron, but she waited inside. To pass the time, she grumped to herself about Diane Blake, whom she was supposed to resemble—she'd heard that before. Yes, they were both the little, pretty type, the kind of women men liked a lot because they didn't carry any load of threat. They both had big eyes, smooth, shiny hair, nice legs. All right. But they really didn't look alike except in these very general ways, she being fair, Diane dark. More importantly, they were very different in personality, which might, of course, be accounted for in part by Diane being younger by some years. Surely, though, there was more to it than that. Diane had a hard streak, something like that. Maren could sense it.

What the hell was bothering her? Derek's tantrum had been upsetting, but he was obviously just a twit, not worth a moment's worry. After he had left, Irina had come and then gone inside with Judy, leaving her on the deck. She had felt fine, enjoying the sun, the paper. But her mood was swiftly dispelled by the descent of Boris from the climbing structure and his mother's gigantic fuss-fuss, suddenly turning into dejection or something like it. Irina had seemed almost afraid. Maren didn't know what to think about Irina, but she didn't feel right, any longer, about simply dumping her into the category "unpleasant parent," along with Derek. And she shouldn't have let Boris fall. She was ignoring Boris. Was she? Was she ignoring Deirdre? She wasn't doing her job. Was that the trouble? But Judy must not think so, or she would have said something.

What the hell was it? Maren knew she didn't like being compared to Diane Blake, but no one could take the comparison seriously. You couldn't liken a teacher to a parent! Different orders of humanity.

In the past, when she had felt unhappy, she always knew why. Aaron. Aaron acting crazy. She loved him, but he could make her sad, and mad, as no one else could. That was the old Aaron, of course. But lately, it seemed to her as she considered, perhaps some of the old Aaron was coming back, working up to the surface. There were no noisy outbursts anymore, his tantrums over nothing, but he didn't always seem really happy. He's pretending, she thought. Maybe. Well, that wouldn't be good. She wouldn't want that. Hard to tell the difference, though, between falsely pretending and just being nice.

At 5:30, his usual return time, her burly, black-haired spouse threw open the front door. After crossing the threshold, he gently deposited his briefcase, a huge, battered object his mother had given him two decades ago, upon the bench in the hall. Once it had been his practice to let it crash to the floor, rattling the house, but lately he seemed to have conceived that this annoyed her. In truth, she didn't care what he did with it. Then he hugged her, she having come forward to be hugged, since she knew he liked it. Unfortunately, he had his corncob pipe, a prop, in the front pocket of his overalls, and it jabbed her.

"Aaron, ease off." She muttered this into his chest.

He backed away, keeping his big hands on her shoulders. His bushy eyebrows were up, raised almost to his droopy hairline. "What's that spot on your chin?"

"Your pipe. It stuck me. Could you..."

She wanted him to go change out of his overalls. After a month of wearing them twice a week, they were beginning to look alarmingly authentic. He was too used to them. Right now he had his thumbs hooked in the straps. Moreover, the overalls gave him the appearance of being fat, rather than simply big, as he was, tall and wide-shouldered. He looked okay in regular clothes.

"Uh," he said, keenly. "I think I'll get the ovies off. They're too hot."

As he went toward the bedroom, she called after him, "How was the taping?"

"Fine," he said, stopping for a minute. "The kids were sort of wild, but I managed. Anything for a fartie."

The California State University system had a new pay gimmick, the Faculty Achievement Rating Terminal Increment, popularly known as the fartie. To get a raise you applied for one or several farties, instead of simply surviving for another year and getting more money because you still breathed and hadn't disrobed in class. Maren didn't really know how the farties worked, but she understood from Aaron that everyone hated them, as an evil import from the corporate world, but would do anything to get them. He, however, had refused to apply, but that was the old Aaron. Reformed, made new by therapy and that serotonin drug the shrink had him take, he decided to give farties a try. His uninspiring student evaluations wouldn't help, he knew that; neither would his meager efforts as a Whartonian, a few articles and notes, the book he'd edited but didn't even like to talk about. That didn't matter, he told her: the big shots who gave out the farties (who passed the gas, people said) didn't care about teaching or scholarship half as much as they did about publicity. It had long grieved them that although far more students took classes on CSU campuses, like San Francisco State, than the U.C. variety, like U.C. Berkeley, the public seemed scarcely to know that the former existed.

Therefore, Maren's husband prevailed upon his racquetball partner Charles, who managed the campus cable television station, to let him have a show. Aaron was a good-looking guy, once you got used to his extremely thick and bristly eyebrows, personally engaging as long as he kept his temper under control, which was no longer a problem, and he had a great, deep voice. Perhaps a time slot where he talked about books, a kind of review show.

Instead, Charles made him Aaron the Tale Spinner, a good ole country boy who actually did no spinning of anything, but read children's stories before the camera every Monday and Thursday. These sessions were taped and then broadcast on Saturday and Sunday mornings. They did quite well, better than most of the cartoon shows, or so Charles thought. It was hard to tell since they couldn't get accurate ratings for the area their station could reach, a vaguely delineated chunk of northern San Francisco, much of which was occupied by Golden Gate Park, and sometimes Kentfield in Marin County, when their signal made it across the Golden Gate Bridge. But children liked the show. Charles got letters from the parents and occasionally from a kid. The latest of these had been kind of discouraging. "Arom [sic] is dum," complained its author. "Let the kids reed." He also wanted more *Freddy the Pigs*. The kids were Juan and Rupert, the photogenic sons of Martin, who ran a campus food stall, and their friend, a little girl named Marcelline. They liked Aaron but teased him without mercy. Aaron enjoyed doing the show, probably, although he talked about it less and less. He must have been disappointed last year, the maiden season of Aaron the Tale Spinner, when he received no farties, although he had put in for three.

Now they were both in the kitchen. Clad in jeans and T-shirt, Aaron was masticating a mango stick. He told her it was a good one. How was her day, he wanted to know. "Oh," she said, "I had a *great* day." He looked at her.

"I did."

"Well, tell me what happened. What was good?"

She got up from the table, opened the fridge and looked inside. She could make fajitas, had the stuff right there. No beer, though; maybe he would want to go down to the little store and buy one.

"It was just good, Aaron. It was sunny. Oh, did you read about Cedric? I forgot his last name. The Wharton guy we met at the party."

"McAulay. Yeah, I know about him. I'm supposed to be in one of those books he does. I don't know. What's the good of it?"

Maren closed the fridge door and turned around. She wanted to ask him why he was being so negative, but she didn't understand what he was talking about. She didn't understand what *she* was talking about.

She tried again. "The *Chron* said—you took it, right?—he left his house but never showed up at his office. He was getting threats, and now he's disappeared."

"Not quite."

"Not quite?"

"Yeah." Aaron said. "No. Whatever."

"Well, did just his head disappear?"

He was being so snitty, or shitty, just like the old Aaron. Time to tell him to go get his beer.

"Hyip-hyip." He made his strange, barking laugh, as if he were a baby coyote. Now, so suddenly, he was the new-model Aaron.

If he'd always laughed like that, she never would have married him, but this...this *yipping* hadn't started until last year. In the old days he hadn't laughed much, being grumpy most of the time and wanting more from her, often, than she wanted to give. He sensed this, even when she gave it, and was therefore all the grumpier. At least he had a real laugh, exercised about once a month. The new one, the yip, was often, though not always, a warning that he was about to give her a surprise, which was always flowers.

Aaron heaved himself out of his chair. Maren watched him go to the bench in the hall and reach for his briefcase, which, as far as she knew, had never contained a flower. Lots of other things, most of which would crush or poison a flower. Hundreds of student papers to grade, broken-backed text books, filthy, crusted coffee cups for her to wash. He took out a piece of paper and brought it back to her. It was a picture, she could see that, and then he put it on the table.

"My God," Maren said.

"Hyip-hyip. Cedric McAulay, dean of the old school Whartonians. The man is mad."

But Aaron was marveling at the man, admiring his nerve. She could tell. There he was, McAulay, looking up from the table at her. A shirtless Whartonian, with a round belly, a little nose, twinkly eyes, and a big, wide-open mouth. He was laughing. He looked like a big baby, though he was at least sixty, or big idiot, nothing to exclaim over, and he wasn't the reason Maren had said, "My God."

He had his arm around Diane Blake, Hillside School mom. Silly, willful (she knew it!) Diane Blake in a red bikini top and no facial expression. And presumably a bikini bottom, but the picture only went halfway down. What an awful person!

"This is crazy," Maren said. "I know her." She explained to Aaron. The daughter's name was Deirdre, and, though quiet, she was cute and smart. Smarter than her parents, and much nicer. The Blakes were jerks, Eastern people with big money. Well, Derek was from the East; she didn't know where Diane came from. And Derek had the money. A line of frozen fish products, things you brought home in boxes and microwaved. Derek was an animal rights activist who had recently negotiated the release of a captured jumbo squid. Had Aaron read about that? It had been in the paper, not the *Chronicle*, one of the weekly throwaways.

Aaron tried to understand. "They were going to freeze the squid?"

"No, just keep it in the aquarium in Golden Gate Park."

But Aaron was no longer trying. He was looking at Diane in the picture, cute, little Diane, whose breasts, not big, nonetheless sat up high in their little scarlet cups. Nice tan, too.

"She's a parent? You know, I didn't notice before, but she looks a bit like you. A lot like you."

She crossed her arms over her chest. "Before? You've met her?"

"Once. At this Wharton tea. She came with Cedric. She's his graduate student. Now she's his girl friend. Remember at that party? He was hitting on you. So he got himself another lit-tle…uh, you know, small, attractive woman."

"Where'd you get this?" Maren said, meaning the picture.

"Www.edith.org."

Grand! A website. Computer voodoo. She got up and started in on dinner, yanking out a skillet.

"It's a website, the Wharton website."

"I know that." Plopping a piece of steak on her cutting board, she seized a knife and hacked it to bits.

"Okay. So I got the picture off the website. The text said they're in Las Vegas, where someone took the picture and stuck it on the net. I don't know who, and I don't know why. There's no Wharton tea or conference going on there, so they must have gone just for, you know, pleasure. Wow! She's—"

"Oh, forget her. Him. Does he, does he do this stuff? Go off with his students for a screw in the sand?"

"He's done it. Usually his wife doesn't tell the cops or the papers. Never went with anyone this cute, though. But always to Vegas; he likes Vegas, although it's the most un-Whartonian place conceiv-able. I'll tell you this: if somebody's trying to embarrass him with this picture, they can forget it. He won't care if people know about him and Diane. Won't care about the *Chron* article, either. He'll just laugh. You know what he is? He's an asshole, but I'm stuck with him if I want to get published, to help with farties. Oh, boy."

"What?" she said, after a moment or two. "What is it?"

"I don't know. I'm sorry she's a parent. That's a little sticky, might be embarrassing for you."

"Why? It's sad for Deirdre, that's all."

That's all? She remembered Deirdre's father that morning, talking about her mother. "She took off. She just took off." To be with a fat old man. But what really bothered him was having to miss a meeting about reptiles. Wonderful parents!

"So," said Aaron, brisking up, "what's for dinner? Fajitas! Great! Think I'll go to the little store and get a beer."

The door closed behind him. Maren stood, knife upraised. What the hell was bothering him? Or her? Why did she care? She didn't. Everything was fine.

Soon Aaron returned, and soon they had dinner. At the little store he had bought two beers, big, black Kirins, both of which he drank. That was unusual, a two-beer dinner. He seemed tense, and he kept yipping. Maren felt like yipping back. Instead, she asked him if he knew anything about the hate messages the *Chron* said McAulay had received. Does this happen? To others besides him? He said that it sometimes did.

"Especially in English departments. The young people, the grad students and the new professors, are all radicalized. I don't mean that they actually *do* anything. They just interpret texts in a radical manner. Most of the time, actually, they read criticism that does it for them. They used to read Derrida and Lacan. Woo! Never understood much of that shit. Hyip-hyip. Is there anything wrong?"

"No."

"You look the way you do with a headache. Want me to go on with this? Okay. What they do now is postcolonialism, cultural studies, and postmodernist, I mean *post*-postmodernist, feminism. Europe bad, rest of world good. Men bad. I mean, I could explain this, but probably not very well, and that's sort of what it boils down to. Needless to say, I don't have a fucking chance with Edith."

Wharton, he meant. It took Maren a minute.

"These fajitas are great! More, yes?"

"Yeah. Why don't you get up and make yourself one?"

"Of course, Maren." He proceeded to busy himself in her kitchen. While eating standing up, he continued to explain the current state of things literary-critical.

Choppy though the explanation was, interrupted oft when Aaron chewed and swallowed, eventually Maren thought she got the point. The latest generation of young scholars, who, her husband mused, all seemed to come from either Long Island or northern New Jersey, had one grand idea. This concerned the famous or infamous "canon," the list of "great works" that English majors used to be expected to read. The idea was that the canon was bad. It was extraordinarily bad, because it made the favorite enterprises of patriarchal, imperialist Europeans and European-Americans seem good. And once you understood how Shakespeare, say, not only justified but largely inspired both the slave trade and the rampant masculinism that still flourished in college English departments, then you were reading Shakespeare right. It didn't seem to matter which play. You could read anyone that way, including writers who were neither white nor male, and therefore not even in the canon, although there was a special twist to that. Aaron didn't express an opinion about all this. It didn't seem to interest him much. The climate had changed, that was all.

"But Cedric"—now he was up at the sink, rinsing the dishes, vigorously scrubbing her pan—"Cedric doesn't care, and he writes about Edith in a sort of familiar way. It isn't appreciated. The younger faculty, the women, anyway, don't like that, but he doesn't care. He's a full professor. He—"

"Laughs."

"Yeah. I've heard of only one time when he didn't laugh, and he wasn't a full professor then. And it wasn't a woman. It was Gregor. Hey, remember him? Little Gregor?"

"Who? Gregor Grosz? Oh, sure."

They had known Gregor moderately well when they and he were undergrads.

"I just heard this. Well, a few years ago I did, but it happened years before that. Gregor accused McAulay of publishing an article plagiarized from a paper he'd written in the Wharton seminar.

It was a graduate seminar, but he was just a junior. At first, Cedric laughed, yeah; but Gregor wouldn't back off. Finally McAulay got him kicked out of school. Didn't he just sort of disappear? But the article, based on the paper, supposedly, got all kinds of favorable notice, launched McAulay's career and all that. I think Gregor was nuts, but he was terribly smart. This story might be true."

She nodded. Well, yes. She remembered Gregor, very well. Smart. Never awed by authority.

"If it's true," Aaron continued, "then Cedric got away with something. After that, I gather, he became a full-time laugher, mocker, and teaser, and he does it in print: you know, makes fun of post-postmodernist feminist readings of *The House of Mirth* and so on. He gets published because he's provocative, and because he's been published so much already, so he gets hate mail."

"At this point he decides to have an escapade with his graduate student, with Diane Blake. All right. But she's young, more or less, and I hear she's a feminist. Why doesn't she hate him?"

"Maybe she just calls herself a feminist. Doesn't look like one."

"Oh, she doesn't?"

Aaron came over to the table and picked up the picture. "Nope," he said, looking at it closely, looking at Diane closely. "Not to me. Also, she looks kind of dumb. What? What's up?"

Maren said nothing.

"Your face! Hey, probably she's smart. How would I know? I never heard her say anything at this tea I went to. Cedric did all the talking. Hate him, you say? She could. But he's been pulling this shit for years, taking his grad students to Vegas, and nothing ever happens to him. Besides the calls and e-mails. Maybe because he gets the grad students good jobs. I should talk. I'm no better than they are. Think I ought to sweep?"

He contemplated the kitchen floor.

"Oh," she said. "Oh, I'll do it. Take me three minutes."

"Okay, thanks. I've got papers."

He graded, out in the living room, and she swept. Then she got down on her knees and wiped the hardwood floor with a damp sponge. There wasn't much of the evening left when they got together again. She told him how much the kids liked the new angora rabbit, Lion, that Judy had brought down from some huge breeding establishment in Napa. He expressed interest, but seemed distracted and also depressed, which was not at all what she wanted for Aaron. He was not himself, she thought, although she couldn't say he was now being grumpy, which was how his depression used to come out. He just sat and looked worried until he showered and went to bed.

Sprawled on the couch, Maren read an old *New Yorker*. After a while she took her bath, donned her nightgown, and finally joined Aaron, who surprised her by being still awake. Then he surprised her even more.

"Could we?" he asked.

"Could we what?" She still had the *New Yorker*, was in the middle of something.

"Could we get together? I just would like to, for once."

Now he sounded a little grumpy. But Maren hardly noticed.

"You mean, fuck?" she said. She almost added, "with you?"

"Oh," said Aaron. "Okay. Don't have to. Bad idea."

He turned away from her; she put the magazine down and touched his shoulder.

"Good night, Maren. Good night and goddammit. Goddammit, I'm sorry. I'm angry at myself."

She doubted that; she'd heard that one before. It didn't matter. She just didn't want him to be upset.

"I was surprised, that's all. Aaron, come on. I was surprised. You know, your medicine, your Aetherion."

Aetherion was a drug that did something to his serotonin. He had too much of this tricky substance, or he had too little, or it moved too slowly, like molasses. Whatever the problem was, Aetherion had proved to be the answer to his depression. He was nice almost all of the time. His view of life was positive, mostly. Much better for them both. There were side effects, but they weren't too bad. He seemed to need more sleep, and he yipped. His libido had gradually diminished to vanishing, to a now and then cuddle.

"Come on. I want to." Again she was surprised, this time at

herself. She was telling the truth. She wanted him. "Aaron," she implored. Her tone seemed to her imploring. Pulling up her nightie, she plastered herself against his back. She put her arm around him, but he pulled away and then got up. Bumping around in the dark room, he found his bathrobe and then he left.

"I'm wrong," he called from the living room, although his voice sounded miles away. "I shouldn't have. Tomorrow it didn't happen. Okay? Okay, Maren?"

"Okay." She was whispering, and he probably didn't hear. Okay. Of course, she was wrong, to be so surprised when he asked her. He would be unwilling to ask her again soon. That was a shame. But it would have been worse if they had gone ahead and he hadn't gotten hard or hadn't been able to ejaculate. She wasn't sure which symptom Aetherion caused, perhaps both.

"Hoo-hoo." Outside—she thought of him as being outside, though he wasn't—Aaron laughed. She had never heard that peculiar chortle before. It was so sad. What was wrong with him?

She became sleepy thinking about Aaron; she kept from thinking about herself.

Chapter Two

In the morning Maren and Aaron said acceptable things to each other concerning the day before them and went their separate ways. Dressed in coat and tie, looking neat, but soon to be disheveled because of the passage of time or the movements of the air, Aaron walked to BART. Maren, in jeans, sneakers, and long-sleeved shirt, although the weather was fair, drove her small and ancient car to Hillside School.

Judy was already on the grounds, sitting on the third step from the bottom. It was her turn for greeting duty, saying hello to kids and parents or au pairs and making sure that only the kids went on up. Maren went up herself. She laid out the toys on the rug in the Big Room; ninety percent seemed to be trucks. A lot of boys this year, and, as it happened, this year's girls seemed also to like trucks, at least so far. Holly showed up, wearing a blue University of California baseball cap and carrying a large plastic cow, a spotted one with mighty udders. She had bought the thing at a garage sale. They positioned it next to a tanker truck.

The kids came. The three C's came, Conway, Crystal, and red-haired Cloelia, wearing her princess dress even though her parents had been asked to send her to school in something else, anything else. When Cloelia showed up in the purple princess outfit, then Crystal felt sad because she didn't have one, and therefore Conway, their friend, a sturdy boy with no interest in girls' clothing, became disturbed. He would try to bop people, pushing them down, exclaiming "Bop! Bop!" Now he looked around for victims. Snapping up Conway's favorite truck, a timber hauler, with logs, that no environmentalist parent had complained about as yet, Holly leaped to head him off.

Moby Leibling appeared. His father was a graduate student in English, but somehow they had plenty of money. No doubt Mariko, the Leiblings' au pair, had brought him in the Volvo. A tiny, elfin child, Moby knelt on the rug by Holly's cow, placed his head against an udder, and appeared to fall asleep. Maren gave him a pat. He always did this, this flop, at this time. It was his way, and she always gave him a pat. When he opened his eyes, after all the racket of arrival had ceased, he always found her and bestowed a pat on her. She often wondered about his state of mind on the day he would learn his parents had named him after a whale.

"Bop! Bop!" Conway had bopped poor Boris Pownall, a hard, frontal bop sending him crashing into a doll's bed that collapsed underneath him. Perhaps Conway was sorry. Since most of his head was engulfed by Holly's blue hat, which he had asked to wear, Maren could see only his chin, which did seem to be trembling. A weeping Boris was assisted from the doll's bed by his father, Anthony, who was not supposed to be there. Conway shrieked and, though blinded by the hat, ran out the door, with Holly right behind him, no doubt intending to place him upon the yellow stool reserved for miscreants. "Stooling," they called it. A few more children trooped into the Big Room. They were suspiciously wet. Had Faucett brandished her hose? Maren waved them to their cubbies, to deposit their lunch boxes. She wiped Boris's nose while smiling cutely at his father. Probably wouldn't work. She had never had the impression that this finnicky limey cared at all for cute.

"Sorry! So sorry! Conway never bopped him before!"

"'Bopped'?"

He was not a friendly man. Maren usually liked dapper, little fellows, and this one was quite little and extremely trim in his dress, certainly so when compared to Aaron. But he was unresponsive, she thought.

What was he doing up here? Irina usually brought and also

picked up Boris. In any case, it was Judy's job to encourage au pairs and parents to stay below unless there was something they needed to carry, and Dr. Pownall was carrying nothing except a terrible frown. His mouth looked like a horseshoe standing on its feet. He was so exasperatingly neat! She wanted to plop him in front of a truck.

But Maren knew she had to take her medicine. Yesterday she had let Boris topple from the climbing structure, and Anthony had probably marched up here—brushing aside Judy, which wasn't easy to do—to complain at her about that. And then Boris was bopped right in front of him. A more mobile child could have moved out of the way, at least partly, so that he would only have been jolted a bit, not knocked into the bed. She gave Boris's nose a final wipe. Poor little guy. Why did she have this terrible trick of not noticing him? He had stopped crying. Holly had already marched past, clutching a flailing, kicking Conway, en route to the stool. There he would stay until calm. The victimized Boris, Maren noted, was already calm, or seemed so.

"Hey, Boris," she said. "Ready to play?"

"Bullshit," he replied.

"Boris!" Anthony sounded mad. She hoped he would make this quick. She had work to do. Where was Judy? It wasn't her way to let Maren cope with people like Boris's father by herself.

"May I take you aside?"

A genteel request. Judy came through the door, her stint as greeter concluded. With both Judy and Holly on the job in the big room, Maren knew she could be spared for a few minutes. She walked out onto the deck, followed by the tiny biologist, or whatever he was. Probably the Big Room was better off without her, at the rate she was going. All that empty talk with Aaron. Have a good day! You too. That always made her feel unsettled, jerky.

"What happened yesterday..." Anthony looked off into the view, westward. The Berkeley flatlands, the Bay, both bridges, the peaky structures of downtown San Francisco. Mt. Tam in Marin. Clean, all of it, in the morning sun. No wonder the site was worth a fortune to slimy contractors who wanted to buy and level

Hillside School and erect a forest of condos. So hard to keep this place for children.

"I'm sorry, Anthony," she said. "I looked aside for one minute."

"Oh, did you?" Anthony fiddled with his glasses. Took them off, looked at them, replaced them. At least he didn't huff on the lenses the way people did.

"As for his saying bullshit, he didn't pick that up from us. We don't say that. At any rate, the real concern here is that Boris may not be relating well to the other children. I think Conway was almost surprised just now when he ran at Boris and actually hit him. A child like that..."

She realized she was about to say that Boris was easy even for teachers to ignore. That wouldn't do. A crash resounded from the Big Room. Perhaps Conway had lunged from the stool and bopped again. Let it not be Boris!

"Mrs. Matthews—I mean Maren. My wife insulted you yesterday, and she is very embarrassed and very contrite. Judy was kind enough to allow me to come up here to say this to you. Irina hopes that you will accept her apologies."

"Oh," Maren said, surprised. "Oh, I wasn't even thinking of that. Irina doesn't need to apologize. Parents yell at us all the time. I never take it personally. And she's under stress. That's obvious."

She stopped talking, because it seemed to her that she had said the wrong thing. Anthony's horseshoe mouth had softened a bit while he was apologizing, but now he looked, once again, quite grim.

"Stress? Stress? What did she say?"

"That leftist parents are prejudicing their children against Boris, because he comes, or she comes, from Russia."

"Well, yes. That." The horseshoe relaxed. "That's a problem for Irina. Russia isn't socialist anymore."

"Yes?" said Maren, wondering where Anthony was headed.

"Oh, it's nothing to you, but Irina believed what she was taught growing up, and now she can't let it all go. Hard for her. Besides that, she's part of a capitalist venture now herself. So she feels guilt on two levels, and Berkeley is supposed to be so radical. She

imagines things, slights. You can understand this causes problems. The remedy, I've been told, is to take her to Chez Panisse."

Ah, Chez Panisse! The greatest restaurant in Berkeley. No, its
greatest attraction of any kind, more celebrated than the Rad Lab
and the Bancroft Library combined.

"Fabulous place," Maren said, although on the one occasion she
had dined there it had not seemed all that great and not exactly a
magic bullet for post-socialist guilt. What else had Irina said?
There was something. Yes.

"There was another thing. She said there was tension in the
lab."

"That's absurd. There's no tension in the lab. What exactly did
she say? Did she say anything more?"

"No. Just that."

"Nothing about the project?"

"No, Anthony." Don't bark at me, Anthony. For a moment she
had thought she could like him; she doubted it now.

"It's demanding work, and Irina may well need a break. She's
taking one now, in fact, but it will have to be very brief. She's
needed. If Boris says something about her not being home, it's
because she's spending a lot of time with friends. She should—I'll
speak to her."

"At Chez Panisse?"

"Right, whatever. Uh…must go."

Abruptly he turned away from her and walked quickly toward
the steps, Maren staring after him. The door to the Big Room
opened, and she saw Judy standing there, giving her a look that
meant, "Get in here! We need you!" She heard Holly saying, "No,
she has udders. Ud-ders! Not boobies!"

Maren hurried in. Holly was holding the plastic cow behind
her back. A few of the boys were circling around behind her, trying to get at it. Stupid cow! Except for its benign expression, it
resembled Irina Pownall. Judy, sitting at a low table with a bunch
of kids, looked at her, then at the door, and said "Okay?"

"Yeah. All settled."

After lunch they groomed Lion, the new angora rabbit. The
children had named him. Because of his profuse growth of silky,

white hair, his whole body looked like an albino lion's mane, or the head of an old man with an Afro, a do popular in the sixties. Maybe it would become fashionable again in Berkeley, at least in the U.C. English Department. In any case, Lion was a good name for this large rabbit, who had a certain majesty about him. Squatting calmly on the deck, he permitted Cloelia, now de-princessed and clad in jeans and sweatshirt from the school clothing chest, to pull a comb through his pelt and work out tangles. Boris watched. After a moment, Maren handed him the comb, which he plied, but too roughly, so that Lion jerked away and she had to snatch him into her lap. Boris sat down again. Poor Boris.

Deirdre Blake came up. Maren wondered. Had she been avoiding Deirdre? She certainly hadn't let her eyes rest on her for long. Poor Boris? How about poor Deirdre? Her mother having a fling with a stupid old professor, her nearly naked breasts plastered on www.edith.org for all to see.

"Hi, Deirdre! Come and groom Lion!"

If Deirdre combed her own hair, then she could probably do an excellent job on an angora rabbit, having quite a flourishing blond mop herself. She was very cute and remarkably polite, though a bit shy. Other kids always wanted to play with her, but when someone plopped down next to Deirdre on the floor, she always seemed startled. With parents so rigid and phony, Derek rigid, Diane phony, she wasn't used to open expressions of friendship. Maybe that was it. She was also on the small side and, although very well-coordinated, a bit fragile, prone to bruise when bopped. It was good that she avoided rough play and tough characters like Conway.

Gently Deirdre stroked Lion, who turned his head and stared, it seemed, directly into the little girl's dark eyes. Light hair, dark eyes. Brooke, Maren's daughter, now almost all grown up, had the same combination. Blond like her mother, but she had Aaron's eyes; Maren's own were green. With the Blakes, it was the other way around: Derek had blond hair, probably thinning; why else would he always wear a hat? And those awful flat blue eyes. Diane was the dark one.

Deirdre noticed a small leaf tangled in Lion's hair, on his side near his right hind leg. She gently pulled it free, then found and removed another. She got up and began to go around the deck picking up leaves and other small debris, so that soon she had two small fistfulls of assorted stuff. She looked around for a place to put it and probably would have gone into the Big Room, where there were several trash cans, had not Boris, Boris!, trotted up with a paper box he had found somewhere. Deirdre dumped her load into the box. Reposing in Maren's lap, Lion watched the children.

Four little boys ran out of the Big Room, waving trucks, yelling. Conway followed them. "Bop, bop," he said, in a reflective tone. Both Boris and the rabbit grew tense, but Deirdre appeared to regard these intruders, who might be expected to startle and confuse her, with something like aristocratic disdain. It was cute in her, if that was what it was, off-putting in her cold-fish father. The boys had their lunch boxes. Pick-up time was nigh. King Lion was escorted to his hutch.

In thirty minutes time, all the children had been taken away except for Boris Pownall and Deirdre Blake. No one came for either of them, so the teachers were stuck. Holly pleaded Kyle's soccer practice. Practice every day? Maren knew that Judy was thinking the same thing, but she let Holly go. Then Judy went into her office and called the Pownalls and Blakes while Maren stayed on the deck with Deirdre and Boris, whom she watched like a hawk. It occurred to her that Deirdre was also the kind of child that one lost sight of. She wasn't likely to fall down and hurt herself, so there weren't any dire consequences. But scant attention was paid her, this pretty, quiet little girl in a class dominated by bumptious boys. Overseeing Boris, once again engrossed in playing with his un-vel-cro'd shoes, Maren tried to talk with Deirdre, determined not to bring up either of her peculiar parents.

"Do you have any pets at home?" That seemed safe, though unpromising. Maren didn't expect that she would, animal rights activists usually being anti-pet.

"I don't," Deirdre said, "but my daddy has a wolf."

"A wolf!" Recently they had read the wolf and little pigs story to the kids, in a modern version, narrated by the wolf.

"Yes! We just got him. His name is Artie, and he's very shy. I don't get to play with him. Daddy says animals are themselves. Not for play."

There we go: the party line, even with imaginary pets. Artie the wolf. Deirdre looked sad. Time to change the subject.

"But you like to play with Lion at school."

"I love Lion."

"I love Lion, too." Boris, looking up from his shoes. "I will sing Lion a song."

He pronounced it "songk," which made Maren smile, but she was quite moved by the sweet and wordless melody that Boris, now standing beside the hutch, proceeded to intone. Seated on the deck, Deirdre joined in, supplying the lyric. "Lion is king, king, king," she sang. "King of our school, school, school."

"I can't reach the parents." Judy was whispering, but the kids noticed her and stopped. Deirdre got up and went to stand by the hutch with Boris. Judy explained that nobody was home at the Pownalls', no answering machine either. When she had called their lab, she learned that Irina hadn't come in and that Anthony was in conference with someone important named George. Judy had left her home number. As for the Blakes, well, she hoped Maren wouldn't mind: they had a machine, and the message she left on it instructed them to pick up Deirdre, ASAP, at Maren's house.

"And I'll hang onto Boris. That okay?"

Maren said sure. It seemed a shame to separate the two kids, that was all. For a moment she thought they were holding hands, over by Lion's hutch, but they weren't, she saw when she took a second look, and probably hadn't been.

She had errands to do, the cleaner's and the library, books for school, and it was fun having Deirdre along. In the library, they looked at a picture book together, a book called *Bored*, about a couple of kids sitting around the house with nothing to do. So they build a plane out of stuff they find in the kitchen and garage and fly around for a while before coming home for dinner. Aaron had had a lot of success with that one on TV, although a parent had called the station to complain about her own kids slapping something together and crashing it in the back yard. Deirdre seemed to respond quite strongly to the idea of nothing to do, which really meant, Maren knew, at least with kids that young, "my parents do nothing with me." Except stick another video in the VCR. She didn't know if the Blakes did that, but they were the type. Like the Pownalls, they did without an au pair, probably because, given their do-gooder politics, they resisted exploiting immigrant labor.

Her own daughter, Brooke, had been sturdier and a bit less Lion-like in the coiffure department, but they looked alike. They really did.

"Want to go to my house?"

"Sure."

Deirdre obviously liked the library and was, just as obviously, a very bright little kid. She thought about the world, just as Brooke had at her age. But Deirdre wasn't in the habit of talking, while Brooke had talked and talked, always saying cute and funny things that she and Aaron never forgot. No such memories for dopey Derek and Diane, who in all probability didn't care.

Thinking these thoughts, thinking of Brooke, who always made everything right for them, Maren drove home. There was a shiny green convertible in front, top up. Cute car. She pulled in behind it. Too close, its driver thought; he honked. But she was by no means too close, and he had parked in front of *her* house. Lucky for him she wasn't Mrs. Faucett.

Now the green car's door popped open. A leg popped out.

"Well, shit," said Maren, softly. By this time she was standing on the sidewalk with Deirdre, who seized her by the thigh and seemed to want to drag her back to the Bug.

"It's all right," she told Deirdre. I can handle this person, she told herself.

"Deirdre!" the person snapped. "Get in the Mercedes. Now!"

Derek Blake. Wearing a big, mannish leather jacket, engulfing his skinny form, and his usual plaid cap. He had narrow little lips. He clamped them shut. He opened them again. "You get in here *now!*"

Detaching herself from her teacher, the little girl, blank-faced, walked reluctantly to her father's side. Snatching her up by her armpits, he dropped her into the car seat, under the wheel, and then he pushed her to move over. He pushed her with his foot. Now Maren felt very weak; now she could do nothing. Placing his foot, the same one, into the car, preparatory to getting in and taking off, he finally focused his blue, fish eyes on Maren.

"I've been here for an hour," he said. "I've been *stuck* here! The message said you were taking her to your house—" Here he broke off to wave his arm at their little house as if to push it from its shallow foundations and into the Bay. "Taking her here. So here I was, but where were you?"

That is what she should be asking him: where were you at pick-up time? We were the stuck ones. But without a word, she turned away and walked across the lawn to her front door. She realized then that her key was in her purse and the purse in the car.

"No recognition of our needs," he said. "Five hundred dollars a month, and I get this. What?"

Deirdre must have said something. Maren continued to face the door; it needed paint, she observed. After a moment, Derek started up, making his car roar unnecessarily, she thought, and drove rapidly away. Now she could go back to the Bug for her purse and keys, and the library books—*Bored* and a bunch of others, mostly about nice people and nicer animals. Gathering these up, she realized she had forgotten about Aaron's cleaning, a jacket and two slacks, so she went to the cleaner's. A parent was in there; it was rather a posh cleaner's. She quite liked this woman, but when she saw her, Maren said, "Oh, I forgot!" and immediately rushed out. Lurking in the video parlor next door, she saw the parent leave, then went in and collected Aaron's stuff.

Derek's wife had run away; of course, he was angry. That's the way a man would act. He had to love Deirdre. How could he not? How could Diane not?

Aaron got home. He looked tired, but went running anyway. When he came back he had a cut on his shin. "Oh, do I?" he said. "Oh, yeah. Oh, well. No, no." He waved her off as she was moving in to examine this minor wound. They ate. Dinner was great, he said. He cleaned up the kitchen and then proposed a walk.

"Aren't you tired?"

"From running? No, I wouldn't say I was tired. Not tired enough, I'd say."

She just didn't want to go, but she thought it would be a bad thing to reject him. Something was bothering him. But she didn't want to.

So she said nothing, until Aaron forced a smile and said, "Be right back."

He left. Judy called.

Maren told her that Derek had come for Deirdre, had been extremely unpleasant. Also, she was surprised to find herself saying, his wife was having an affair with her professor, Cedric McAulay.

"Was that his excuse for being late?"

"No, he offered no excuse. I just know that. Derek was mad at me for being late, the way he figures. What happened with Boris?"

"What usually happens with Boris? Boris sat in my house. He watched me work out on my Health Strider. When I got off it, he tried to get on when I wasn't looking, and fell off on his face. Poor Boris! Why does he always pick the moment you're looking away? Finally his dad called, after he was through being with George, and then came and got him. You talked with Anthony today. Did he mention this George person?"

"No. You mean the guy he was conferring with?"

"Yeah. Must be his boss. He impresses Anthony, who would seem difficult to impress. The *idea* of me calling and wanting to talk to him while he was with *George*...well, he was trying to apologize for not taking the call, but that's how it came out."

"Maybe George is the head scientist on this mysterious project the Pownalls are in. I don't think Anthony wants people to know about that, judging from the way he talked about it yesterday. Judy, I wouldn't take him too seriously. He's a twit, and he's weird. How about Irina? Did he mention her? I think he said this morning she wasn't home much. What's up with her?"

"He did talk about Irina. Said she was with friends, some people she met. Probably she's staying with them, not just hanging out, or he wouldn't be in such a stew. 'These people,' he said, and he looked all pissy. Probably doesn't want her to have friends. Boris was playing with his shoe during all this. I thought he wasn't listening, but he asked, 'What friends?' Anthony just said, 'Let's go,' and yanked him away."

"He's a jerk. Boris is sweet. I think Irina cares about him."

"She's all right. She's doing her best. Better than some, like Derek Blake. Asshole! Pushed her into the car with his foot, you say? And what's with Diane?"

"I told you: having an affair."

"But how is she relating to Deirdre?"

"I don't know."

"You don't?"

"No! Judy, I don't know *her*. She's said ten words to me, at most."

"Sorry."

"No, I'm sorry."

"Well, I'm glad it's Friday."

That's right. It was Friday.

And then it was Sunday, with football on the television in the morning. After the game, around one, Aaron went out running and, two hours later, still hadn't come back. This was what he used to do on weekends, one day or the other, just take off and go for miles, sometimes walking most of the way back from places like Richmond or Emeryville. He wasn't sleeping much then, so that when he finally lurched back into the house after such an outing he looked as if he'd spent a ten-hour shift breaking up rocks. After a few months in therapy, he'd broken free of this routine, but Maren had had a feeling today, when he went out the door, that he was going to backslide. It was a shame. She wanted to garden, and he was good at planting things, could get them out of their pots and into the ground without traumatizing them—a strange talent for Aaron. Anyway, he wasn't here. Maren drove to the nursery and came back with some red and yellow chrysanthemums. She went into the back yard.

She was talking over the fence with Mr. Guignan when she

heard the front door slam. Then Aaron put his face to the kitchen window. Maren assumed that he didn't come out because he didn't want to chat with Mr. Guignan, who was a bit boring and sometimes rather incoherent. Nice, though. Eventually Aaron appeared and was all right, mostly ignoring their elderly neighbor, and doing all her planting. Mostly ignored her too, though. Shirtless, sweaty from the run, he became somewhat caked with dirt and looked damned primitive. Mr. Guignan became nervous and went in.

In the evening they walked up to Solano Avenue and had dinner at Cactus. Good Mexican food, made with Niman Ranch beef, but not Maren's first choice. A family place, it sometimes attracted school parents and kids down from their homes in the hills, and she just wasn't in the mood. "Look, Melody! Here's Maren!"—as if she were a rare bug who rarely strayed from her native grove or bush. And then they might want to conduct a mini-conference on the spot. But Cactus was fast: you got in line, ordered the food, and by the time you hit the register, your burritos were ready, or almost so. She didn't want Aaron to have to wait, didn't want to sit with him while he said nothing and kept turning his head, looking for the food so he could eat it and get out.

None of the school families came in. Aaron and Maren walked down Solano to Front Row Video, where they picked up a film, a drama set in Sarajevo; they hadn't heard of it, but it seemed interesting.

"If you do," Aaron said. "I'd like to see it."

"It doesn't sound funny." Aaron favored funny videos.

"Oh, let's try it. Looks fine to me."

Good for Aaron! He certainly hadn't been rude or crazy in Cactus, although he hadn't said much.

The movie was all blood. Everybody died. Maybe he liked it.

Finally, after that, he wanted to fuck. He asked her.

"If you do, sure."

"Really all right?"

She took her nightie off and put her arms around him in the bed. Soon she discovered that her old husband had some new ideas, new but not interesting.

He started with a series of nuzzles and lickings that were foreign to her experience and, as far as she knew, to his. She felt like a tooth being cleaned. After his last lick, he began shifting her around, putting her in various positions whose common characteristic was an awkward and extreme elevation of her buttocks. These he occasionally slapped or pinched.

"Ow," she said. "Will you not hurt me, please?"

At some point they actually had sex, as she understood it. She wasn't sure if he spent himself or not, but at least it was over, and he lay down next to her.

"How was that?" Aaron asked. His tone was dry, as if he sought some kind of numerical rating, a fartie for sex.

"Aaron," she said, couldn't help saying, "*what* was that?"

"Just trying," he said. It was too dark to see, but now he sounded as if his jaw were quivering. "Trying something new, just to get started again. Long time, you know."

"Yes," she said. "I know. But you didn't have to do any of that...that stuff. Just a—"

She didn't know what she wanted to say. Suddenly he grew loud: "Just a good, old, straight-on fuck, huh? That's the ticket, huh?"

"I don't know," she said, alarmed, confused.

HUMPA HUMPA HUMPA...suddenly, from outside, a monstrous drumming. No, a throbbing. Maren was glad of the distraction.

"Damn kids," she said, thankfully.

Just some teenagers in a car, with a really loud sound system. These noisy cars often pulled up on their street, no one knew why. Maybe to plan which party to hit next. They didn't stick around. She wondered about that red sports car she kept seeing during the day, but it never made any noise except with its motor.

HUMPA HUMPA HUMPA.

"Fuck fuck fuck!"

Aaron appeared to be dancing next to the bed, stomping up and down. "Not this time! No! I tell you fucking NO!"

And with that second thunderous "No," he rushed from the room.

In a moment, the throbbing suddenly ceased. Then she heard Aaron bellowing something about asses and kicking and little fuckers. Mr. Guignan's lights went on, probably a lot of other lights too. She heard a scream. Then the car blasted away in a hurry.

"Hah! Hah! That didn't take long. Didn't even give me an argument. Hah!"

Silent, Maren waited.

"Hey," he finally said, "I've got no clothes on. Oh, boy. Oh, boy."

"Yes," Maren said.

"Ahh," he said. "So? Hmm…well."

He had pulled the sheet back, revealing an equally unclothed Maren, Maren incredulous. When he put his hand on her right breast, she swiftly rolled from the bed and grasped her nightie. Turning her back on Aaron, she put it on.

"What? What?"

Over her shoulder, she said, "Put your bathrobe on, or something. I want to talk to you."

They went into the kitchen. Aaron gnawed a mango stick while she interrogated him.

"Are you still taking your Aetherion? You're not, are you?"

"No." He shook his head and, for some reason, closed his eyes. "Uh-uh."

"Well! So what does Jerry say? Did he say it was okay?"

Jerry was the shrink. She thought Aaron liked him.

"I sort of stopped with Jerry, so he doesn't know. I imagine it would be okay with him. He knew I didn't want to take that shit forever."

"You said it was all right to take it. You said you felt the same, just more stable."

"Short-term, yes. Long-term, no. I did feel different, not me, not myself. And I missed sex. You didn't, obviously. Well, I'll just have to accept that. But I would still like to try life without drugs, if it's okay with you."

She *did* miss sex, real sex, but knew he wouldn't listen. What could she say about anything that he'd listen to? She wasn't even sure if he was being ironic or not with that "if it's okay with you." Possibly his mood would be easier to interpret if she could see his eyes. She watched him chomp his mango. It looked like a slimy orange root.

"Can you take something else?" she asked. "Some other pill? Can you do something else?"

"Sure, probably. I'll look into it. See Jerry."

He sounded bored. Enough with him! "Well, do it!" she said. "You've been acting crazy."

"Really?" Finally, he opened his eyes. "Besides that one thing just now? Really?"

She wasn't sure, wasn't sure how bad he was getting. Maybe not so bad. The problem was that just recently he'd been the nice, new-model Aaron, and then, so quickly, she had the old one back, maybe even worse. Which made her think.

"Did you do it gradually? Or did you cut it off all at once?"

"My business."

"Oh, is it?"

"Yes, dammit! All at once. Cold turkey. I hate it!"

He got up from the table. "What do I do?" he said. "What the hell do I do?"

She had no idea. He had never been as bad as this, in the way of being unpredictable from moment to moment. It touched her, though, that he thought she might know. Poor Aaron.

"Go to sleep," she said.

"Oh, God. Me out here?" He pointed toward the living room, the couch.

"No, come to bed. But no, you know."

"Oh, no, no. Not after that."

"Come to bed. It's okay."

He flopped around in bed quite a bit, then got quiet. Sleeping, finally. Then, suddenly, it seemed, he leaped right out.

Maren, left alone, gradually realized she'd been asleep but had been awakened by something before Aaron had started up and shaken her into full consciousness. Then she knew it was the door bell, for it sounded again.

"Boy," Aaron said. Evidently he hadn't gone anywhere, he was standing by the bed. "I didn't expect this."

But, she thought, he'd expected something, a not quite this.

They rang again, whoever they were.

"Coming," he shouted

"Bathrobe," she called, her eyes still closed.

"Got it."

Maren got up and groped for her own robe. She was exhausted. "Fine Monday," she said, looking at the clock, which said 6:15. Cops rousting Aaron for his street mime of the night before? No, they wouldn't come this early, not in Berkeley, which demanded that police work be subtle and decorous.

She heard voices, one vaguely familiar, and then, quite distinctly, Aaron saying, "Sparkle?"

Sparkle?

This was followed by a dismal bray: "Haw-haw." Worse than hyip-hyip. She walked out of the bedroom.

Looking around Aaron's broad back, Maren beheld a tall, fattish, sixtyish man. A few papery, crimson blooms from their bougainvillaea had drifted down upon his hairless dome and stuck.

"Haw-haw. Well, anyway, we're here. Sorry about the hour. I thought we'd stop on the road, but we didn't. Eli, Eli, I'm so glad to see you. And grateful." The man winked at Aaron, then commented, "They have no Peet's coffee in Las Vegas."

"It's Aaron," said Aaron. "Maybe you should go see Eli, whoever he may be."

"Maren! What are you doing here?" Diane Blake, Hillside School mom, had appeared from behind the fat man's back.

"Diane! Diane, I live here. My house."

"You live...this is your *house*? Why, that's amazing! Deirdre just loves you! But do you think she's entering in enough? She only talks about this Boris. Is he real or did she make him up?"

"Come in, come in," Maren said, and Aaron backed up a bit, giving their callers just enough room to get into the house. So now Aaron was standing next to her in their little entryway, facing the dean of the Whartonians, Cedric McAulay, while she was lined up opposite big-eyed, ebon-banged, petite, stupid Diane. Cute gazed on cute, or perhaps cuter, being younger. Aaron, though considerably younger than Cedric, was too big to be cute and looked, in fact, quite grumpy.

Aaron began talking to her. He didn't seem to care that their guests, for it appeared that he had invited them, could hear every word he said.

"I told him they could come. Just to regroup before they went home to face their spouses. Cedric e-mailed me from Vegas, and I e-mailed him back, said okay. Should have asked you. Trying to do myself some good. So now I have to sparkle."

"You will, you will," assured Cedric.

Maren didn't understand about "sparkle," but she could see that it had Aaron upset. He might indulge himself in a major fuss-fuss. He might not. She couldn't tell what he might do. There was absolutely nothing she could think of that he might *not* do. And they had a parent here.

Aaron more or less grasped her concern. Ignoring Cedric, he said, "Now I've embarrassed you, because of her."

He pointed at Diane, who blinked at his large finger.

Maren tugged his arm down. "I'm not embarrassed," she said, softly, and then: "Come in! Put your pack down, Diane. I'll make coffee. Peet's house blend okay?"

"Oh, thanks, dear. Karen, dear Karen."

"Ma—" corrected Maren, cut off by a big smack from the big Whartonian, always a kissing fool, she now recalled.

"Ugh!" said Cedric, whom, while recalling his penchant for kisses, she had reflexively kneed in the balls.

"Foo," said Maren, again without thinking. He tasted like dirty rubber. "Sorry," she added. "God, I'm so sorry!"

Cedric seemed to be making an effort to smile. "My fault," he said, wheezily. She knew she hadn't gotten him hard. Aaron didn't laugh, as she had feared he might. She steered Diane and Cedric to the kitchen table and started coffee. "How was Las Vegas?" she asked.

Cedric said it was great. "Dismal," opined Diane.

Maren joined Aaron in their bedroom. He was sitting on the bed, with his hands on his knees. They were shaking a bit, either the hands or the knees or both.

"Patronizing asshole," he whispered. "He told me he'd put my essay on *The House of Mirth*, this close-reading thing I've had around for years, in his next Wharton book. That's got to help with the farties, right? He just wanted to regroup here, he said. So he shows up at dawn—I'd figured by now he wasn't coming at all. I was glad! Fuck him! Fuck farties!"

His whispering had grown emphatic. "Easy, Aaron," she said.

"And the first thing he says to me is, do I have anything else? He doesn't like the old one any more. 'Surely you must have something with a little more sparkle. Haw-haw.' Sparkle, my ass. I'm glad you got him in the nuts."

"No, we just moved at the same time. Look, Aaron, I know you're upset, but you don't really want to alienate this guy. You'll feel bad if you do. Be nice!"

"Ah, he'll never give me anything."

"He might. At least he won't go out of his way to screw you. And there's Deirdre to consider."

"Deirdre? You mean Diane."

"Deirdre is Diane's child at school, and this mess with her parents is very bad for her. This crazy affair. I don't need you erupting, making things worse. Don't…just don't say anything to them! Just get your overalls on and leave. I'm sorry, Aaron, but I have no idea what you're going to do next."

"You think I'm as dumb as he is," he said.

"Don't you have brown sugar?" Diane Blake from the kitchen.

"No, Diane. Sorry! No, he's so dumb he's amazing. No one could be as dumb, I would have thought. But let them regroup, okay? And then they can get out of here. They have the coffee, they go. Poor Deirdre."

Aaron puffed up his cheeks and blew the air out, signaling reluctant consent. He went to shower. She gave the professor and his student half a grapefruit each, at their request, Diane still moaning about the brown sugar, still wanting to confer. She told her Boris was real, who his parents were. Diane was quite surprised. "Those people," she said. "The mammalian biologists. They're Deirdre's friend's parents?"

"Yes, he's so nice." Maren guessed it was biology they did. She didn't remember either Pownall ever saying, exactly. Odd that this English graduate student, such a silly little thing, would know, would care.

"Aaron!" Cedric, able to breathe freely again, calling out to his fellow, if lesser, Whartonian, who was back in the bedroom, banging around. "When are you going to show me that article, the one I *know* you can write? Can't wait to see it! Eh? Why are you dressed like that?"

Monday was a taping day. Aaron had emerged, clad as the rustic Tale Spinner. "We got a little farm at State," he said. "To supplement our miserable wage. We're manuring today. Nope, nope."

Didn't want the coffee Maren hurriedly offered, to distract him. Didn't want a grapefruit half. But at least he was silent. He opened the fruit jar and extracted three large phallic slivers of dried papaya; they were out of mango. Maren had to shower. As she left the kitchen, she heard Diane. "Are you really Maren's husband?"

"Yes!"

"A farm? We should have a farm at Berkeley, but I guess we're all too busy with research. Those women who keep harassing me…they should be working on a farm. Milkmaids. Right, Diane? Haw-haw."

Maybe all Whartonians were a bit dim, although Cedric was more than a bit. Another dismal haw-haw. He didn't sound too sprightly. Then Maren turned the water on and so missed Diane's reply, if there was one.

When she and Aaron were about to leave for work, Diane was in the bathroom, Cedric still at the table in the kitchen. He appeared to be asleep. They had made a deal; that is, she had made it with Diane. Wash up, change clothes (they had all their stuff in a white 4X4 in front of the house) and then, please go. She hoped they would do it. The parents didn't always take the teachers seriously. There had been that issue about Deirdre bringing soup: "Yes, I read the note," Diane had told Judy, "but I just didn't believe…"

Maren stepped out the front door. She saw four deer and was amazed.

Sweet and hot. The smell came out of her house like an evil

guest. She walked in, got in the middle of it, and then couldn't smell it any more. And then she couldn't hear either. Not anything. There were cars running up and down the street, there always were, but she couldn't hear them, or the loud ticking of the wall clock when she walked into the kitchen. If you could call it walking. Gravity had increased; she was clumping. I couldn't run, she thought. She looked at the clock, which said 2:35, watched the second hand sweeping across its face. Then she lowered her gaze.

A chair was knocked over on its side. There was blood on the floor, all dried up, staining the wood. It had run under the fridge. Half of the body, the top half, was under the table. Somehow she thought it was Diane, but no, obviously, not with those large shoes: black sneakers of some kind, old man's shoes, with crusted blood. She knew the blood was the smell.

Maren bent her knees, slowly, feeling very old herself. Peering beneath the table, she regarded the top half of Professor Cedric McAulay. She regarded his broad stomach, ballooning down over his khaki trousers, which might have been partway unzipped. She regarded the roundness of his head, its top half, the crown, for the whole of it appeared somehow folded down upon the neck. As if, without moving his right shoulder, he had managed somehow to apply his rubbery lips to that. There was that and that: Cedric...he was just parts now. She remembered how he'd kissed her that morning, when she was telling him her name was Maren, not Karen, and jerked up, lightly tapping her head on the bottom of the table. She was under it, on her knees.

Why am I under the table? What is this woman doing under the table? Feeling the dried blood under her knees making them sticky.

The professor's head was folded down in that funny way because the back of his neck had been deeply, savagely, cut. Chopped, cleaved, but not tidily, the way a skilled executioner might do it, although the man's head was practically off. She reached out, not thinking; all she could think about, at that moment, was the cougar. She saw him nosing the bits of apple in the street.

Maren touched Cedric's chin, felt beard bristles. TOCK-TOCK-TOCK. Something went by in the street outside, a roaring circus truck full of roaring animals. Her refrigerator cut loose with a growl. The hot, sweet smell hit her in the face. She crept backward, made it out from under the table before she suddenly felt too hot and sticky to move.

She realized, with wonder, that she was going to pass out.

Chapter Three

She just wanted to say it, but the 911 operator wanted her name and address, with the cross street.

"All right, then," the operator said. "Now. Describe the situation."

"I have a dead person in my house. In the kitchen."

"You have a dead person. Yes. And otherwise you are alone."

How did she know? There seemed to be no reason to say anything back. Why did they still have a phone with a cord? It only let her go a few feet out of the kitchen. Angling her head, she managed to peer down the short hallway from the dining room, where she was standing, and glimpse a bit of the street through the living room window. Framed in it was a neighbor man talking to his dogs, who were too low for Maren to see. He and his wife had a flock of five or six collies, long-nosed, gentle animals. Suddenly the neighbor was gone.

The 911 operator said, "Oh, that one. You're covered. We got it covered. Hello?"

Maren pushed the button down, got rid of her. Then she pushed it again, picked out a number she was surprised she knew.

A woman answered. "Tammy speaking."

Aaron had mentioned that State had hundreds of part-time teachers now: as soon as a regular faculty member stepped out of his office, a lecturer would pop in and hold office hours.

"Aaron. Is Aaron there?"

"The guy who has this office? Matthews?"

"Yes. That's...yup."

"Uh, I haven't seen him today. But I have on other Mondays, and I think he said this is about when he videotapes his kids show, in the pee em. I do a show too. 'Climax with Tammy'? Good sex."

"Good sex. Yes."

"Want the studio number?"

It turned out that clever Tammy knew not only the television studio number but also how to transfer calls, a skill unknown to Aaron. Thick Aaron, who likes phones the way they used to be, and, it turns out, isn't in the studio either.

Yeah, he was supposed to be. This was the taping time for Aaron the Tale Spinner. Yeah, we had the hay all ready. Maren had once seen a tape; he'd brought home several. He and the kids sat on bales of hay. But over the weekend Aaron had called and left a message saying he couldn't make it. So they called the kids, Marcelline and the Nunez boys, and called it off. You there?

"Yes."

"You're welcome."

The guy hung up, or maybe she did. Cedric's body made a sound, a sort of shlup, as if rolling over soggily. She couldn't see under the table. The phone dangled by its cord.

When she got outside, the cops were already there. She bumped right into one of them. Door left open behind her, walking as fast as she could—would have been running but her feet were stones—she tried to get around him. But he was a very wide man, if rather short, huge in the shoulders. She found herself pressing her nose into his white shirt. After that, he was holding her.

"Hey, hey," he said, sympathetically. "Maren. Maren, it's me."

"Just go in," she said. "Jimmie, Jimmie. It's in the kitchen. Jimmie?"

She had thought he was all done with this, with police work.

He said something to one of the two uniformed cops he had with him. There were three Berkeley police cars in front of her

house, blue ones for the cops, while Jimmie's detective car was
tan.

"You, Steingroot," Jimmie ordered. "Handle this woman."

"Don't want to be handled!"

"Well then, could you just stand here with the officer while I
see what's inside?"

She didn't see where she had a choice. Suddenly his broad
back was poised in the doorway. It caused her distress, this seeing people framed, like still shots, and missing the motion, the
process, from shot to shot.

"Hi, dear," said Officer Steingroot, suddenly right next to her,
an African-American woman somewhat younger than Maren.
"Would you like to sit in the car?"

"Wait," Maren answered. She looked around, saw the light
bands on top of the blue cars flashing, saw the people on the
sidewalk. The man with the flock of collies, all gracefully reclin-
ing. Other locals, including several neighborhood kids. She
knew the names, but that was all. Old Mr. Guignan was standing on his own lawn. He appeared to be holding a rifle at port
arms. He was easily frightened, she knew.

Maren pointed out the rifle to Steingroot, who said, "What
the hell!" and marched next door. She ordered Mr. Guignan into
his house.

Now Maren realized she was seeing normally again, not in
those jerks. People were moving. At the moment, they were
moving away, because Steingroot and the other cop, a big man,
taller than Jimmie, though not as wide, were ordering them to
decamp.

"Okay, one more time, dear. Wanna sit in the car?"

"No, thanks."

Maren was thinking, trying to think, about Jimmie, Jimmie
Greenlee the detective. He wasn't that anymore, she had
thought, but here he was, inside her house with Cedric, all in
blood. She saw Cedric's head with crimson bougainvillaea blossoms pasted to it. No! She shook her own head so hard that her
neck made a little snap.

"Hey," said Steingroot.

"No," Maren said. "Please." She didn't want to go sit in the car, not with all the neighbors watching. She was thinking about Jimmie. Yes. That was better, tricky but better. He was an old boyfriend from college, but the relationship was sort of funny because Jimmie was African-American, and that wasn't quite normal then, even in Berkeley. Another thing was that Aaron was supposed to be her boyfriend at the time.

It annoyed her that Steingroot was holding her wrist, but there wasn't much she could do about it. Eventually the cop let go.

Maren saw Jimmie walking slowly out of her house and tracked him—he didn't even look at her—to his detective car, where he got on the radio. And then, with a terrible look on his face, he virtually jumped out of the car and jogged back into the house. Steingroot called out to him, but he just waved.

Jimmie had come back into her life, Aaron's too, when they had a murder up in the school, a parent, not a kid. After being a pro football player, and some other things, Jimmie had become a cop. At first she thought she still had feelings for him, but then she discovered she didn't. Although Aaron and he hadn't been friendly in the old days—she had never been sure how much Aaron knew then about her and Jimmie—they seemed to bond, in an oafish, male way, while the murder was being settled. They didn't stay friends for long. Jimmie stopped being a Berkeley PD detective and became a psychotherapist, specializing in masculine guys like himself, cops and jocks, who needed to get in touch with their feelings. Maybe Aaron and Jimmie fell out because, when Aaron needed a shrink, he didn't consult Jimmie, or perhaps he had, but was turned down as not being macho enough. That would piss Aaron off. Where was Aaron?

Jimmie. Jimmie was a detective again.

"This is a bad one. This is one hell of a bad one. Go, do it."

Jimmie, standing next to her on her lawn, was talking to several men wearing windbreakers that said Berkeley PD on the back. One had a camera slung around his neck and was carrying several boxes of something, some kind of equipment.

"The techs," Jimmie said. He was wearing a gray suit himself, his standard detective suit, and seemed to have a bit more gray in his hair, on the sides, than the last time. His eyes looked big through the lenses of his glasses. He was getting old, she thought. She smiled at him, and he stared at her, for a moment, as if she'd lost her reason.

"My car, okay?" She went. He opened the back door for her, then sat down in the front seat, the passenger's side, twisting himself around so that he could see her. They left the car doors open, onto the sidewalk.

He asked, "What am I doing, doing this again? You want to know?"

Maybe she did. He thought she did. "Okay," he said. "I had retreat rights when I quit, and it turned out I had to use them. The therapy business went bad. The insurance companies won't pay. They think we're all Freudians, which is ridiculous, and Freud's finished. Well, everyone knows about Freud."

She didn't.

"Now it's all drugs."

That she knew about, from Aaron.

"I'm not an M.D., so I can't prescribe drugs. I know all about them, the new serotonin adjusters, which some of the psychiatrists don't. They have to look them up in the manual. My hard luck. When I started averaging two clients a week, I came back to the department. It was embarrassing, and they weren't real glad to see me. So, how are you?"

"Fine."

"Aaron?"

"Fine. He's at school right now. What are we doing?"

"What? Oh, you mean talking? I thought you wanted to know about me. I'm sorry."

For a moment they just sat. Jimmie was so big that Maren couldn't very well see around him; nor was she really trying to, but she kept noticing all this vehicular motion, over his shoulder, through the windshield. Another tan car, like his, and a couple of vans. Looking to the side, she saw a crew of men in white uniforms who were pushing a gurney toward her front door. A cop came out and stopped them. Then he walked to the car, leaned in, and whispered something to Jimmie.

"Okay," the detective said. He had a hard time levering himself out of the car, being so broad.

A man in gray coveralls walked by Jimmie's car, saw her in there and handed her a printed card. She read:

TI-DEE CRIME SCENE SERVICE
1-800-392-6530

GREETINGS

**Ti-Dee Crime Scene Service is a specialized cleaning agency for biohazard, be it accident, suicide, or homicide.
We are PROUD of our success in eliminating the unpleasant odor associated with DECOMPOSITION.**

Maren dropped the card in the gutter. Across the street she saw the Ti-Dee Crime Scene van, and on the lawn, getting quite a trampling, the Ti-Dee crew, in gray, talking with the ambulance guys, in white. Jimmie came out of her house. He didn't get in the car, just squatted down on the sidewalk. She pointed at the van.

"They're early," he said. "They're good. And the city pays for it. A service. Do you guys have a dog now, or what?"

"They're going to clean my kitchen?"

"Yes, when I tell them to. But there's this paw-print on the floor I just noticed, a partial, like two-thirds of a paw. Do you have a dog now?"

"No. The print's in blood?"

"Yeah. Yes, it is."

"So some dog...some animal got in there after he was killed."

"Some animal? What else? The paw of a fairly large dog. Yeah, Maren. After, or during. So we'll ask around and see if anyone saw someone walking a dog."

"Everyone walks dogs around here. There's a guy who has five. I just saw them."

"It's a lead, okay? Why are you always so—no, forget it. Let's talk about him, the guy, the victim. He has Cal faculty ID that says he's Cedric McAulay, from the English Department. That's who it is? All right. So, what was he doing in your house? Wait, I'm coming into the car."

Jimmie sat down with her in the back, after she moved over. He was so big. Seated next to him, she couldn't tell that he was short and felt, herself, the size of a child.

In about six sentences Maren told Jimmie who Cedric McAulay was, why he had come to their house, and whom he had been with.

She then said, "Oh. Where's Diane? Diane Blake. Oh, no."

"She's okay," Jimmie said, quickly. "She's okay. We got her."

"Got?"

"Yeah, one of the traffic units stopped her for erratic driving, thought she was drunk. She was having hysterics, really. She told us that a guy was dead, all this blood, couldn't remember where. But she gave your name, and they looked it up. Then they sent me, and after that your 911 came in. I was just told."

"I called," she said. "I called as soon as I could."

"Right. Now she's—Diane Black?"

"Blake."

"She's been talking about it. That's what they wanted me for just then. She went away by herself, leaving McAulay, who was taking a nap. She went to see her husband. I don't get this. He wasn't home; she thinks he was out in some marsh, a wetlands. That's where he is now, maybe. So she came back here between noon and one, it seems, and she saw the guy, saw the body. Then she drove, just drove around."

"Poor Diane."

"The sergeant says she's all broken up, she's trying to comfort her. We may have to take her to the emergency room. She's just a kid."

"Well, no. Not quite. She's a mother at our school, believe it or not."

"Yes, she told Sergeant Hata you were her child's teacher. 'She lives in that house,' she kept saying. Appeared to amaze her."

Thinking about Diane, Maren made no response. She wasn't sure what to think. All broken up? Maybe, but maybe not.

"She tell the sergeant why she and Cedric were here?"

"You call him Cedric. How well did you know him?"

"Just met him once before. Aaron knew him slightly."

"Aaron did, huh?"

"Yeah, slightly. Professionally. But you knew why they were here, yes? They came from Las Vegas."

"I know what she said. Now I'm asking you."

"Are you? Jimmie, I don't like this! I don't like this…this playing around. You did it last time."

She meant the murder case at the school. Jimmie lied in that, to her and to others. He was extremely sneaky, that old boyfriend, even though he claimed later to have had good reason.

Jimmie didn't get it. "Last time? What last time? Look, I didn't talk to her. Sergeant Hata did, and she told me. I know essentially what Diane—Diane? okay—what Diane said, which is essentially what you said. Yeah, Vegas, which seems odd for an English professor. I'm corroborating. You get one story, you get another, you put them together. That's what I liked about therapy; of course, in the therapeutic encounter one person's telling all the stories. Hey, wait."

Maren was getting out of the car. She didn't wait.

"You people! Get the hell out of my yard!"

There weren't as many as before. Only the Ti-Dee Crime guys, who were smoking and leaning against her house. The ambulance guys must have gone inside.

"So where do we go? They called us early," said "Al," according to the name over his breast pocket.

The ambulance guys suddenly thundered out of her front door, two on either end of the gurney. It bore a large strapped-down bulk under a sheet, a sheet so white it seemed to blaze. The techs emerged right behind them, carrying their stuff. "All right," one said. "We got it all."

"Hey, lady," Al said. "Just want to get to it, okay?"

"The longer that odor sits," elaborated a colleague, "the harder it is to get out."

"Wait, wait." Jimmie. They looked wounded, such an eager bunch.

"I want one more look," he said to them, and then he said, to her, "Can you go in there too? Maybe you'll notice something."

Maren was surprised by the clutter on the floor, a couple of broken plates and cups, two spoons, a scattering of paper napkins. There had been a small pile on the table; she made a lot of fajitas that generated drip. Some of the napkins were crusted, with blood. At first she felt dully angry at the technicians for making this mess; then she realized it must have been there all the time and that she just hadn't seen it. She asked Jimmie what she was supposed to be looking for.

"Is there anything you can't explain? Anything weird?"

This isn't weird? But she knew what he meant. Big, important things, not that she could imagine anything he wouldn't notice, too. A message on the wall in gore: "Fascist termite!"

"Nope," she said. "Nothing."

"The weapon, the weapon. We're interested in that. Whoever did this couldn't have done it with anything small. So I gotta ask you."

He stopped. "Go ahead," she said. "Just don't be cute, that's all."

"Oh, Maren. Okay. Do you own a very large knife or cleaver?"

A cleaver? For a moment she imagined herself hacking up sides of beef. All she had was a large knife, which she never used, the largest knife in her rack. She pointed at it.

"Well, maybe. I mean it might be possible, but I doubt it."

He took a handkerchief from his pants pocket and used it to slide the knife out of the rack. "Looks a little funky," he mused. "As if it had been sitting there for a while. No, I don't think so. Too small. How about tools, something on the order of an axe? See, whoever did this used something pretty big, and it's more probable that he found it here than that he walked in with it slung over his shoulder. Not that that's impossible. So, what do you have here? Aaron must have some tools around."

Jimmie walked into the living room. What, did he think that Aaron had a work bench out there with a collection of huge planes and drills? The detective seemed to have a new way of

walking, as if it hurt him to put his feet down. He was also getting a belly, she had noticed, and seemed to lack dash. He'd had
plenty of dash, but now he struck her as prissy. Absently, Maren
gazed down at the floor; she was standing next to a plate-sized
splotch of dried blood. Aaron would be home soon. Screwed-up as
he seemed to be, she didn't want him to see this mess. Didn't
much like it herself.

She called out to Jimmie: "Hey, can they clean now?"

"Yeah, how about it?" One of the Ti-Dee guys, calling from the
front.

Jimmie's voice came from the rear of the house, possibly the
yard. "What? Oh, yeah. Go, do it! Maren, don't you have any gardening tools?"

The guys piled in. She went out—he was in the yard—and led
him into the garage. The side door was just a few steps from the
back door to the house. They stepped around the litter, much of
it consisting of boxes of books unread in decades. No cars. Their
garage had never had room for a car. They stood before some
shelves attached to the wall with brackets and screws.

"This stuff here is just bottles and other little crap," he said.
"Well, here's a spike thing, for weeds, it must be, but it's way too
small, and...ow! Dammit. Maren, could you help me move this
can? My back's no good this week."

She helped him push aside a small garbage can, next to the
shelves, full of little rocks that Aaron once thought he needed
for some project involving drainage. As they pushed, several
large, clunky objects, having been propped against the can, gradually descended to the concrete floor. When they touched down,
they clanked. A shovel, a pick, a maul, which resembled the pick
but had a broader blade. She remembered a cursing, sweating
Aaron battering a tree stump with it, long ago. It seemed to her
most unlikely that whoever did this had had the cool to take one
of these big things, do what he did, then return it, pushing the
can back so that everything appeared just as it always did.
Jimmie looked at them anyway, without picking them up.

"There's dirt on this one." He was pointing at the maul. "Been
gardening?"

"Yeah, yesterday."

"He must have had the weapon with him," he said. "It doesn't have to be that big. Something like a machete would do it, especially if he was a big, strong guy."

Jimmie bent over, very slowly, to pick up the tools.

"Let them lie," Maren said.

She noticed that the lid on the can of rocks was sitting askew; she was going to push it on straight, but Jimmie was leaving the garage. She hurried after him.

They walked past the Ti-Dee crew, scrubbing like lost souls condemned to cleanse a kitchen in hell. Jimmie sat in his car and did something. Maren sank down on the stone steps in front of her house, beneath the door. The man with the dogs came walking down the street, without his dogs. Mr. Guignan appeared, without his gun. Kids on bikes.

"What?" Maren said to this mute assemblage. "What?"

But she didn't say it loudly. When Jimmie came back out to her, they all moved away again. Maren got up.

While sitting on the steps, which were cold and hard, she had thought: Jimmy said, "Whoever did this"—that's wrong. There was a killer here. We should say, "the killer".

She was sitting with Jimmie in the living room, having just gone through it all for the third time. Everything she knew, anything that would make sense to him. She was drinking wine, a fancy Chardonnay they had, given to her by one of the Hillside School families last year. The grapes came from the family's vineyard. Ti-Dee Crime had done their job and taken off. Probably they had done it very well. She hadn't been in the kitchen yet.

She wanted to find out about Diane. How was Diane? Pretty shocky, probably. And what was it that Diane had said about all this? Jimmie said he didn't know exactly, because he hadn't talked to her, just to Sergeant Hata, and briefly.

"Did she say when Diane came back here and found him?"

"Around twelve o'clock. Maren, I think I have everything. I think I can go."

He got up. She motioned to him to sit down, but he kept standing.

"What about the threats? You know about the threats?"

"'Essentialist'? 'Termite'? Yeah, they filled me in." He laughed, he had a stupid chuckle. "Oh, we'll check that out with the University Police, possibly. This doesn't sound like a post-post-modern job to me."

"You know about that?"

"Sure. Minor pain in the ass. Rallies."

Rallies? Maren wasn't sure if post-postmodern meant to him what she thought it meant to her. They were feminists, yes? She wasn't sure, not sure of anything. What the hell were she and Jimmie talking about? For a moment, sitting there in her own house with a man she used to know extremely well, Maren asked herself whether she might be dreaming. It was so embarrassing, this hackneyed question, but she couldn't easily make it go away. The deer in the morning, long ago, the rabbit, the cougar. Maybe the cougar was a dream. Should she tell Jimmie? Detective, a suggestion: possibly the cougar I saw in the hills, if I didn't dream it, got all the way down where I live and killed an Edith Wharton expert. What do you think?

"No, no."

"What? You okay, Maren? I have to leave now, really."

Of course cougars didn't do that; she knew they killed people once in a while, tore them up, but not in houses, not in kitchens. But didn't Jimmie already think that the killer had walked in with a dog? Let's go in here a minute, Bosco; I have to kill somebody. That was almost as dreamy. She didn't like this.

"She got back here around twelve?" Maren asked. "Is that what you said?"

He was standing by the door. "That's what Hata told me she said."

"And Aaron and I left around eight, so it happened in those four hours or so. You can ask the neighbors if they noticed anything. The kids are all in school, of course, and everyone else goes to work, I think. There's him." She pointed through the window at the neighboring house. "Mr. Guignan. But he sleeps a lot, he says."

"Ask the neighbors? Don't worry, we're canvassing now. In fact, we're probably done by now. If anything important had shown up, I would have been told. But this isn't the end of it: people often remember things later. We'll keep coming around. Guignan the old coot with the rifle? Yeah? Hey. Don't you do any poking around, asking the neighbors and conducting your own little investigation. Just screws things up."

"I have no intention. I don't even know most of them."

"Get back to you soon. Don't go anywhere, okay?"

"Jimmie, don't go yet. Wait, the kitchen."

She wanted him around when she went in there. For Aaron. Aaron had to eat. Jimmie shrugged, and she entered the kitchen, observed her floor. Seemed fine. Smelled fine, looked fine. Good work by Ti-Dee.

"Okay," she said, coming out. "It's all right. You can go, Jimmie. Bye."

But Jimmie seemed confused. Instead of taking his leave, he simply waited by the door, which at that moment opened, almost clipping him. Thud! Down crashed the briefcase, shaking the room. Before them stood Aaron, in his overalls, looming like some redneck wrestler from the golden age of television.

"Ti-Dee Crime Scene Service? Odor of decomposition? Greenlee? Greenlee! Maren, what the hell is this?"

"Hey," Jimmie said. "Aaron, man."

"Hey what? You a cop again? The guy with the dogs was out there. He told me there was big trouble. What the fuck is this with the card on the door from Ti-Dee?"

He waved the card.

"Ti-Dee! A joke? What?"

"Aaron," Maren said. "Just sit down."

"All right." He deposited himself on the bench. Maren glanced at Jimmie, who seemed to be contemplating Aaron, taking him in. Now it seemed to her that he hadn't really wanted to leave, but had been waiting for Aaron. She never was sure about Jimmie. Although he sometimes acted dumb, he wasn't. And once, a long time ago, Aaron had scared him, probably without knowing it. Aaron could seem...could give an unsettling impression. They made each other nervous, something they handled with a show of male-bonding, macho bullshit that made *her* nervous.

Jimmie explained. He was professionally concise.

"I don't believe this," Aaron said. What else would anyone say? Then he went on for a bit. "You're telling me, you're saying, Cedric got killed in here, in the kitchen? Who could have done it? Oh, this is absurd! Good God! Where's Diane? Where's Diane?"

He seemed genuinely concerned about Diane. They were able to assuage his fears. He gulped a glass of wine. He went into the kitchen and looked around.

"Everything seems okay. Right?"

"You mean our stuff? Yeah. Right."

"Aw, fuck. What a day! I wish those people had never come over."

Jimmie sat down at the dinner table. She joined him. The detective cleared his throat. "Professor McAulay was an English professor at Cal. Maren said he was a Wharton specialist. First name Edith, right? Yeah, I remember her. Some survey I took once. You know, if I'm not mistaken, you do Wharton too."

"Sure, that's why I knew him. That's why he and Diane Blake were here. She was his grad student."

"Maren said. She explained."

"She tell you about those threats? Crazy people, couldn't think they really meant anything. Good God."

Walking past Jimmie and herself, he didn't look at them. In the living room, Aaron let himself drop heavily upon the couch. He seemed to be comprehending, finally. Death in their house. But Aaron wouldn't know how horrible. She was the one who had to see it, while he was at school teaching and taping. But he hadn't taped.

There were some shrieks outside, distant, down at the junior high field. The ululations of young female warriors. Bemused, Aaron didn't seem to hear them, but Jimmie turned his head.

"Soccer," Maren said. "Girls' soccer."

"Really? What do they want, blood? I never heard guys sound like that. Say, Aaron!"

"Uh, what?"

"What's with the...uh?"

Man talk. She noticed that Jimmie was plucking at his own lapels. Apparently it went against the rules to use words to ask why another guy was wearing whatever he was wearing. Of course, she was wondering too. Why today?

"Oh, these overalls," Aaron said. "I do a kids' show at school, in our cable station. I'm supposed to be kind of a country type, you know. Doing it for farties."

"Farties? You mean, like for kicks?"

"No, a raise. Not that I don't enjoy it."

"How was it today?" Maren asked. "What happened today?"

"Oh, it went okay. Ah, no. I'm all mixed up by this. We didn't do it. We didn't tape today."

Aaron rubbed his head with the palm of his left hand, then scratched his head with his fingers. He let the hand drop into his lap. He looked stupid, extra stupid.

"They cancelled," he said. "Don't know why."

"Oh," she said.

"Last minute."

Aaron sat on the couch, mute. Somehow, as Maren watched, his thick eyebrows and the hair down on his brow appeared to be growing closer together. She had a feeling he was about to emit a mighty burp.

Jimmie broke the silence. "Hey, Aaron. Somebody pop ya? You got a ding under your eye."

That brightened him up. "I do? Hah! Let me check that out."

He got up, headed, presumably, for the bathroom, where the light was good. But he wouldn't need the good light. The mark was pretty conspicuous, a red spot under his left eye; Maren had noticed it when he came in the door, but hadn't thought about it. An irritation, she would have said. But when Jimmie said that about someone popping him, she saw that the mark didn't really look like an ordinary skin problem. Something made it.

Aaron was back; he pulled up a chair and sat at the table.

"Well, I guess I got that last night. Making a fool out of myself with those kids. There were these damn kids with the humpa humpa noise in the car, in front of the house, so I got pissed. Went out there."

He'd begun this explanation by talking to Maren, then switched to Jimmie. Now, pausing, he gazed at Jimmie, as if expecting a sympathetic response, like "I know, I know. Sometimes a man is just pushed too durn far."

When Jimmie said nothing, Aaron went on. "Well, there was no fight. They took off, that's all. And then, then I walked into the damn school crossing sign. The one with the two little kids? I thought I'd fucking blinded myself."

He waited so that Jimmie could say, perhaps, "Well, we all do stupid things. Long as you're okay."

Instead, Detective Greenlee replied, "Was that you out there, dancing around? We got a complaint on that. Two lesbian lawyers. They live in your neighborhood. Said a naked man was shouting homophobic epithets at them in the street."

Maren couldn't help herself. "Aaron, really!"

"I did not," he said, stoutly. "I didn't shout any epithets at all."

"They also said you were seven feet tall and black."

"Well, see?"

"I should arrest you, huh-huh."

"Go ahead, dude."

He didn't sound mad; he sounded amused, as if he knew Jimmie, who was laughing in his stupid way, was just kidding. She wasn't sure, though. Jimmie could be a very tricky guy. As for Aaron, who she wouldn't have thought possessed a secret or even an opacity in his entire personality, now she wasn't even sure about him. That damned Aetherion!

"I would, I'd haul you in, but you'd get a lawyer who would claim you were doing some kind of ritual dance in the street. In this town, you'd probably end up screwing—I mean suing—the lawyers, the lesbians, for desecration."

"Really?" Maren asked.

"Oh, we get those, we get those. Naked people all the time. Broad daylight, usually. Dancing on Telegraph Avenue. But you gotta watch it with the epithets. Then I'd have to come down on you."

"I did not use any epithets, okay? I think I said fuckers."

"That's okay."

"All right. God, now I feel embarrassed. I thought they were punky kids. Kind of funny, though, huh-huh."

"Huh-huh. Aaron, fuck."

"Jimmie, man."

They were bonding. They were bonding! She hated that. A cop and an English teacher. Was it because of McAulay? Does violent death make men feel closer together? Do they like it somehow? If she were to hear other women asking these questions, she would have thought they were stupid. Post-postmodern feminism, she would have thought.

Now both men were looking at her; they seemed to be beaming, as if assuming she'd approve of their toughness. Or worse. They were almost the only men she'd ever slept with, and each knew about the other. No, not that. Probably not.

"Got what you want?" she said, abruptly.

They looked at each other. Then Jimmie said, "Who, me?"

"Obviously you."

"Well, yeah. I think for now I'm done. I think, also, we're having a little hysteria here, after what happened. That's normal. It's a form of post-traumatic stress disorder, in the short term. And it can crop up later, in the long term."

"What are you doing," Aaron asked, "scaring up business?"

Aside from looking pained, Jimmie ignored the question. He told them that they would have to stay in town, if they had happened to have planned otherwise. They hadn't, but they didn't say so. At least she hadn't. Jimmie said they would be interviewed again. He said goodbye.

"He," said Aaron, "is a bit of a prick, you know."

Later on they saw two men stalking around in front of the house with videocams on their shoulders. Aaron, now wearing jeans and a T-shirt instead of his Tale Spinner outfit, declined to go out and chase them off. "I'm in enough trouble already," he said obscurely. The collie people came out, both the man and the woman this time, with their dogs, and the cameramen taped them. At some point everybody left. It got dark, and the house was dead quiet.

Aaron graded papers. She sat, hoping for a call from Brooke, but knowing that she wouldn't tell her about this crazy business today, the dead man in the kitchen. Maybe it would be in the news on television, but probably not in San Diego. Brooke didn't call. Nobody did. How solitary she and Aaron were! No brothers, no sisters. All four of their parents gone. They had friends, each of them had, from work, but the friends didn't know one another.

"I called you today," she said, "after I came home and found him. Talked to Tammy."

"Tammy? Oh, just a sec."

He put a grade on a paper, probably a C-, his standard grade.

"Hardly know her. We're always in the office at different times, and in the studio too. She does a sex ed show. I see the crap around, the vibrators and whatnot."

"I called the studio, and you weren't there."

"That's right. I wasn't. These papers!" He waved a sheaf of them at her. "Worse than ever. Junior-level composition. Once you just assumed juniors could write."

He put the sheaf down on the coffee table in front of the couch. Glancing at the one on top, he sighed and transferred it to the bottom. "Stupid bastard," he said. Looked at the next paper. "Not her, always whining." That went to the bottom. "Oooh," Aaron whined. She kept her eyes on him.

"All right," he finally said. "I wasn't in the studio, as you know. And I told Jimmie that they cancelled, but they told you it was me. Right? All right. This worries you? I forgot, and I told Jimmie the wrong thing. So what?"

"Just wondered, just curious."

"What are you, a cat? I felt like an idiot, because this morning, with Cedric and Diane popping in, I just forgot, forgot we weren't taping, and got dressed for it. I'm not going to call Jimmie and say it was me who cancelled. I'd feel even more stupid. Just a useless detail. Where you going?"

"To turn on the TV, watch the news."

"Then I'm gonna go grade in the kitchen. No, I'm not. The bedroom."

He wouldn't grade papers in the kitchen, but it was all right for her to cook in there, although all she did was warm up some soup from Andronico's.

"What did you do?"

"Huh?"

"Instead of the taping that you cancelled."

"Just stuff, just little crap."

He said this walking away from her toward the bedroom, not even turning his head.

Usually he said somewhat more than that when she asked him about what he was doing on campus, although she hadn't in a while. Well, the library. English teachers had to go to the library. Maybe he belonged to a committee or two now, although she thought he hated committees, in pursuit of a fartie.

Oh, it didn't matter! What difference does it make what anybody did in the afternoon? The morning...that's when it happened, when Aaron happened to be in class. And certainly she believed him about being absent-minded, which he certainly was, and putting on the overalls without thinking. Why, after all, would he want her, or anyone else, to think he was taping when he wasn't?

Maren had been standing in front of the television, having walked up to it to get the remote, which they kept, irrationally, on its top. As she backed away, she pressed the power button, which seemed to activate a voice inside her head. It was a little whining voice, which said: "You saw him last night. You saw him this morning. He didn't have any red mark by his eye."

Then Paige Fuji came on, at the top of the news. Beautiful Paige, newscaster without spot or stain, telling Maren what was what. She did some politics, since there was an election coming up, and a little foreign news, then got into the local rubbish. Much violence, as usual, particularly in the high schools. Some poor kid at Castlemont High in Oakland was stabbed in the buttocks. "Stabbed seriously," Paige added, in case anyone thought that was funny. It wasn't gang violence, though, which was a mighty good thing. Another kid, visiting a high school in Fremont, in the South Bay, was beaten senseless with golf clubs.

Evidently students at Los Lomas High carried putters for self-protection. Or, wondered Paige, did the visitor get into a clash with the school golf team? School and district spokespersons declined comment. Likewise regarding a big fight out in the Contra Costa suburbs after a football game. Rich kids. Always interesting. Paige smiled and was replaced by a commercial, itself followed by the man who did the sports. Then another commercial.

They were running out of time. If Paige was going to talk about what had happened here—Maren turned her head toward the kitchen—it would have to be now, and this news usually didn't end on a serious note. Of course, Paige could make anything seem funny, smiling the way she did, regardless of whatever she was talking about. And there was some potential here: college professors are naturally funny, and one could well smile to think of a cloistered academic suffering a violent death, if not burst out laughing. Maren thought about this as she absently watched a young woman experience a Tammy class orgasm while eating a potato chip.

Paige smiled, each tooth a little work of art. Then she said, "Some cute animal stories today."

Maren stared.

Albert, one of two alligators rescued several months ago from the chilly waters of Stow Lake in Golden Gate Park, wasn't eating well in his new home, an aquarium in Louisiana; the experts there thought he might have gotten used to his diet in San Francisco! Alberta, his mate, had already died. Paige smiled. She then said that a cougar, or perhaps two, had been seen in an upscale neighborhood in the Berkeley hills.

From the bedroom her husband yowled, "One more of these fucking papers! Goddammit, I thought I was through."

"Oh, relax," Maren said, too softly for him to hear.

No one had a name to give the cougar. Paige reminded Maren to look big if she saw him and, above all, not to run.

Paige laughed. She made a very curious yuk-yuk laugh, most unlike her usual crystalline tinkle. This was because her final animal item, and the final bit of news on the whole show, concerned hyenas. It also concerned Berkeley, dear, bizarre Berserkeley, always worth a laugh just by itself. It seemed that Berkeley had recently become the only city in the world with two enterprises devoted solely to hyenas, whereas until now, it had had only one. Of course, no other city in the world had even that. Paige smiled.

"Now, along with the University of California Hyena Project, Berkeley also boasts the Ultima Hyena Research Facility, stocked with clan members obtained from the U.C. Project. Hyenas congregate in clans. Hoot mon! Why this interest in hyenas? Well, the Project, of course, is for scientific study of these happy hooligans of the animal kingdom. As for Ultima Hyena, they're not talking much, but we understand that maybe, just maybe, hyenas may be good for something in the medical world's search for treatments for new disease."

"New disease" couldn't be right. Paige stopped talking for a second, but she didn't look flustered. She never did.

She mentioned some man with an unlikely name, very British-sounding. He owned or managed this new facility and was the source of the hints about medical uses for hyenas, for hyena substances. "Good night," Paige said, and she went into her closing routine, wherein she briskly gathered the sheets of paper on her desk and made them into neat little stacks. Then she and the desk were suddenly replaced by an animated cartoon, which showed two silly hyenas dancing side by side in what appeared to be a jungle clearing They were orange with purple spots and had huge snouts. They twirled canes. When their big hind ends collided, with a *boomp*, both hyenas fell down. Bananas and other fruit rained down on them, flung by monkeys, as they writhed on the ground laughing. Close-up: crazy eyes, big tears.

Maren clicked the TV off and returned the remote to the top of the set. Ugly, ugly, she thought, thinking mostly of hyenas. She knew what the real ones looked like, the *Chronicle* Sunday magazine having recently published an article about the Hyena Project, only somehow the name had registered with her as the University of California Hyena Colony. She had heard of the California Men's Colony, which was a jail, so she was probably just mixing them up. The hyenas in the pictures with the article looked like convicts, big, thick-bodied, mean. They were terrible animals, who loved killing; hyena babies began to attack each other as soon as they were born. She remembered that. The women, the female hyenas, had a lot of male hormones, so that their clitorises were as long as penises. And they were twice as nasty and aggressive as the males.

"Aggh!" bellowed her resident male. "Fuck, fuck! I hate this shit."

A man had been murdered in their house that morning, and Aaron was raging about another paper found ungraded; but he happened also to be expressing, in his own professorial fashion, how she herself felt about the world just then and everybody in it over the age of, say, twelve. Except Brooke, who deserved a better place. Ugly, ugly. Too damned so.

She called Judy

After Judy picked up and said hello, Maren said, "I'm going to talk for, I think, about five minutes, maybe less. You won't believe it, but it's true."

Five minutes later she was finished.

Judy said, "You done?"

"Yes."

"Well, I believe it. Parents! I can damn well believe anything. What are we going to do about Deirdre?"

That, of course, was the point of the call. Little Deirdre Blake. Because of this zany, murderous business, her mother, already a major flake, would be even crazier, her angry dad even angrier. Deirdre wouldn't understand why: she might even think that she was the reason. They knew they'd see her tomorrow, at school; the Blakes were always busy. Classes, squids. Sometimes they did-n't have time to dress Deirdre completely or to fix her a proper lunch.

"Bet she'll bring soup again," Judy said. "Won't be the worst of it. What'll we do?"

As they both understood, the question had no satisfactory answer. There's little that nursery school teachers can do if a child has bad or crazy parents. They would be alert to Deirdre's moods, would try to keep her involved in the group, make sure she got a lap to sit on during story time.

"Just watch her," Maren said.

"Yeah. This is the worst damn thing we've had, almost."

Judy was thinking about the time a parent was killed. There was a tremendous mess, and at the end of it the surviving parent, the mom, disappeared with the kid. People told them, told her and Judy and Holly, not to worry about this child, because children are resilient. But they're not. Teachers know. Children are good at surviving, yes, but they don't just snap back into shape.

Then Judy said, "Anthony Pownall called before you did. I don't know why he didn't just wait and talk to me tomorrow. Irina's feeling better, but she's still on vacation from the lab, and she's spending a lot of time with friends. He doesn't like the friends. Boris doesn't get to see her enough. He's a bit upset, so we'll have to watch out for him, too.

Well, okay. They would. Something made Maren ask about the friends. Were they scientists also? Other...what were the Pownalls? Mammalian biologists. That's what Diane had said this morning. She told Judy this.

"That's what they do? No, he didn't say anything about these people Irina knows. Maybe they're Russians, émigré's. There's a ton of them in San Francisco now. He doesn't care, really. He just wants her back in the lab. Or George does. That George. These parents! Poor Boris!"

Yes, poor Boris! Again, poor Boris.

"Well," Judy concluded, "He and Deirdre seem to be hanging out together, so that's a good thing. Maren, I'm sorry. I'm sorry this stuff happened to you today."

"I don't know," Maren said. "All I am now is tired. The truth is...oh, I don't know."

She was going to say that the truth was she didn't care anything about Cedric McAulay, whom she'd met only once before today. It was too bad he'd been killed in her house, but Ti-Dee did a great job. Already she couldn't remember what he looked like under her table. These things were the truth, yes, but there was more to it. What she had told Judy was right. She didn't know.

"Aaron okay?"

"Sure."

She couldn't hear him doing anything. After she said goodbye to Judy, Maren went into the bedroom, then the bathroom. There he was, stretching the skin under his eye with his fingers, looking at the spot. When he noticed her, he moved his hand to his chin, which he rubbed, as if essaying the state of his stubble.

"Want the first shower tonight?" he said.

"No, you can. Have a good one."

The water came on. Maren was sitting on the couch. She was thinking about him. With all that had happened, she was thinking about Aaron.

Chapter Four

Now she was thinking about Derek Blake. How could she not have thought of him? Jimmie said that yesterday Derek was supposed to be off in some marsh, an alibi the police would surely check out. You had to consider him, the husband, the cuckold. The cuckold in the marsh. He was mean; she had seen that.

But, Maren thought, not big or at all strong-looking. Cedric was old and fat, but considerably larger. Even if the Wharton scholar had simply lain on the floor, if he'd been stunned, say, and let the animal rights activist hack away at him with something, it was hard to imagine Derek doing all that damage. He seemed, however nasty, to be pretty much of a wimp. She couldn't be sure, though; all she knew for a certainty, right then, was that she didn't want to face either him or Diane that morning. So far, it looked as if she wouldn't have to: school was about to start. Deirdre hadn't come. Nor, she realized, had Boris Pownall.

On Tuesdays Maren had greeter duty. She always did it on Tuesday, so she was doing it now, hanging out at the bottom of the steps. Most of the kids had gone up already, and she had succeeded in dissuading the parents and au pairs who wanted to go up too. They just wanted to postpone the separation a bit, but it led to much fuss-fuss, this postponing.

The Cedric story had made the *Chronicle*, page nineteen in the front section, along with some other murders with just single, rather than group, victims. She and Aaron had tugged the paper back and forth at breakfast. Unlike good nursery school students, they declined to share or to use words. She read it first, then dropped page nineteen in front of Aaron, who read, grunted. Nothing much, neither their house nor themselves, no mention of anything, really, except: Berkeley professor dead, expert on writer Edith Warton (sic).

Aaron grouched. "Never get it right, dammit."

Cause of death? No hypotheses, said the *Chronicle*, not yet.

Aaron said, "Hey."

He had leaned over the paper again, same page. Getting up from the table, going out, Maren focused on it herself. It was just a brief article about a new pep-up tonic called Green Guzzle. This product was being introduced in the Bay Area, you could buy it in some markets; but people were starting to complain it made them sort of dippy. Tests were being run.

Just the thing for Aaron.

It was time for her to go up. No Deirdre. No Boris. Someone else was missing, too, but no. Just now he came, walking around the curve in the road with his mother, the sleepy little boy who always had his morning rest and pat. But something was different.

"Why, Moby!" Maren exclaimed. "You have a whale!"

Moby Leibling, the English grad student's son, held in his arms a large, plushy, purple whale. He extended this object to Maren, who made much of it. Behind Moby stood his mom, Louise, beaming idiotically.

"He knows," she said. "He knows! The neighbor girl told him he was named after a whale. We always dreaded the day, but he's so proud!"

"I'm big," declared Moby, the very smallest child at Hillside School. "I *mash* you!"

He attempted to hit Maren with the whale, succeeding only in rubbing it across her thighs.

"No, no," entreated his mother.

"Oh, it's fine, it's fine. Go right up, Moby! Show your whale to everyone! Bye, Louise, bye!"

Anthony Pownall was dragging Boris up the street. Behind those two, Diane and Derek Blake stood next to their Volvo wagon, probably having a hell of an argument; Maren got the impression that they were hissing. Maybe they didn't want Deirdre to hear, or maybe they just liked to hiss; each parent held one of their daughter's arms, but they were talking straight over her head. Deirdre's expression was blank, which was not natural in children.

The two Pownalls reached the steps. Anthony relaxed his grip on Boris, who promptly fell to the ground. Maren helped him up, noting that his scrawny body felt tense, rather than slack, the usual condition of little bodies after such a flop. Boris was a twig about to snap, and Anthony looked awful! Usually so neat, so groomed, such an anti-Aaron, this morning the tiny Brit was a mess, all stubble and pallor and tangled gray tendrils and wisps. He was saying happy things, though, about Irina, as if he thought Maren were particularly concerned about her.

"How silly I was," he continued, "to become so alarmed. It's good...ah."

Anthony appeared to have lost the thread. "My," he said, and he rubbed his hand across his face. Looking over his shoulder, Maren spied the Blake family marching her way, Deirdre still blank, Diane the same, and lean Derek, looking grim. Indeed, under his silly cap, Derek looked quite hateful. His lips had virtually disappeared.

"Good? Good? Yes, Anthony?"

"Oh, ever so good that Irina's with friends and can relax for a few days from the atmosphere in the lab, where we're having quite a bit of difficulty. Because the work is so demanding, you know. Of course, without Irina, the team is incomplete, and she has removed a subject...a subject...ah. But not the most important one. George knows. Ah. Must go. Goodbye, Judy."

"I'm...right. Bye. Careful there." Spinning away from her, Anthony had tripped on a pavement crack, but managed to maintain course.

And then Maren had the son to deal with. "Boris! Must go! Up the stairs, quick! No, not that quick. Up. Get up. Careful!"

With Boris on his way, she was now alone with the Blakes. Diane smiled at her. Diane's teeth were almost in the Paige Fuji class. She was wearing shorts, sandals, and a sweatshirt. So was Maren, who for some reason looked down at her own legs just in time for the arrival of Deirdre, as the little girl stepped forward and embraced her teacher's right thigh. Gently Maren touched her fluffy hair while watching Derek, who was looking at her, or through her.

"Get up those steps," he said. "Now!"

He was addressing Deirdre, although Maren assumed he would talk to her in the same way if he had some request. What a jerk! Just a jerk? Of course, he had good reason to be upset with his wife and perhaps his life, but Deirdre had done nothing and didn't require an order to ascend the stairs. She called out to plodding Boris, who turned, making Maren fear that he would fall, but he didn't.

"Deirdre!" he fluted, in his odd Russo-British accent. "Hi! *Privet!*"

Presumably, he was saying "Hi" in Russian.

"Is that Boris?" asked Diane.

"Yes," said Maren. "That's him."

"All right, you." Maren was you. "You know about everything. They were in your house, and he turned up dead in your house. Well?"

Derek had a very thin nose, which now seemed to dip in her direction, like a little dowser's rod. She thought, I bet you have a tiny prick. Why am I thinking that?

For some reason, Diane was nodding vigorously in her direction. Yes, yes, he *does* have a tiny prick.

"It's funny, isn't it?" Derek went on. "I hear your husband, she tells me" —he angled his sharp chin at Diane—"has quite a temper. That he was quite unreceptive when she and McAulay dropped by. Well?"

First he looked at Maren, with his flat, insolent blue eyes, and then at his wife, whereupon his expression subtly changed. Now he was seeking approval, although it seemed to Maren that he was mad at himself for doing it. What other messages could he send with that face, which seemed to her now one of the most active— nose, eyes, lips, and chin—she had seen? Since Derek rarely spoke, he had struck her as uncommunicative; but evidently he relied on visual signals, as the lower orders must do, including the marine species he so much resembled. As she marveled at Derek's face, the fact crept in upon her that he was also employing his voice and that what he was saying had very unpleasant and certainly ridiculous implications. As ridiculous as he was!

"My work day has begun," Maren said.

"Mine, too," he stuffily replied. "Mine, too. I shouldn't even be here." He made his lips wiggle like worms. "We're meeting at the pony ride dumpster at Tilden Park."

"Derek, she doesn't need all that."

"The Save the Red Fox Committee is meeting. You're saying we don't need foxes? Diane, you bitch!"

"Fuck you, Derek, you...you fish!"

"You whore!" he said. And now his wormy lips drew back, revealing many small gray teeth.

"Must go," said Maren, brightly.

"And you," he said, meaning his wife this time. "You pick up the kid! I have a conference call scheduled with Baton Rouge. Albert won't eat!"

"Well, you know why," his wife said.

He must miss Alberta, who had died. That was Maren's thought and also, evidently, Diane's.

"No, no!" Derek insisted. "He doesn't give a damn for her. I told you! They're not people. They're themselves! They shouldn't even have names. I'd like to kill the fool who named them!"

He spun around and walked off, not to the family Volvo, but across the street where, Maren noticed, he'd parked his little green Mercedes. Unfortunately for Derek, he had parked it across the sacred driveway of Camilla Faucett. Having evidently lain in wait, crouching on the sidewalk, now she rose up, swaying like a python, and blasted him in the face with a jet of water from her hose.

"Teach you!" she said. "Do it again, and I call Eugene Spain!"

Mr. Spain, whose name and influence Faucett occasionally invoked, had been mayor of Berkeley from 1955 to 1959. He no longer counted for much, even if he were still alive, but Derek

Blake, new to the city, didn't know that, so perhaps he was cowed. He said nothing to Faucett, who flounced victoriously into her house, but merely scooped his cap up from the street—Maren wasn't surprised to see that he was bald on top—and threw himself into the front seat of his car.

"Yah!" he shouted. "It's sopping! Diane? Diane, what do I do? My bottom's all wet. Those fox people will think I'm a fool."

But Diane wouldn't help him. She ignored him. As Derek drove off, hunched forward so as to raise his bony buttocks above the wet seat, she was talking intently to Maren.

"We have to get together. I have something to tell you, and I need your help."

"Help with Deirdre?"

"Yeah, Deirdre, how she's responding to Derek's craziness. You saw it."

"Sure, I'll talk to you, but not now. I have to go up."

"I didn't mean now, Maren. I have to go, too. Meet me on Telegraph, after my class. Threeish, okay?"

When she said "class," Diane suddenly looked young. For a moment Maren pictured this bitch, this whore, seated at a seminar table with other grad students, dark eyes fixed on her book.

"Where on Telegraph?" she asked. "Look, Diane, hurry!"

Diane named a coffee place, on which Maren drew a blank. No wonder. She couldn't remember when she'd last been on that scruffy street, main stem of the region south of campus. The people there, the panhandlers—they made her nervous.

"Chancellor's? Does that ring a bell?"

Yes, she knew Chancellor's Books, of course. It was huge, famous. Okay then, in front of Chancellor's.

When Maren ran up the steps and entered the school, she found everything in good order. Holly was doing art. The kids had aprons on and were pasting together a collage made out of little animal figures she had cut from cardboard. She was very good at art projects, and the children always liked to see Holly wearing the burgundy baseball cap she put on when feeling arty. Judy was reading the other kids the new wolf and pigs book, with the wolf telling the story. Aaron had read that one on the show. Deirdre and Boris sat on the floor with the rest of Judy's listeners.

As Maren watched, Moby Leibling crept, holding his whale under him as if he were riding it, from Judy's group to Holly's. There sat apron-wearing Conway, the school bopper, frowning over his art.

"Mash, mash!" Moby shrilled, shoving the whale, which he seemed not strong enough to throw, into Conway's back. His little chair went over, spilling Conway, who responded to all this whale fu by laughing his head off. Moby and the whale descended upon him, and they commenced to roll.

"Conway!" admonished his friend, Cloelia. "Conway, paste!"

But the guys were making friends, the way guys do. They were also screwing up the art session, and Holly couldn't take action effectively: the burgundy hat made her not only arty, but also genteel, too much so to keep rowdy kids in line. With her green A's hat, signifying assertiveness, upon her head, she would have stooled Moby in an instant, although that might not have been the wisest thing.

"Hey, Mr. Whale," Maren said, bending over the purple cetacean and the boys. "Time for a break."

The whale went to Judy's office, to take a nap. No outcry from Moby, who trusted her, knew he'd get it back. Conway resumed art, which he liked. Moby lay on the floor, his eyes dreamy, no doubt contemplating his new life: life as a guy. A whale guy.

The morning, though warm, had been cloudy. Now the sunlight was coming through the windows, and it lit up the kids' hair. They all had such pretty hair, even though at the moment some had unusual coiffures, by reason of paste. While Maren applied a damp towel to heads, Holly gave her table the same treatment, and Judy came to the grand finale of *Framed by Pigs!*, by H. Owling Wolf, in which the hero-author goes gonzo and screams threats at all those of the porcine persuasion. This energized the children, who all tumbled around for a bit, then went outside. Lion was brought forth and groomed. The kids climbed and slid. Conway bopped Moby, who, though bereft of his totem, instantly bopped him back. Cloelia frowned. "Disgusting!" she said.

A lot of action, in the middle of which sat Boris and Deirdre, conversing in the sandbox. Maren approached and knelt in the sand herself. Deirdre was talking about her daddy. Her daddy had "growled." Was that it?

"Then Daddy got mad at Artie. He kicked Artie!"

Ah, Artie the wolf. Maren had found out about him last week. Boris looked horrified. He gasped something in Russian.

"Yes. And Artie growled again. Loud! So Mommy put him in his cage."

"Your daddy?"

"No, Artie! She pushed him in with a broom. Want to pet Lion?"

"Too many people."

Deirdre left. Boris noticed Maren and scooted toward her on his rump. Without realizing what she was doing, she had lowered her own rump to the sand so that she was now sitting with her legs spread, and Boris seemed to want to get into her lap, but he stopped. She scooped him up and held him; gradually he relaxed. She cradled him like a baby. Conway and Moby tumbled into the sandbox, and she worried for a moment that they'd sneer, that Conway had given his new pal a sneering lesson. But they didn't. They merely grappled.

Boris said, "Is my mommy coming today?"

"I don't know, Boris, but I think it'll be your daddy this time."

"Irina is very upset. The atmosphere in the lab is very hard. And she has removed...removed..."

Maren patted his black curls. "Boris," she said, "don't worry. She's fine."

Boris straightened his legs out. He almost kicked her, and he began to struggle the way a cat does when held against its will. Instantly she put him down on his feet.

"Then why can't I see her? Why can't I go, too?"

"Your daddy goes?"

"Yes, when I'm here."

"To San Francisco?"

"What? Where's that?"

"Do you talk to her on the phone?"

"Yes, a little. Maren, Daddy said I can't...I'm not allowed."

He turned away and began to run.

"To do what?" she called. "Boris, look down!"

His shoe was loose. As she should have known he would, Boris tripped over the wooden edge of the sandbox. He lay upon his face. Hastily turning him over, remembering his plunge from the climbing structure, Maren readied herself for another monstrous howl, but Boris didn't even cry. Examining his face, she wished he would, for he had scrunched it up in what seemed to her a terrifying manner: eyes and nose and mouth all squeezed together— as if he never wanted to see, smell, or speak ever again.

Moby strolled up, holding the liberated whale. Pick-up time was nigh. "Ah, he's okay," said Moby. "Here."

He handed the whale to Boris, who clutched it to his chest. Maren was astonished.

Across the yard Deirdre sat with Lion. Girl and rabbit. Just the two of them, both so quiet.

No one came to pick her up. Maren remembered. Derek had the foxes. Diane had a class, and then, in about an hour's time, a date with herself. Deirdre had been dumped. When Maren didn't offer, Judy took Deirdre home, to her own home. At least Anthony Pownall, his grooming unimproved, came for Boris.

As Maren drove down through the hills, she wondered about Artie the wolf. Was he a real animal? He certainly wasn't a wolf. No one would kick a wolf. But even a pet gerbil in the Blake household would be unlikely. Animals are themselves, Derek said, and that credo seemed to rule out pets, which are, or could be seen as, mere property. Artie was probably a pretend animal. If anyone was growling in the Blake household, it was Derek, if a fish could growl. She didn't like that about the kicking. Was someone actually getting kicked? She remembered Derek in his car, shoving Deirdre with his foot. It would be wise to check for bruises. Poor Deirdre! And Boris too, with his crazy mother, his father not much better.

Speaking of crazy, Maren had now arrived in the South Campus area, having steered herself there on automatic pilot. This showed how often she had once been in the habit of going there while an undergraduate at Cal and for some years after. It was always interesting: political activists making speeches before excited crowds, craftspersons selling their goods, a great variety of cool-looking people. Everybody had seemed so confident, so much at ease, in the "cradle of the counterculture." The phrase came to her; she'd heard it or read it. But not recently.

Ah, there! A space. She cut her wheel to the right, started to reverse.

"Hey, lady! Hey, bitch! I'm saving this for my friend. Get the fuck out!"

It was a nice space, near the corner of Blake and Dana. Small, so that only very little cars, like hers, could fit in it. But that was a mean-looking …what?…street person standing on the curb screaming at her, waggling his scruffy blond beard. He might have been a student. These days, they weren't very nice either. So Maren moved on. I should just go home, she thought.

Instead, she drove around the district, finally returning to Blake and Dana; there the tiny space remained, with no sign of its guardian. She zipped in. Suddenly Scruffy Beard appeared on the sidewalk and, before she even got a chance to turn her car off, started banging his fist on the right side of her windshield. He banged, the tiny motor rattled, the Bug shook. At first Maren looked away from him, then at him. Who was his friend? Was it an imaginary one, like Artie the wolf? She turned the key. The car settled.

"Uh-uh," she told Scruffy, shaking her head. "Uh-uh. Stop that!"

"Oops!" he said, staring at her and then down her, perhaps checking out her legs. "Oops!" And he backed away. Maren calmly got out of the car and ignored him when he spoke.

"Want a cappucino?" he asked. "Wanta go to the Med? How about Intermezzo?"

She walked the block to Telegraph and then turned north, in the direction of the university. In a few moments she reached Chancellor's and was surprised to find no one hanging out in front of it, no disreputable persons lounging on the pavement before the door. Terry Rubenstein, the owner, had been complaining about such loungers for months. There were articles in

JAKE FUCHS / 89

the *Berkeley Voice*. Maybe the cops had driven them all away. North Berkeleyite Maren wasn't up on Telegraph Avenue news. She didn't care. She was only over here to meet dopey Diane Blake, who was late, if she was coming at all. A young woman who let her own daughter go pick-upless at school. And sent soup for lunch. But caught in such a mess!

Maren looked through the open doorway into the bowels of Chancellor's, lined with books in which she felt not the slightest interest. She walked. She walked two blocks, up to Channing Way, passing Cafe Intermezzo, which was jammed. A line of people stood in the street, waiting to get in, even though the time was appropriate for neither lunch nor dinner. Some of those in line looked grubby and streetish, some didn't, but they all knew where the food was good. That was Berkeley. The common denominator for the whole town was a deeply serious, soul-involving desire for the best cooking to be had. And damn the expense! She would bet that Cafe Intermezzo was three times as expensive, at least, as Giant Bootie Burger, which, having crossed the street, she was now passing; this establishment, serving the people's food, boasted not a single customer.

"Hey, lady! Gimme some spare change!"

A kid in a filthy overcoat, yelling, the way she'd heard the Telegraph panhandlers did now. On Solano Avenue, where she shopped and ate, they still just muttered. She wondered what the kid would say if she offered to take him into Giant Bootie and buy him a burger. Of course, she said nothing to him at all.

Then Maren turned around and headed back toward Chancellor's, thinking, as she walked, about her favorite restaurants in North Berkeley. Ajanta on Solano had the best Indian food in the city. And there was always Chez Panisse, not that she and Aaron could afford it.

On Telegraph vendors' stalls lined the curb, most of them selling things for women, men too, probably, to loop around their necks or stick in their noses and ears. And many of the stores, the establishments that stayed in one place and opened their doors in the morning and closed them at night, sold cosmetics and beauty things, soaps and oils. There was a big tattoo and piercings place.

Food and display! The passions of Telegraph! And not a speech-making activist in view. Marijuana was big. Odd, that. The head shops, the cannabis cultivating manuals for sale on the stalls—these reminded Maren of her sometimes tiddly youth when pot was relatively new. Here they were still making a big thing of it, presumably for the tourists. She didn't see anyone who looked exactly like a tourist.

She had come to Amoeba Music. She knew about the place, but had never been inside it; when Maren wanted a CD, not often, she hit Rasputin's, further up Telegraph, beyond where she had just walked. You could get anything there, and it was nearer the university, where the neighborhood was saner. Amoeba must be the competition. It was big, sprawling. Perhaps it had grown like an amoeba, slopping up other structures as it spread. She saw a lot of street people there, sitting and lying on the sidewalk, putting on the same show that Terry Rubenstein had complained about at Chancellor's, right across the street. She looked over there. No Diane. Do we care? She examined the street people. White teen-agers and young adults, both genders with close-cropped or shaven skulls and lots of piercings and tattoos. One skinny youth had a dragon tattooed upon the crown of his head, or her head. There were a few dogs that didn't seem like any particular breed to her, but they might have been pit bulls. They were supposed to have them.

She was staring at these kids, reputed unfriendly. "Aggressive" was the word most commonly applied. Staring was not what one was supposed to do. But they were nothing to her. Whatever they were saying, it was nothing to her. Still no Diane. Was she really meeting a school parent on this ridiculous street? It seemed like a movie set for a film aiming at big grosses from dazzled yokels in the prairie states. The last two days…what the hell *was* real? A dead man under her kitchen table. She remembered looking at the top of Cedric's head. She regarded Dragon Skull, who opened his/her mouth and said, approximately, "Yagh!" That woke Maren up a bit. She realized that several of the others were saying or, rather, shouting "Yagh!" or similar expressions, and that most of them seemed to be getting up.

Little Maren Matthews walked rapidly across Telegraph Avenue, she in her shorts and sweatshirt, hooked over her shoulder a large bag containing, along with her own things, small toys and some books for children. She was followed by twelve or thirteen shaven-headed kids dressed chiefly in black leather or ragged denim, along with several medium-sized dogs. She turned around in front of Chancellor's, saw them coming, and made ready to dash inside the store. But she waited, and saw them all flop down on the pavement, so that the doorway was blocked. They disposed themselves in poses, as if they'd rehearsed everything, and looked a bit like the children at school when waiting for a promised story.

They wanted more, though: they wanted money, to buy prime eats and beautifying oils.

When two neatly dressed customers, a man and a woman, came out of Chancellor's, they stood still for a moment, then began to step over and around the assorted forms that blocked their passage.

"Spare change? Hey, you! I'm talking to you." Dragon Skull had a high voice and was probably female.

"Sorry, sorry."

"We know you got it. Up the butt. Up the butt."

The man looked at the woman, who was high-stepping over a recumbent pet. Their eyes met. Berkeley, they were thinking. Berkeley! And the next time we want a book, we'll go to Barnes and Noble in Walnut Creek.

A small, round man stepped briskly out of Chancellor's and looked about him. He was going to say or do something, obviously. Maren didn't think he was Rubenstein, who was supposed to look like Woody Allen; this guy resembled a sawed-off Oliver Hardy.

"Hey, lady," he said. "Hey!"

He was speaking to her, shouting at her. Everyone did down here. Why?

"What?"

"Don't let me see you lowering your ass to the sidewalk."

"What! Are you crazy?"

Maren found herself gesturing at her sweatshirt with both hands. Do I look like *them*? Her bag slid down her right arm and dangled from her elbow.

She pulled it back up.

"Hey," he said. "So sue me. Some of those grad students and junior professors cause me more trouble than all the regular street people combined. You cause me no trouble, I'm fine with you. Okay? Yeah, up yours, Natalie."

Dragon Skull, indeed a female, had flipped him the bird.

"Especially in English. Especially the women. I've been a doorman in strip clubs, and you meet some real peaches doing that, but never anyone as bad as them. Last week there were some sitting out here talking about clitorises and Emily Dickinson, very loudly, making people sick. When I asked them to leave, they called me an asshole. Them you can't talk to. Hey, Natalie! Git! I'll confiscate your dog."

"Take Groucho? Oh no, Zipkin, you wouldn't."

"Animal Control is on the way."

They got up, yanked the dogs by their leashes, and all crossed back to Amoeba. Zipkin waddled back into Chancellor's. Maren stood alone. Finally, Diane.

"I'm sorry I'm late. I had to have coffee with Mr. Tugbenyoh. Want to go in here? They have good tortes in the cafe."

Diane meant the espresso place inside Chancellor's, which was supposed to have excellent baked goods, but Maren shook her head.

Zipkin stuck his head out the door, looked at the two of them. He seemed unfriendly.

"Asshole," commented Diane. But Zipkin had withdrawn. They walked.

After a moment, Maren said, "This isn't about Deirdre. You left Deirdre."

"Did I say it was about her? Well, it is. Indirectly about her. It's Derek who's causing the problems, of course."

"Deirdre was left. Judy had to take her."

"She did? That's nice. I'll tell you this. No matter what else happens, we are perfectly happy with Hillside School, Maren, believe me."

Diane stopped walking, so that Maren had to stop too, and pointed south."Maybe we can get a table at Intermezzo," she said. "It's back there."

Maren was not interested. "Look," she replied, "I don't go out like this with people, to talk. I don't want to be your...this is not a social occasion. There's something you want to tell me, so tell me. But no food."

They wound up on campus, passing through Sather Gate. Diane complained: "I just came from here." Finally, they sat down together on a bench in Dwinelle Plaza, a space where students rarely lingered. Dwinelle Hall was big, gray, ugly, and airless; the Plaza picked up some of its vibes.

They turned toward each other, Diane sitting on Maren's left. Each had her right leg crossed over her left knee. They both wore baggy shorts of a fashionable olive shade and sweatshirts, although those were different colors. Maren uncrossed her legs. So did Diane, but she kept uncoiling, as it were, so that she pushed gently into Maren. Then she flung her arms around Maren's neck and kissed her on the cheek. Maren sat, stunned. No parent had ever done that to her before. Their bare legs were touching. Maren gave her a little push. "Okay," Diane said. "I'll get off you."

"I feel very strongly about you," she added, settling herself.

Maren made no response. She watched a gray pigeon pecking at something on the ground, perhaps a dirty old candy wrapper.

"I did that," Diane said, "because I feel very close to you, as if you were...I don't know. Not my mother, exactly. She wasn't a very nice person. Hi, John!"

A John had approached their bench. He was wearing khaki trousers, a snappy blue blazer, and a tremulous grin. His upper body swayed forward over Diane, as if he wanted to descend upon her and nibble her thighs.

"I have an interview," he breathed. "The University of Texas, Permian Basin. Oil money! They want a postphallic discourse person. Cappucino? Intermezzo? You, too!"

Now John was swaying over Maren, who promptly swung her large bag from her shoulder and into her lap. Probably John thought it was full of books on postphallicism, instead of little trucks and cars and several volumes by Rosemary Wells about the rabbit sibs, Max and Ruby.

"We're doing girl talk now," Diane told him. "But I'm so happy for you."

John departed, stepping light.

"Asshole. No, not my mother. The thought of hugging my mother, ugh! Of course, she was stuck with Dad. Who was indescribable. But you…a sister. Maybe."

Because they looked alike, were supposed to? That was nothing. But Maren felt, not for the first time, that there was something about Diane she recognized, as if she had known her long ago. Diane did what she wanted to do. That was obvious, but hardly special. A lot of the Hillside School parents were like that, and their children paid the price. These people, however, were dull and stupid, and Diane wasn't. She was more complicated, and whatever Diane had, this familiar something, well, it intrigued her. Diane intrigued her.

But not that much, not enough to sit here all day. "What is it?" Maren said. "I can't stay here too long. What do you want to say to me?"

"All right, fine. That Derek killed Cedric. That's what. Well, I'm sure this isn't exactly a shock. Who else?"

Maren thought of Derek buzzing off in his soaked sports car, hunched, elevating his bony bottom.

"You're surprised? He's got that alibi about going to look at birds and lizards in these wetlands. Did you know about that alibi? It's pretty good, but it's false. What? What are you thinking? That he just couldn't do that? He could, believe me. It's obvious that he's a prick, right? Yeah. Believe me, Maren. He's very, very mean-spirited and terribly possessive. Oh…so why did I risk going to Vegas with Cedric? That's what it is, I can see it in your eyes. Why are you staring at me? You have very unusual eyes, that green."

Maren looked down at the bench. She hadn't been thinking that, about why Diane had gone with Cedric. She was thinking, for no good reason, about Aaron. Diane's eyes made her do this. They were practically black, like Aaron's. To him, when he felt friendly, they gave the look of an amiable crow, but they seemed to lessen in size and, through some odd physiognomic trick, to bounce around crazily when he got mad. Diane's black eyes seemed sad, which was odd, since she never seemed sad in any other way.

"I went off with Cedric because he was an enjoyable old fart, and it was fun being with him. Sure, he's always defending the canon, all those dead white men. He did do that, I mean, but he never meant anything by it. He just thought he was being funny. Other people didn't understand, so I had a lot of explaining to do about being friendly with him."

Diane paused for a moment, then resumed. "And I had never been to Las Vegas. People say it's the perfect postmodern place. You *have* to go to Vegas, right?"

Maren had never been. It seemed to her, from what she had heard, the dumbest place on earth.

"Well," Diane continued, "I thought it was simply stupid. Stupid little families and rotting old men! Oh, Derek. Yes. The thing is, I've done this before a few times, just taken a break with someone, and Derek never did anything. He'd yell at me when I got back, then go off and do one of his animal things, leaving me with Deirdre. Now he's getting all worked up about those hyenas they've got in that new place in Berkeley. He's—"

"I don't believe he killed him."

"He did. He did! I know, it isn't easy to believe. Tell me. Do you even really believe Ced's dead?"

"Yes. No."

"You have to admit: the whole thing's crazy. Who do you know who dies? But he did, right in your kitchen, and who else could have done it? Think about that, Maren. Well, there is somebody else, and I'm going to tell you about that in a minute. That's really why I'm here, for you. But I'm going to tell you what happened, how it happened, because you have to understand. You will listen, and not just look at me?"

"Yes. Okay."

Diane leaned back against the bench. She had no bag, no books.

"I don't know how Derek found out we were at Aaron's house.

I mean, your house. That was such a surprise, seeing you. So, anyway, he just walked in, without knocking or ringing the bell. I think it was around noon. We thought it was one of you, coming back, although it was way too early. Ced and I were sitting in your kitchen, having coffee. We'd both showered and changed our clothes. He'd taken a nap, too. The drive from Vegas really knocked him out. Well, suddenly Derek's just there! And just no fucking understanding at all of the situation, no effort to communicate.

"'Get outta here,' he said. 'Go to the car, bitch!' Ignored Cedric. That would cause trouble, I thought, because Cedric didn't like to be ignored. I mean, he could have said something to him. So I said, 'Derek, don't you want to sit down? I know you probably have to vent, but do it later, can't you?' I can't remember if he sat down or not. Then I said, 'How's Deirdre? How's her school?' How is she, by the way?"

"I'm sorry? Oh, fine. Fine, all things considered."

"That doesn't sound too good. We'll have to talk. But then, *then*, Cedric got into it. He always acted as if everyone was a grad student, and he never took anybody seriously. He was even condescending to Aaron, who's a great guy and also, you know, so big. And, you know, excitable. You could insult Ced, threaten him, he just laughed. Those post-postmodern feminists—you know, Maren, we could blame it on them!"

"I thought you were one."

"No, I wouldn't say that. They're just talking, but I know from life. They're little frauds."

Maren also wanted to ask how Diane knew that Aaron was a great guy and excitable, but what she said was, "Hey! Let go!"

Diane was clutching her thigh, which Maren jerked sharply away. Slowly Diane unclutched but then grabbed her by the arm, not so hard, but still firmly. Diane had a hell of a grip. Their faces were only a few inches apart, too close.

"Oh, Maren," Diane said. It sounded so much like "Oh, Mom," as if there was some point Maren just couldn't get into her head. "You have to help me! Derek is Deirdre's dad. She needs her dad. And besides, he's got all the money, from the fish sticks company.

His parents hate me. Deirdre. *She'd* suffer."

"Yes, I see. I...wait." Maren set her feet and pulled away. Diane's hand detached, and Maren pushed it down.

"Wait," she said, again. Something had been bothering her. "Are you going to tell me you saw Derek kill Cedric?"

"Is there something wrong? Did I leave something out?"

"Jimmie told me you said you went out in the morning, early. You came back and found Cedric dead. Detective Greenlee, I mean, told me."

"Oh. I talked to him last night, for a long time. Yeah, I told Jimmie that, I had to."

"Didn't you tell him, or someone else, a sergeant, that you went looking for Derek, but that he was at these wetlands? That's the alibi. You helped set it up, if it's false."

"Of course it's false. Well, he did go there, but later. Help set it up? He's Deirdre's dad. I hardly had a choice. You'll see that even better if you'll just let me finish with this."

"All right then, finish!" Diane had a point about Deirdre. You had to think. A little child was involved in this.

"Okay. I was just saying about how Cedric got into it. He said something—some stupid line or another, I forget—and he laughed at Derek. Derek said...he said 'Fuck you' or something and turned around and walked straight out the door. 'Hah!' Cedric said. 'Hah!' As if he'd bested my husband in a big, manly quarrel, so that Derek had to beat a retreat; but I told him: 'Asshole! He's coming back!'"

"I heard that," said John in the blazer, who had come back. "Just what have I done to offend you?"

"Oh, John! I'm telling her a story about someone. See you tomorrow, okay?"

He turned away, muttering, shuffling toward Dwinelle Hall. "No tits," Maren was sure she heard him say. Gripped by her "story," Diane didn't appear to notice.

"Derek has a bush knife he takes on wilderness trips, and he always keeps it in his car, so he can feel like an eco-warrior. It's just a machete, but not quite as long. So in a minute he's back, holding it, dangling it by his leg. He's not saying anything, which is a real bad sign with him. And Cedric laughed! They should put that on his tombstone: 'Cedric laughed.' He went haw-haw-haw in that really irritating way he had and said something like, 'Do you work with that on Aaron's farm?' Which made absolutely zero sense."

"Something Aaron said. I guess you missed it. It doesn't matter. Just go on."

"All right. It seemed to piss him off, maybe just the tone of it. Anyway, Derek picked up, I mean, he raised the knife, and then he said something. He yelled, actually, 'You fucker!'"

When Diane said this, repeated what she was claiming Derek had yelled, she actually lowered her voice, to a hiss. No one could have heard her. Nonetheless, Maren looked around the Plaza. All she saw was a man sitting on another bench who was talking to himself and waving his hands a lot. Maybe he was doing it to keep warm. There was a wind, she noticed, blowing up from Sather Gate, from Telegraph. Pages from the *Daily Californian* were blowing around. From the heavens, otherwise clear and blue, a dark cloud had descended upon Dwinelle Hall, squashing that grayly dismal structure even further into the ground. The man on the bench said, loudly, "Give us people! Give us someone to talk to; we're always alone." He had people, walking by, but they looked away from him, obviously nuts. They talked on their cell phones. Maren looked at them while Diane talked, but they looked away from her too.

"I lost it," she eventually told Diane. "I lost it with 'you fucker.' So you want to back up a little?"

"Oh, Maren! What does it matter? Derek yelled all these terrible things. He waved the bush knife over his head, and then he rushed at Cedric, who put down his coffee and jumped up. Excuse me? Do you want to ask a question?"

"No."

"You were doing something funny with your eyes. All right. He jumped up, he knocked the chair over. I don't know. He tried to get away, but he couldn't get out of the room. Derek was swinging the knife, not touching him yet. He got turned around so that he was facing a wall. Then he kind of pushed himself against the wall, and the thing hit him. It was like an accident. It seemed like an accident. I don't think Derek expected it. He seemed shocked. But Cedric collapsed; he fell down on his knees, on the floor."

This Maren could see, unlike the preposterous sketch of plump Cedric daintily placing his cup upon the table and leaping to his feet. Kneeling, with the side of his face pressed against the wall, and his hands on the wall—that was a real picture. Diane was seeing it, too. She wasn't smiling. Like Paige Fuji, she smiled most of the time, although her eyes were sad.

Now she was talking again, back to the story, but she sounded tired. This was the bloody part: Derek, evidently recovered from his surprise, hacking away with the bush knife, right into Cedric's neck. Maren couldn't see it. She couldn't see Derek, that is; she had no trouble with the blood. Like water from old Faucett's hose.

"I was surprised by all the blood," Diane said. "Never thought of necks as having a lot of blood. But of course they do. Then Derek threw down the knife."

She hugged herself. Maren wanted to hug her own self. This was no good, this feeling. This silence.

"There was no knife on my floor," she said.

"It went somewhere, I don't know."

"How did he get under my table?"

"The body, Ced's body? I guess Derek pushed it with his foot."

Then Derek went into the living room, while Diane stood in the kitchen. She felt terribly cold, she reported, and couldn't make her legs work. When Diane gripped Maren's thigh again, she didn't ask her to remove her hand, not then.

"I could barely move," Diane said, "but I began to think. I found I could think very fast about how screwed I was. Everything was going to go to hell now. For us. I don't mean Derek! Fuck Derek, as a person. But he's Deirdre's dad, and now the whole family was going to be ripped. My whole life was going to go wrong because of what this asshole did. So I came into the living room, where Derek was lying on your couch with his eyes closed, and said, 'We have to do something.' And he just attacked me for being with Cedric and causing the whole thing. Of course, if he were nicer, probably that never would have happened, but I didn't want to discuss who was responsible. You can't win with Derek.

"But then we did plan, as well as we could, given all the stress. Yes, Maren, yes! I admit it! I helped cover up a murder. I'm still helping. What do you think I am, a megabitch? Don't answer that. I'm doing it for my daughter and for you too. You'll see! What, what? Oh, sorry. But is it so awful to be touched? By me? My God!"

"You're grabbing me. It hurts. Please, finish up. Aren't you cold? It's getting cold out here."

A nun walked by. A person in nun's clothes, with a wimple. Sister, what do you have tattooed on your head?

"He said we should go different places. He told me to find the key for the 4X4, and I got it out of Cedric's jacket. Then he said to drive, just drive anywhere. And he was going to Hayward. You know Hayward? I never heard of it either. It's down south somewhere, he could get there in forty minutes. They have this coastal marsh, this wetlands area, and Derek happened to have told some people that he wanted to go and see it some day soon. So it was really kind of easy.

"Nobody checks up on us. We keep our cars in the garage, and with all the trees, the neighbors couldn't see what we were doing if they tried. That's what we like about the hills, the privacy. So no one knew when he left yesterday, and no one was expecting him at this wetlands place, which I think is pretty big and pretty much deserted. He went there right then, so he can describe it if he has to. A few people were hanging out there, watching the birds or whatever, and he talked to one of them and said things to indicate he'd been there all morning. And I told the cops that. Also, by saying I was gone when it happened, I don't have to make up any stories that they could break down. Derek ought to be okay, then, unless someone saw him near your house, and he doesn't think anyone did. I guess everyone works where you live, huh?"

Not Mr. Guignan, Maren thought. He's home a lot, but watching television, napping, and, she suspected, drinking. So she didn't mention their elderly neighbor. She wondered what Derek did with his fancy car.

"What about the car?" she asked. "Did he park it in front of the house? It's not a Mercedes neighborhood."

"I didn't see it, and I went out before he did. He's got some special place down there for when he goes to run on the track at the junior high. It really pisses him off that there's no track for the people in the hills. So until he found this place he worried that the kids who live down there would trash his car, key it. Oh, they wouldn't, I know. I wish *I* lived in the flats. I'd prefer it!"

Maren had heard that line before, from hill dwellers simulating guilt. Coming from Diane, it sounded exceptionally phony.

"Okay," she said. "So he went to the wetlands. And then?"

"That's right. He got Artie and left, and I did what he said. Just drove around in the 4X4, went to Emeryville and back on the surface streets. I was thinking about going to the police station in Berkeley, but I didn't know where it was. Finally, a bike cop stopped me for driving erratically, which I'm sure I was. I acted all undone, cause I certainly was. I was coming apart! Maren?"

"He got Artie. Did you say that? I've been hearing about him. He's real? What *is* Artie?"

"Artie! He doesn't matter! He's just an animal we're boarding, one of Derek's projects. He's been squiring this…this weird, exotic dog around, looking for a suitable mate or habitat or something, and somehow he got into your house. The second time, when Derek came back with the knife. Hope it didn't pee on anything."

"What kind of dog is it?"

"I don't know. I think, a corgi."

"That's not exotic."

"Then it isn't a corgi! That's not important. What's important is that my husband went crazy and killed someone."

Maren imagined Derek jumping up and down and yanking at his scanty strands of hair. She was still curious about Artie, the non-corgi. But Diane had something else to say, something else important.

"And he's putting all this pressure on me to implicate Aaron."

"Aaron?"

"Yes, Ms. Green Eyes. Mother Green Eyes. That's a good name for you. Maren the little Mother of Hillside School. Oh, you're just adorable and good! All the kids love you. But if you care about your husband, and you know he's a really great guy, you'd better start thinking. Don't worry! I'll help you. Now listen."

Having listened, Maren moved on, leaving Diane on the bench in Dwinelle Plaza, and walked down Telegraph to her car. She thought Diane was probably angry—well, hurt—that she'd just gotten up and walked off without saying anything. The Bug had a green envelope stuck under a wiper: twenty-two dollars for parking on a day when the street-cleaning machine was coming. "Thanks," she said. "Thanks, scruffy man."

She got home before Aaron, as she hoped she would, and got out the phone book. She wanted to call his former psychologist, Schlinker. Jerry the shrink. The man's name reminded her of the sidling cougar she had seen yesterday. Just yesterday? So much had happened.

Maren found the number. She remembered that if Aaron called him right on the hour, between appointments, there was a chance of getting him instead of his machine. It was five, and she got him. She explained who she was; he said sure, he remembered Aaron.

"But what?" Schlinker asked. "But what?"

"You had him on Aetherion."

She had intended to go on, but paused, not knowing quite what to say.

Schlinker said, "I didn't have him on anything. I'm not a drug doctor."

Evidently a terrible thing to be.

"He got the Aetherion from a psychiatrist, Doctor Schlott, with whom I work when drug therapy seems indicated, as it was in your husband's case. For drug questions, call Schlott. He's up in Pinole. Odd place for a psychiatrist."

"Well, just let me ask you this, Dr. Schlinker. Suppose Aaron just stopped taking it? All at once."

"Abrupt cessation? That I wouldn't advise. It's destabilizing:

you get mood swings. And everything comes back at once, all the depression. But it doesn't go inward, at least; it goes out."

"Out? Out?"

"Yes, out. You *act*. You do and say things, different things. Everyone responds differently to abrupt cessation, and I think it has a lot to do with diet. He didn't do that, did he? Just stop?"

"He might be thinking of it," Maren said.

"Well, tell him to call Schlott."

"Yes. Thanks."

Maren sat for a minute, then went out the back door.

After dinner she told Aaron that she thought the night was turning cold and she was worried about Lion, the rabbit. She was going up to school to bring him indoors. They had an indoor cage into which he would fit, big as he was.

"Want me to come with you?"

"No, no. I'm going to clean, too. There's a smell I don't like in the kitchen."

"A smell?"

"Sour milk."

Aaron was not interested in sour milk, and he let her go out into the night without protest. She needed, she told him, some cleaning rags from the garage. After that, walking down the drive to her car, she looked through the window and saw him watching TV. It was good to get away from Aaron. He confused her thoughts.

Coming up through the hills, she saw several small groups of deer.

She parked near the school in front of George Jackson Park, maintained by the city for the benefit of the citizens in its wealthiest neighborhood. It was just a small place. They never seemed to use it. She had something to do there, but first she walked to school.

Lion frisked behind his chicken wire. He seemed happy in his hutch, not cold. To chill an animal as thickly pelted as an angora rabbit, arctic temperatures would seem to be required, and it really wasn't cold at all, even for Berkeley in October. There was no reason to stuff him into the cramped indoor cage, and Judy would wonder why she had put him there. Maren entered the school.

She sat on a little chair, a kid's chair, in the Big Room. Everything was small in the Big Room, except for some large picture books standing on a shelf. Bad things didn't happen in the books or in school, not usually. Usually nothing happened that was even hard to understand. Once, when her life was very difficult, she had come in here at night and hadn't liked it, because the room was too quiet. She had missed the sounds the children made, their little sounds, probably because they would have distracted her, and she wanted distraction. She had a gun with her and didn't want to think about what she might have to do with it. In the event, she didn't shoot anyone. Now she found the quiet restful. She was glad she had come here. If only she could stay.

It was a good opportunity to think, but she didn't. She could do that tomorrow. Diane's story was crazy; well, there were two stories, both crazy and unbelievable, but somebody was dead, so she couldn't not think about them. But now she needed to sit. After some time, the phone rang in Judy's office. Maren let it ring. She heard the answering machine's message, something the daytime noises usually covered up, and then Aaron's voice. Was she there? He was just wondering when she might be coming back. Then he said: "Hey, dammit, are you there? Fuck it." And then he hung up.

After erasing the message, she left the building, walked across the yard and most of the way down the steps. At that moment, the automatic warning light went on just below her, by the cans. Maren stopped and looked but didn't see anyone or anything until the cougar stepped into the field of light, from which it must have just darted. It then sat down upon its haunches and blinked at her. It had a very round head, as round as a ball. Maren looked at the cougar, the cougar at her. What do you say to this imposing carnivore, imposing though, in fact, no larger than a collie dog? Hello, kitty?

The carnivore opened its mouth, exposing its fangs and some lesser teeth; fearing its piercing, paralyzing scream, Maren illogically shut her eyes. With her unclosed ears, she heard a mere screech, not even that. It was a "mweep," the cry a cat will make when it wants something, like food or to be let in or out.

The cougar commenced to...to croon? Perhaps that was the right word. It made a variety of raspy, high-pitched utterances, such as a mother cat might produce when showing off her kittens. Although she had never seen this, Maren thought that was what they did. The cougar fell silent. Maren saw her shift her head a bit so that the light got into her eyes and made them shine. The round head seemed full of light.

Maren took a step, down, not up. The cougar seemed to pull her head down into her shoulders. She crouched and looked all around her.

"Hey," Maren said. "Hey there."

The light seemed to twist. The animal was gone. Then the light went out.

Maren waited a minute on the steps. She stamped her feet a few times and might have shouted if she hadn't feared to disturb their snotty neighbors. The cougar might be out in the dark somewhere, near her car, and she didn't want to walk into her, startle her. Startled, she might attack. But Maren didn't really think so. The cougar was too smart.

She knows where I am, but it's all right.

Then she went to her car, took out her bundle, and entered the park.

Chapter Five

When, in late afternoon, after Diane in the Plaza and Schlinker on the phone, she had turned the maul over and had seen the papery bougainvillaea blossom, faded to pink, she became briefly worried. It was stuck there, adhering with the dirt, and, despite what she'd told Jimmie, she knew Aaron hadn't used the maul on Saturday. They were just planting flowers, work requiring no mauling, and the bougainvillaea was in front of the house, not the back, where they had been. She couldn't push away her first sight of Cedric McAulay, the silly, tired face, the red blossoms on top of his hairless head.

No, no. It was old dirt and an old bloom, Maren had remembered, from the day months ago when Aaron tried to dig a trench in the front, alongside Mr. Guignan's split rail fence. He wanted to put in something, involving large pipes, that he called a French drain. But it wasn't easy, there were roots. Hence the maul. And when Guignan came out and started giving advice, Aaron had quit. And, anyway, who, after committing murder with a large tool, would try to conceal it by means of dirt and a little red flower? She didn't have to worry about that, not that.

Maren was making this mental review in Judy's office, going over what Diane had told her yesterday, Tuesday, and what she herself had done after that. She was alone. It was supposed to be Cozy Time, their euphemism for after-school day-care, and Judy had the duty; but Judy couldn't stay. She didn't explain. There had been a phone call. She asked Holly, who started talking about

Kyle's soccer practice. Since Holly was wearing her green A's hat, which meant she couldn't be budged, Maren volunteered to do Cozy. "Oh, okay," said Judy, who seemed far from happy, but possibly was merely distracted by whatever she had to go and do. Or she might have been thinking about the dead raccoon, quite torn up by something, they had found that morning in the yard. The raccoons were no good: they went after the school rabbits. Still, it couldn't have been fun to bundle that one up in a big paper bag, as Judy had, and sneak it into the contractor's dumpster down the road.

At any rate, Judy left Hillside School, as did Holly. The parents and au pairs came, and when pick-up time was over, not a child was left. A miscommunication somewhere. They had Cozy only when parents, who had to pay, requested it, but every kid had gone home with someone. Deirdre came and then went with her mother, from whom Maren hid. She thought Boris Pownall went with them, but couldn't be sure.

Yesterday, after talking to Schlinker, Maren had gone out into the garage and moved things around so that she could examine the maul. The maul was okay, she then realized, so she leaned it and the other digging/hacking tools back up against the wall and dragged the garbage can back into place. Full of little, rounded rocks, it took some muscle to move. She looked away from it, glanced around at all their litter. Running along the wall, draped over boxes, were the long white pipes with holes in them that Aaron had intended to use in his French drain project. The rocks were to line the trench, she remembered, around the pipes. Suddenly Maren turned and yanked the lid off the can. It was easy, the lid being loose on one side. She had noticed this when in the garage with Jimmie. There were the rocks, and there was the bush knife. The handle stuck out at her after she scooped away several handfuls of rock. She grasped this, pulled, looked at the brown stain on the blade. After standing there for a time, she saw a bag hanging from a hook. She put the knife in the bag.

Now it was buried once again in rock, in a little tunnel she had found last night at George Jackson Park. The park had oaks all around it. Nobody could have seen. She had never seen anyone in the park except city maintenance men, who would find no grass to cut around the place where she had hidden the knife. Most of the parks in the hills had large boulders in them; probably that was why they stayed parks. The boulders were usually quite pitted, Maren had noticed, and in one of the George Jackson boulders she had discovered her tunnel. She put a lot of leaves and gravel on top.

Diane hadn't known what became of the knife. It had just disappeared, she said, in either of her versions.

Ah, the versions. They were driving her crazy. Diane was the real Tale Spinner. Which tale was true?

On Judy's table Maren had found a pad of lined yellow paper and a new-looking gray ballpoint pen. "VERSION A," she printed at the top, and below that heading she scrawled some notes: "Derek appears. How? Nasty. Leaves, comes back. Attacks. Their plan."

She looked at her words, thought about them: Derek appears. How does he know where they are? Nasty to Diane, ignores Cedric. Leaves house for car (parked where?), returns with bush knife and Artie (?). Attacks Cedric. Both Blakes leave after Derek forms plan, which Diane agrees to follow. The plan hinges on "VERSION B."

Below that heading Maren wrote: "This is story for Jimmie, cops, intended to incriminate Aaron (innocent). Derek, Cedric shout. Aaron crashes in. Shouts too (??). Threats, but odd. Goes nuts, as usual (?). Sparkle. Dinner. UGH UGH UGH!"

Maren considered the yellow pad, reflected on what she saw there, Derek's story intended to incriminate Aaron. Derek and Cedric are shouting at each other (Derek probably hissing), and Derek is waving the knife. Aaron crashes in. Aaron shouts, too. But if the whole story is just Derek's attempt to put the blame on Aaron, this is a dangerous detail. Aaron has a very deep voice and is loud even when whispering. At full volume, he's audible for miles, so Version B becomes doubtful if no one hears him. Of course the Blakes don't know that Jimmie knows Aaron and how loud he is. In the Plaza Diane even repeated some of the things Aaron supposedly shouts: "I'll take you apart! I'll knock you down into little pieces!" None containing the word "fuck," these don't sound like the kind of threats Aaron might make.

At this point Aaron goes nuts, the way he does. What is this? How does Diane know about Aaron going nuts? Does he attack people at Edith Wharton conferences? Terrified, Diane and Derek rush into the back yard. With Artie? Yes, dammit, with Artie! In the kitchen, Aaron going on about "sparkle" and exclaiming, "I'll have you for dinner!" Have you for dinner? Couldn't hear Cedric, presumably laughing. Suddenly from Aaron: UGH! UGH! UGH! And the Blakes go in and there he is, holding the knife that Derek didn't remember dropping. Horribly, Aaron is stuffing his face with awful dried fruit things, actually drops one on the corpse but recovers and eats, and trying to talk. Claims self-defense, Cedric hit him or pushed him. Don't believe it. Cedric wasn't the physical type, and Aaron so big and crazy-looking. Like an animal, with those eyebrows and all the hair. Said he'd—but where are you going?

Maren had left at that point in Diane's story, left her in Dwinelle Plaza. Now, in Judy's office, she thought, Did he do it? Did Aaron do it? It was just a story, a stupid, desperate story Derek had made up. Diane said so. Still, although she hated to, Maren had to ask herself the question. Did he? She considered the timing that would have been involved. They had left together at eight; after seeing the deer that Aaron hadn't seen, she had driven off and he had started walking to BART. In this version, he wasn't supposed to have come in until after Diane and Cedric had showered, Cedric had napped, and Derek had arrived. Did he go to San Francisco and teach his class? Probably the class began at ten, so he couldn't have made it back to Berkeley by noon, at which hour Cedric, in all conceivable versions, appeared to have been some time dead. Even if for some reason Aaron hadn't gone to class, he would have been seen somewhere. How many big, shaggy men, wearing overalls, gripping moldering briefcases, could there possibly be? Surely someone would come forward, assuming there was a need. He would have an alibi.

He couldn't have done it! There were too many holes in Version B. But that was the trouble: holes, holes in everything.

Where had he been all afternoon? He hadn't told her, and she hadn't pressed him. Now, maybe she'd better. And how had he gotten that red spot under his eye? She pulled the sheet of yellow paper off the pad and wadded it up. A lot of good that had done! She tossed the wad into Judy's basket, then bent hurriedly down, and plucked it out. Her head below the surface of the desk, she thought, He could do it! He's crazy, crazier than ever. Quickly, she sat upright. No, he was never violent, just noisy. Sometimes he would shove someone, but that was before his therapy. Yes, before. She shoved the paper wad into her pocket, stood up.

"It's a story," Maren said, aloud. Diane said it's just a story Derek made up to incriminate Aaron. But Diane got into it, this Version B, when she told it; she made it seem real, more real than Version A. Who was the more likely killer, Derek or...? No, stop.

Conceivably, Diane and Derek had planned this torment she was going through as a strategy to make her worry that Aaron *had* done it. If Diane had said, "Listen. Aaron did it, and here's how," the story would have seemed ridiculous. She could have dismissed it from her mind, possibly.

Well, assuming that the Blakes were really this tricky, although Derek, at least, seemed far too dumb, what would they want from her? She had left Dwinelle Plaza before Diane could tell her, if she'd planned to. Perhaps help cook up a third version, so that both Derek and Aaron could stay out of trouble. They could blame Cedric's death on...on whom? The tottering Mr. Guignan? He preferred rifles to bush knives. The collie man? Not with only one paw print. Diane had said something about post-postmodern feminists, but they were even less likely as candidates for a killer's role than the neighbors. Oh, presumably they could kill, if need be; but no activists of any kind ever went into their part of town, scorned by guidebooks as spiritually part of dumpy little Albany, Middle America by the Bay. Indeed, North Berkeley was much closer geographically to Albany, with its Rotary and Little League, than to the U.C. Campus. If there was any place in the city a white masculinist, essentialist, whatever-the-hell-else-he-was could be safe from hotheaded academic radicals, it was the area she called home.

Okay. Aaron hadn't killed Cedric, no matter what. He just wouldn't. Then Derek must have, but he was such a fish! Although cold and nasty, he was too silly and ineffectual. Maybe. She needed more. She needed to know more, especially since half of what she did know was probably bullshit.

"Bullshit!" she shouted in frustration. "It's just bullshit."

"Helloo?" Someone was in the building, a woman. Maren went to see.

"Where is my baby?"

"Oh, Irina. Boris went home with Diane Blake and Deirdre."

"Was that the plan today? I thought tomorrow Boris goes with Deirdre. Ah, well."

Irina was disappointed, obviously, but she didn't explode, as she had been in the habit of doing even over tactful notes about kasha and velcro. In fact, she seemed relatively calm and happy, and her complexion was a healthy pink. Previously, Maren now realized, her skin had been starkly, unnaturally white, denoting terrible strain. A new woman she looked. Together they walked outside, into the yard.

The new woman was now waving her arm in the direction of the steps. "Come, Natasha," she said. "Come and meet my Boris's teacher."

Evidently, the scientist—what was she again, a mammalian biologist?—had finally acquired a friend. Anthony had said she was staying with friends, presumed Russians. But Maren didn't think this young person was Russian.

Slowly, shyly, the girl approached, with her dog.

"Natalie, isn't it?" inquired Maren. She was quite sure she was right. How many people have dragons tattooed on their skulls? Besides, she recognized Groucho, the dog.

"Yeah, but I don't mind 'Natasha.' What do names matter? You were on the Avenue yesterday, weren't you? Talking to Zipkin."

"Yes." Maren patted Groucho. Was he a pit bull? He wasn't demonstrative, but he seemed friendly enough.

"He's all right, really. Don't let him scare you."

Zipkin? Groucho?

"He's got a job to do, and he thought you were—hey! That's the biggest angora rabbit I've ever seen!"

"She luffs all animals," said Irina, considering Natasha, now standing rapt before Lion's cage. "So nice. They all live together, in digs, with dogs, a skunk, rats."

"Rats? Wait, Natalie, don't unlatch the cage, okay? He gets out."

"I just wanna hold him. Oof!"

Lion had kicked her in the chest with both hind feet. He had a powerful boot and employed it on Natalie/Natasha because he didn't like being plucked up by a stranger, not out of fear. Now, staring down at Groucho, he scrambled in her arms—as if he wanted to get at the dog and either fight or frolic with him.

"Hey!"

"Yes, Natasha, please put bunny back in cage. He doesn't know you, dear."

"Oh, that's silly!" But she replaced Lion, then walked to their climbing structure and sat on one of the mid-level bars. She slumped. Perhaps she was tired. The girl was very thin, and her leather jacket looked as if it weighed about thirty pounds. The sun beamed down upon the dragon, which was red, silver, and green. Looking concerned, Groucho curled up at her feet.

"Oh," said Irina, cheerfully, "the rats. Not street rats. Hooded rats. Nice. Nice companions."

"Pets. I remember. Brooke, our daughter, had one of those." It was in the back yard somewhere. The interment of Robert Redford Rat, a digging job for Aaron.

"Well, not pets, really. They don't like 'pets.' Is 'companions,' companion animals, all of them, not just dogs and cats. Even rats. And the predators. Innocent killers. We are all innocent, all togedder, on this earth."

Irina looked about her, beholding this earth.

"But they give them names." Maren didn't know why she was interested; it occurred to her that she would never give the cougar a name. Artie. That was a silly name.

"Natasha can't help it," Irina explained. "She was raised that way, a nice family in the Middle East, Indianer. They named the animals—KoKo, Captain. She has pictures. Oh, Maren, I like these people! They live together and do everything together, and they are…warm. What I have been doing! That Saxon!"

Suddenly Irina strode across the yard to the climbing structure. She gave N/N, whose eyes were closed, a gentle shake. "Come, dollink! Maren wants to go home."

"Aw, fuck," grumbled the dollink. "Oh, sorry. G'by, ma'am."

That Saxon? Somehow Maren doubted that Irina was simply condemning white men as a class, no matter how much they deserved it. She said, "That Saxon?"

"George Saxon," Irina said, boosting her friend from the structure. "Big boss, at the lab, but so little. Funny man. Says he is English, but I don't know. I asked Anthony, he says he doesn't know either; but Anthony is afraid."

"Why?"

"Can't say yet. I have a problem with him, George, legal. He can deport me, he says. Natasha is getting me a lawyer."

"Yes, I saw an ad on TV."

"Oh, very good."

The women left, with Groucho. Maren made sure everything was locked up. They got vandalized sometimes. Should get dog. Maybe the cougar would patrol. So much with animals. Derek did animals. There was the mysterious Artie, who Deirdre thought was a wolf. And the Pownalls did mammals.

"Ah, nuts." Walking down the steps, she saw a sports car, arrogantly red, on the street below. Derek. She didn't want to see him. But, she instantly assured herself, she would. For some reason, she knew it was important. As she descended, however, she realized that the sportster was not, in fact, Derek's Mercedes, which she now recalled was green. She remembered the red car from someplace, though. Where? Suddenly it rolled away, as if the driver had been waiting for someone else to come down from the school, not her. Or perhaps this person had simply discerned that the man in the gray suit in the tan car that had pulled up and parked behind the red whatever, was a cop. It was Jimmie.

"Hey, Maren! How ya doing?"

Was she supposed to think that the detective, out driving in the lovely Berkeley hills, had impulsively decided to drop by and say howdy? Well, whatever the game, she'd play. Around my school, she thought, I feel strong.

"Hi, Jimmie! Just passing through?"

"Yes. No. Uh. Gotta talk to you."

She stood there. His place, her place? Her car, his car? No more games.

"Where?"

"Here, if it's okay." He reached over and opened the door for her. Maren got in, but then told him to drive somewhere else, go a few blocks. The detective cars were unmarked, entirely nondescript, but anyone could tell what they were. Faucett would be out, nosing around.

Jimmie understood the problem. When he found a place, he said, "Okay? No neighbors."

They were parked in front of George Jackson Park, which made her feel a little twitchy. But, yes, it was okay.

"What?"

"What what? I mean, let's go slow here. This is kind of difficult." Jimmie took his glasses off, removed their case from an interior coat pocket, cased the glasses, pocketed the case. He cleared his throat. "It concerns Aaron," he said.

He waited. She said nothing.

"I don't hear you saying what."

"Fuck you" is what she wanted to say.

"All right, Jimmie. Tell me."

"Guignan, the old guy next door to you. Now he remembers he heard Aaron yelling that morning. He didn't see him, but he heard him. He was sort of asleep, he says. He had to think about it."

"Aaron was in class. He has class on Monday morning at San Francisco State."

"I know where he teaches. But, Maren, I called his department office and checked his schedule: he has no class on Monday morning. He has no classes at all on Mondays."

"But he goes. He goes every Monday."

"Not to class."

"Well, then," she said, "he must do something on campus before his kiddie show. He leaves with me every Monday at eight."

"And goes to BART, while you come up here."

"Yes. He's doing something at State. He never told me he had a class. I just assumed that. You know, we don't always talk."

"He needs to do some work," Jimmie said, reflectively. "That's one angry guy. He should consider medication. I can't prescribe, but I can suggest—"

"Schlott?"

"Say what? Anyway, none of my business. As far as what he might have been doing, I can check around at State, but if he's not there regularly, where people can see him, he may have a problem. Because he needs an alibi."

"Guignan's a drunk, and he doesn't like Aaron."

"I wouldn't say that. He seemed sorry for him, and he was awfully clear about what Aaron said."

"All right, Jimmie. Tell me."

"Odd things. They seem weird, but given that it's Aaron—well, what's weird? Like, 'I'll tear you into pieces,' something like that. And, this is really nuts, 'I'll have you for dinner.' Maren? Maren, hello?"

Just what Diane had said.

"Guignan tell you this?"

"Yeah, Guignan. Who else?"

"You were there?"

"When he said all this? Yes! He called, and I went over. And then I came here. Now I guess I'm gonna write it up and report it. So, maybe Aaron needs a lawyer, today. Or maybe I'll hold off a bit and do some more investigative work, such as going to State. Listen, Maren, I don't think he did it. He's not *that* nuts, unless he's really changed, gotten way worse. And at least I know where he got that ding."

"Ding" somehow came over to Maren as "dog," or as a breed of dog. The Australian ding. Then she got the word straight in her head and remembered that Jimmie had used it Monday to mean the mark by Aaron's eye. Didn't matter. She wanted to talk about the strange threats that Aaron was supposed to have made to Cedric McAulay before falling upon him and nearly hacking his head off.

"Isn't it conceivable," she began, and then stopped. There had to be something she could tell him. She realized she was smiling, which made her feel moronic, but didn't try to take the smile away.

"Isn't it conceivable—I have reason to think so—that someone may have gone to Mr. Guignan and, oh, persuaded him to say those things? He's a nice man, but he's very old, and we all know in the neighborhood that he's not quite right in the head. You remember, he had that rifle out."

"Don't remember that." Jimmie was shaking his head. He looked worried. It was nice to know that he had so much concern for Aaron. Maren felt pretty good about the story she was telling. It made sense! it was probably true.

"He has Alzheimer's," she said. Probably did. "You could make him believe anything."

"We can check on the Alzheimer's. He seemed pretty stable to me."

"Oh, he can seem that way."

"And there's some verification, at least possible verification."

"There is? Another neighbor?"

"No. Diane Blake, in a way."

"In a way? Well, tell me what she said. Jimmie? Jimmie!"

"My God!" he said. He was gaping at her. "Did you know? You look exactly like her! Like Diane!"

"This is important?"

"Except for the coloring, you being lighter. But it's not just the looks: you've got the same style or something. And I gotta tell you: she really turns me on. This is getting worse and worse. I...Look, this is official stuff, so don't tell anybody. Here's what happened."

"Let go of my leg."

"Oh, sorry. Didn't realize. All right. You wanna hear?"

"Yes, I want to hear."

"Last night I went to their place. The husband, Derek, told me he wanted to see me, that he had information. He said, on the phone, that Diane had some new stuff to tell us. That interested me, and, of course, *he* interests me."

"Derek? As a suspect?"

"Sure he's a suspect. He's got an obvious motive. I have to say, though, that I can't see him taking someone apart, doing that...that butcher's job. He's an obvious jerk, with terrible people skills, but he's not up to that. Oh, you never know, but I kind of trust my instincts. Besides, he's got an alibi. He's supposed to have been in this marsh in Hayward, bird watching or lizard watching, and we found some guy who thinks he saw him down there. We're checking that out, of course. Anyway, I arrive at their house when they're putting the little girl to bed. Cute, huh?"

"Yes. She's a bit more than that."

"All right. So I sat there. Then they came out to where I was, obviously mad as hell at each other, hissing...like lizards. Huh-huh. And he said that the real story was that Diane had come back to your place *twice*. The second time we knew about: she walks in, sees McAulay, deceased, and drives off, half out of her mind. In fact, she was so shocked, Derek said, that she forgot about the first time. What happened then was that she just stood outside and heard Aaron shouting."

"Aaron shouting."

"Right. He sounded angry, real angry, so she got scared and left again. It's Derek telling me this, now. Then he said to her, 'Tell him. Tell him what you heard.' Meaning the first time, of course. But she just said, 'Not much.' She was very reluctant, didn't want to talk. 'Goddammit, Diane,' he said, and then she admitted she'd come back and, when she heard voices, she decided not to go in. They were men's voices, her professor's, of course, and someone else's, Aaron's, really deep. Only nobody was shouting. She couldn't make out what they were saying."

What was this, Version C? Apparently so, but still aimed at Aaron. Maybe they—Derek—wanted to be more subtle. Well, Derek wasn't so smart!

"But," Maren said, "Guignan, half-asleep, heard every word. Does that make sense?"

"She might not have been there right when the other person made the threats. When Aaron made the threats, really shouted them out. That would be most improbable. Am I an idiot?"

"Why do you ask?"

"I mean, if she had reported hearing exactly what Guignan said he heard, then I'd have to suspect collusion, a put-up job to take suspicion off Derek."

"Which it still could be."

"Well, how? What do you think, the Blakes hypnotized Guignan into thinking he heard those threats? Or bribed him?"

"I don't know." Actually, that wasn't impossible. "They have lots of money. From fish."

"Oh, I don't think that's..."

He didn't even bother to finish the sentence. She had another thought, something she'd been wondering about, though she didn't know if mattered. "How about a dog? They have a dog? You see an animal up there?"

"No. Why? Why do you say that? Guignan heard a growl."

"Growl?"

"Yeah. I said, specifically, 'you mean a bark, or barking?' But he insisted. Like a lion, he said. Maybe he *is* a little off. I'll check on the Alzheimer's. But there was that paw print. So you gotta consider. They, the Blakes, didn't say anything about a growl. Why'd you ask me, though, if they—shit!"

Someone had banged on the car window, behind his head. They both stared at the banger, a big white man in a brown uniform, astride a bike.

"Hello, brother," he said to Jimmie, ignoring Maren. "Suppose you move along now. The locals don't like sitters."

"Suppose you—" Jimmie broke off, started up again. He volunteered to the man, obviously a private security guard hired by the people who lived around George Jackson Park, that he was a city detective. He reached into his jacket pocket for his ID, but the guard said not to bother. The nondescript car was no doubt sufficient to tip him off. He didn't care that Jimmie was a cop. He didn't care about the name of the park.

"They'll be calling me again," the guard said. "My clients. Eventually they'll call your people. I suggest you roll, brother." This time he pronounced it "brotha."

"I will," Jimmie told him. "I will. Be rolling right along. But first, may I see *your* ID? Let's just check if you're all squared away with the city regs and other such things. Eh, my brother? Break it out!"

He had very clearly enunciated the last syllable in "brother." Jimmie got out of the car, as did Maren, who started walking, leaving them to yammer. Perhaps Jimmie would sign the man up for his dwindling practice: he seemed sufficiently macho. Rather than heading straight back to school and her car, she took a walk through the hills.

Since she had been driving up there every weekday for years to get to her job, she knew the streets, but hadn't ever walked them. It wasn't her part of town. No security people were likely to bother her; she hadn't even known they had guards up here. But, nonetheless, her home was in the flats.

It was interesting now, what she saw. Not all the houses were big and fancy. Some would have fitted into her neighborhood. Indeed, a few structures resembled cabins; Maren guessed that they were the oldest houses in these hills, probably built before the streets were paved. That might have happened in the twenties; until then it was pretty wild up here. Still was, maybe. The animals certainly thought so, the deer, ever on the increase, and the others. Maren arrived at an intersection into which four narrow streets curved, rather than meeting squarely. She looked down each of the three ways before her, as far as she could. There was a lot of foliage, too much and too close to the houses, which were constructed mostly of redwood. Dangerous when the dry weather came, and fires could get started. Now, though, the vines and shrubs seemed impressively fecund, flourishing. Did no one tend them? She noticed several very old American cars reposing in the street; Aaron would have known what they were. The green stuff was draped all around them. Soon the cars would be hidden.

Some people were out, standing by the front doors of the brown houses. Maybe they had just come out. They were old. Maren walked on, eventually circling back to Culloden Lane, where Hillside School was. She kept looking, but all she saw were more old people and cars, more fresh foliage. No animals today, but she knew they were there.

At home, a few hours later, she fed Aaron. It was a very quiet dinner, not that they ever said a lot. He asked her if she'd seen either of the Blakes. She said no. At one point she said "Jimmie," just the name.

"Jimmie what?" asked Aaron.

"I wonder why he hasn't gotten back to us. He hasn't contacted you, has he?"

"No, and I'm not wondering. We've got nothing new to tell him. We weren't here. I'd like to know what he's asking the Blakes. Diane said she wasn't here, right? I mean, when Cedric got chopped. One of you told me that, you or Jimmie. Yeah. Well, that's awfully convenient for Darryl, or whatever his name is."

"It's Derek."

"Stupid name, either way."

True, she thought, as she watched Aaron munch on a circular piece of dried pineapple.

"Oof," he said, putting it down. "Too sweet! Uck!"

He flipped the thing into the sink.

"But," he went on, "the real, sad truth is it could have been anybody. They say crime is going down, but I think there're more crazy people around now than ever. Some nut coming in here, maybe with burglary on his mind. Drug-addled, probably."

In their neighborhood, so near Albany? No druggies here. Nothing ever happens here.

Aaron had a question: "Did you look around?"

"Look around?"

"For stuff that's gone, that was taken. I did. Also I think he took a nap. The bed was messed up."

"I think it was Cedric who took the nap," Maren said, "not a burglar."

Then she cleared the table.

Crazed burglars who slay and snore? She doubted this hypothesis, she really did. She had her doubts on various subjects. At least Aaron seemed okay. A bit stupid, yes, but that was nothing to worry about. Right now, tonight, he seemed okay, like himself. While taking the Aetherion, he'd become a little too eager to please, as well as somewhat smirky, giggly. And he did everything as if he were older than he was. She realized that she didn't really want to see him that way again. Then he quit the drug and got all screwed-up and unpredictable, screaming at those lawyer women in their car, for example. But now he was calm, or was he too calm? Stupid. Too stupid?

He asked her to take a walk with him.

"I took one today," she said, knowing he'd think she meant in their neighborhood, so that she wouldn't want to do it again. He put on his jacket and left. She went to the phone to call Jimmie. Next to the phone, in the kitchen, was Aaron's dried fruit jar, which, she observed, was empty. She should get him more. Maybe he would get some on his walk, from the fancy market on Solano, Andronico's. It had quite an assortment of those gummy treats he craved.

They had Jimmie's home number. She called and got his machine, but after a few minutes, Jimmie called her back. She wanted to know about the ding, the mark under Aaron's left eye. At dinner, while he had paid close attention to his food, Maren had briefly regarded him with similar care. When he sensed that she was staring, he raised his mighty brows. The mark under his eye had faded; she might not have noticed it if she hadn't known it was there. But it was, and Jimmie had said something about it in his car today.

Should she bring up the security man at George Jackson Park, ask what had finally happened? She chose not to. That was guy stuff. She didn't care. She wanted to know about the ding.

"The ding," Jimmie said. "Oh, sure. I think Aaron must have gotten into a fight in a bar. Monday afternoon. After the professor died, when they cancelled his story time. The bar's in San Francisco. He hasn't been named, but who else? Big guy with black hair, much black hair, dressed in overalls? Very deep voice. Who else? Someone in the bar asked if he sang."

People often asked him that, but although he could usually begin to sing a song, such as "My Boyfriend's Back" or "Let's Spend the Night Together," so that people could recognize it, his performance would then collapse into a tuneless rumble that sounded like the grinding of tectonic plates. He couldn't dance either. But it was him, Aaron, in this bar. Which one? Where in San Francisco?

Jimmie talked fast, in a hurry for some reason. He didn't seem much interested. "An Irish place, the Wee Shamrock, Eighteenth and Guerrero. The Mission, the trendy part: Mission Deluxe, they're calling it now. Maybe it's a Latino-Irish bar, or a Gay-Latino-Irish bar. The Castro's pretty close. Maren, I gotta go."

"How—"

"How do I know this? The bartender called San Francisco P.D. the next day, made a report. Nobody hurt, not bad. A little guy, a medium-sized guy, and the big guy, who got punched. Cause he was strangling the medium guy. No one's made a complaint so far. Oop! The door! She's here. Bye, Maren."

"Company, Jimmie?"

"Just a friend. I don't...bye."

A lady friend, no doubt, no doubt younger than he. He wouldn't want anyone his own age. At least Aaron didn't do that. He merely strangled people! Why? Who the hell were the little guy and the medium guy? The Mission was practically at the other end of the city from SF State, a long trip by bus; if she knew when Aaron had been seen at this Wee Shamrock place, she might be able to tell whether he'd been on campus at all.

Suppose...suppose he'd come back to their house in the morning? Was there a connection between whatever happened then and the tussle in the bar? She couldn't think of any reason at all; but, then, she couldn't imagine any reason why Aaron, assuming he wanted a drink, would travel all the way to the Mission, deluxe or otherwise.

Aaron returned from his walk, fruitless. Flopping down on the living room rug, he did sit-ups, then push-ups. He told her that he had walked over to the parcourse that ran beneath the BART elevated tracks and had failed there, despite much effort, to do even one pull-up.

"I weigh too damn much."

After his exercise, he lay on the floor. She could have told him that he was just big and that big guys had a hard time with pull-ups, since she believed that was the case, but she wasn't sure that he wanted her to say that. Wary of pissing him off, she said nothing. He stared up at her.

"You okay?"

"Sure."

"You and your silences."

"Aaron, are *you* okay?"

He gave her silence. Eventually he fell asleep, or he seemed to. Maren turned off the light; he didn't move. She took a bath and came out into the living room in her nightie. She stood next to Aaron, over him. Usually a noisy sleeper, a nocturnal emitter of grunts and whimpers, he now seemed entirely at peace. He sleeps sweetly, she thought. Sweetly. What an odd word for Aaron. She took her eyes off him for a second, and when she did his hand snaked out and gripped her by the right ankle. She let out a shriek and kicked him with her left foot, square on the side of his face.

"Maren," complained the shadowy bulk on the floor. "Maren, my God! I didn't even grab you hard!"

As if she liked being grabbed at all. True, he had grabbed her soft, but that was why it had scared her so much. She looked at the front door, looked at it with longing.

"I'm sorry," she said.

"You just got me in the cheek. It doesn't really hurt. How's your foot?"

"It's okay."

Aaron started to laugh, but she ran, though not through the front door. She ran into the bedroom and closed that door behind her. Sitting on the bed, she heard him plodding up.

"Maren, what is it?" he said, his voice deep and thick. "Look, I'm all right. What is it? Is it everything, the week?"

"Yes!"

Aaron punched the door. The noise made her jump off the bed.

"Goddamn fucking McAulay! Motherfucking son of a bitch! Goddamn farties! Goddamn all!"

He hit the door again. She said, "Go!"

In the morning he didn't seem crazy. After spending the night on the couch, Aaron moved purposefully around the kitchen. He prepared his usual soggy bowl of bran, squeezed some oranges she had brought home recently from Monterey Market. He didn't say anything about his hitting the door and yelling. He didn't look at her. Maren was sad. She thought of how much he liked her legs; he liked to hold her small feet, although she never liked being held at all, in any way. When had he last done that?

Now Aaron was ready for school. "See ya later," he breezily said, striding past her as she rooted in her bag. He was headed for North Berkeley BART, about half a mile away.

"Have you seen my keys?" she asked, although she knew he never would have noticed them, even had they been dangling from his nose. They were in her bag anyway, most likely, under all the other crap.

"Uh, on the bench?" He picked up some of the items that accumulated on the bench by the door, where she often left things.

"Oh, I got 'em," she said, plucking them out of her bag. "Oh."

Aaron was dressed. That is to say, he was wearing cords, a tweed jacket, and a tie—not overalls. And it was Thursday, a taping day.

"Eh?" he said.

Somehow she felt it was a touchy subject. She plucked at the sweatshirt she was wearing. Aaron looked dumb. Then he saw what she meant.

"Oh, the overalls. They're in here." He patted his case, that ancient, shabby thing. She wished he would open it and show her. He didn't, never having been particularly astute at reading her mind.

He said, "I think they've been freaking the students in my comp class, the one I have on Tuesday and Thursday morning. That is, they keep staring at me on Thursdays, and acting confused, and they don't on Tuesdays, when they just don't give a shit. They're from Asia, all different parts; overalls must be alien or sinister or something. Who knows? I explained about the show, but I'm sure they don't watch it. Oh, hell, now what? Your face! Maren, out with it!"

"What do your students think on Monday? Of the overalls, I mean."

He turned and opened the door, to let himself out. "I don't have classes on Monday and Wednesday. I mean, I've just got a seminar on Wednesday afternoon. Nine people. They almost cancelled me. Had to beg. See ya later, okay? Gotta catch my train."

"Wait, Aaron. What do you do in the mornings then? I mean on Monday. Office hours?"

"Office hours? No, I hang around, go to meetings, work in the library. That sort of —"

"Stuff," he was going to say, or, more probably, "shit," but the door closed behind him.

Chapter Six

O n Thursday, at Hillside, Maren lacked focus, although she went through the motions of being a nursery school teacher. At one point she took Lion out of his cage, plopped him on the deck, and forgot about him. When she went back inside, the rabbit got away, necessitating a three-teacher search around the school's periphery with the children tagging after. In the evening, Aaron walked, while she stayed home, without even hinting at an excuse for not going with him. He sighed. She wanted to talk to him then, but he would have to start it, and he didn't; he just left. At eleven, after showers, each offered to take the couch. "I won't be able to sleep anyway," he said. "It doesn't matter with me." This sounded reasonable. Everything he said sounded that way, but he didn't say much. He got the couch, she the bed.

At school the following morning, she saw Boris Pownall and Deirdre Blake next to Lion's cage, huddled together, looking miserable. Lion sat close, up against the chicken wire, his aspect full of concern.

I'm going, she thought. That Shamrock place. Eighteenth and Guerrero. SF State. Go there, or go crazy. Do something. She told Judy she had to leave. All Judy said was "well," and she looked quizzically at Maren, who then turned around, descended the stairs, and made for San Francisco. There was no reason to drop by her home first; there was good reason not to: Aaron was there. He had Fridays off, so he usually graded papers in the kitchen and worked, ever more languidly, on articles about

Edith. Or perhaps he just kept rewriting the same article.

The trip over the Bay Bridge and into the Mission, Mission Deluxe, was easy; actually going into the bar was another matter. She stood on Guerrero, steeling herself. A man in a leather motorcycle jacket walked up. If he had just vaulted from his Harley, the machine was not in sight. He gave Maren an incurious glance and proceeded through the open door. Dark in there.

Maren had never enjoyed bars. At least she could enter this one in the daytime. At night it would be crowded and some man might try to hit on her, make some buffoonish pick-up move. That's what used to happen, even though she was always with friends. Instead of getting pissed off, Aaron, if she was with him, seemed to enjoy watching her cope with these dim-witted overtures. All this was years ago, of course.

On Guerrero, she saw people who looked Latino, many families of such, and quite a few men who appeared, to her, gay. Nobody seemed distinctively Irish, but when she finally went into the Wee Shamrock, she heard the brogues before her eyes adjusted to the dimness. Then she saw the guys, sitting in booths toward the rear of the bar. They wore tweed caps, for some reason. It wasn't cold or wet outside. A lot of Irish in San Francisco, she'd read, Irish-Irish; they were illegals, generally, and worked construction on the cheap. She thought about this while standing by the bar. When the bartender came over, she asked for a Coke.

She sipped the Coke. The bartender, who seemed nice, was very busy. A lot of people were drinking their lunches. Some of them had a sleek, wealthy look. Yes, Mission Deluxe. And someone hit on her, finally. It took all of five minutes.

"Buy you a drink?" Spoken without brogue.

"Got one," she said. "Thanks anyway."

When he didn't go away, she looked up. "Agh," she said, sputtering out a bit of Coke. For a moment, she thought it was Aaron. But the guy, big, dark, was actually much younger, and he was already talking to someone else, one of the leather men. They were having a very jolly, animated conversation. Everybody was talking. The atmosphere in the Wee Shamrock, although irritatingly smoky (in violation of a city ordinance she was not about to invoke), was downright convivial. Jimmie had said something about the Wee Shamrock's clientele being mixed and, other than its being mostly male, he was right. There were Latinos in here, as well as outside, gays, rich people, and an astonishing quantity of highly vocal Irish. Everyone got along. Any kind of aggression would be quite out of order here. Aaron, you jerk!

"Another Coke, Miss?"

"Sure, thanks."

"But there's still a lot in your glass," the bartender said. "I should have looked. Uh, like some peanuts? Chips, I mean crisps, with vinegar?"

What a nice kid, very young. An American boy. He was slightly built and wore glasses, and at just that moment no one in the booths was shouting at him to bring drink.

"No," she said. "Thanks, no. But could I ask you some questions? You could tell me some things."

"Well, I'll try. This is a famous Irish pub here in San Francisco. What can I tell you?"

"There was a sort of a fight in here Monday, right?"

"Was there?" He said this in a squeak. He seemed genuinely surprised.

"I think there was. You weren't here?"

"No, no. I was just hired for the day. I'm a temp. But this doesn't seem like the kind of bar—"

"That's enough. I'll talk to her. Customer over there wants an Anchor Steam."

Suddenly she was looking at another bartender, old, graying, and beefy. She smiled at him. When he didn't smile back, she took a slug of Coke. He took a slug of something from a glass of his own. Suddenly the Wee Shamrock had grown quite devoid of charm.

"Okay," the man said, his accent straight out of Brooklyn. "You're not from *Pub World*, that's obvious. When you told Chad, Tad, whatever his name is, that you had questions, I thought maybe. First I heard you guys—well, it isn't you. First *Pub World* was coming, I heard, to do us for their Irish issue, and then it was supposed to be off. Only I'd hired that kid, also a bunch of supposed Irish people, for free drinks. But you want to know about a so-called fight."

"Yes," Maren began. "Please."

"Just hang on. Hey, Chad, Tad, stay away from those booths. No more for those guys. No, sir, you will not get another drink today. You had your three already, I'm positive!"

This last he whispered fiercely to a blond young man now standing on Maren's left.

"Oh please, sir" said this new arrival, in a burlesque East Indian accent. "Give me yet one more tiny sip of Bushmills. Then I will return to the ashram, I promise!"

"You're just an actor," said the bartender, loudly now. "I knew it. Worse than an actor! Another voiceover guy, with the stupid accents. No, you don't get nothing! Beat it!"

This instruction was ill-received. The man who did the Indian imitation retreated to a booth, where he climbed up on the table. "I'm Captain Toyota," he bellowed. "Follow me to Greenbrae Import Auto!" Then he leapt to the floor and began to march around the room. Several other "Irish" followed him, also bellowing.

"Put you some of thet thare Glunk 50 in your tank. Ah did!"

"Glotz Noodles! You get'em, you like'em!"

"I'll set you aflame, Blue Buzzard!"

The leather men and the Latinos, who may have been real customers, began leaving the Wee Shamrock. They seemed bewildered, disgruntled. Maren waited for the crowd of them to make it out the door before trying the bartender again. The sleek people—tourists?—begin to drift away as well, including the guy who had wanted to buy her a drink. Chad/Tad left. Perhaps the real bartender had fired him. He was yelling at the Irish, the actors. Or voiceover guys, who must do commercials.

"Get out, get out! We're closing for the day, for the weekend!"

"Oh, very good, sir! Extremely so."

"See what I'm up against?" he said to Maren. "If *Pub World* ever comes, I'm better off closed. But they won't, they won't. I should find real Irish. I tried in the Sunset, up near Golden Gate Park. They're supposed to hang around there, but I found only Chinese."

Now the bartender seemed to like her.

"I'd like to talk with you," Maren said. "Is this a good time?"

"Is this…yeah, it might be. It might. You're not a cop, right?"

He smiled, she smiled. "Oh, no," Maren said. "Not a cop."

"You want to know about that ruckus we had in here? So sit down."

They sat together in the booth from which Captain Toyota had made his lunge. Monday. What happened on Monday? She waited for him to tell her. He lit a cigarette.

"Why?" he said. He turned his head and blew out some smoke. "Why?"

"Why do you want to know about the fight?"

"It's personal." She sounded stupid to herself.

The bartender laughed. "So is my bar personal," he said. "Why?"

"Listen, please. I heard there was a little guy in here and a medium guy and a big guy. They had a fight."

"Not really, not a real fight. I reported it anyway. I'm the only one who got hurt. I mean, in terms of business. The little guy was a regular customer. At least he'd been coming in here the last couple of weeks and bringing people with him, okay? From the studios. I need people in this place, as you can probably tell."

He flipped a hand back over his shoulder, indicating the empty state of the Wee Shamrock. Of course, he'd just kicked everybody out. Maren knew about the studios he'd mentioned because one of the parents had been a filmmaker. The woman was dead now, part of that big mess they'd had a few years ago. Her old studio, really just a couple of rooms, had been in the area they called Video Gulch. South of Market, west of Fifth. Or was it Media Valley? Something.

"But he hasn't been back," the bartender complained. "Greg."

"Okay," Maren said. "The big guy. Was he wearing overalls, and did he have black hair?"

"Yeah."

"And, if you heard him, he had a very deep voice?"

"Yeah."

"I think…look, the big guy is my husband Aaron. I want to find out what happened to him. He doesn't want to tell me."

"Oh, you poor fish." Maren thought he was really sorry for her. "What is he, some nutty organic farmer? Or just another actor, like those pseudo-micks? All right, I'll tell you. Greg. That's the little guy, who used to come in. The medium guy I saw a few times, with him. I never saw your husband before. By the way, I told him never to come back to this bar. He said, 'Think I'd fucking want to?' Not a nice person, your husband.

"So they're sitting in that booth, right next to where we are now, and they're drinking beer. They all must be talking, but your husband *rumbles*; that's all I can hear, the rumble, not that I'm trying to eavesdrop. Just before they blow up at each other, some character in here walks over and asks him if he can sing. I believe the guy was serious. Aaron—you said Aaron?—must still be in a good mood then, because he tries. It's awful and kind of scary, like an organ in a horror movie. People walk out."

Maren interrupted him. "What time was all this?" The narrative was fascinating, but she had to know when.

"One, one-thirty. That matters?"

Yeah, she thought. Early afternoon, and he had to get here, so the time he's got left in the morning to do anything gets smaller.

"You seem relieved. Should I go on with this?"

Maren nodded.

"Suddenly he gets angry and yells like a bull ape, yells Greg's name, I think. My other customers, the ones I have left, they run out. I go for the phone, but I wait; usually these things blow over. Anyway, Aaron's trying to get at Greg, reaching across the table. Swearing away, saying—well, he sounded flat-out *nuts*. Your husband? Yeah?"

"Yes. Yes, of course."

"Okay. Making all this ruckus. Greg's saying something, but I don't know what. He's hard to understand, funny accent, like an English accent, but not quite. He slides down under the table to escape, thank God; wouldn't have a prayer, he's a shrimp. The medium guy punches Aaron in the eye. It doesn't seem to hurt him, he doesn't touch it or anything; but he grabs the guy by the neck and starts shaking him. I thought, 'Jesus Christ, what if *Pub World* comes in *now*?'"

She was supposed to say something. "Oh, yes," she said.

"But I don't believe they're ever coming."

"And then? Did he, did Aaron, keep on?"

"No, he just dropped him. He just stopped everything. Suddenly it was real quiet. He says something, and Greg comes out; well, his nose and eyes do, you know, sticking up above the level of the table. And I do hear what Aaron says then, which is something like, 'We're through! It's finished!' That mean anything to you?"

"Not right now. I can't imagine."

Greg. Had she ever met or heard of this antlike person? Something. There was something, maybe. She wanted the bartender to be quiet while she thought, but she decided, think later, and said, "What else? What else did they say?"

"He said, 'Leave my family alone, or I'll fucking kill you!' Nice guy, your husband. Your...no, you're not. You're not married to that guy. His wife, this Aaron's wife, would be a wreck."

"What? Of course I'm his wife."

"Prove it. Break out some ID."

"No," she sniffed. "Sorry."

"No? I think you're a private investigator, working for the guy who got choked. Or Greg. Or their insurance companies! Making me responsible for some trumped-up injury. You're good, you're good! Very good at playing dumb and helpless. Oh, the poor little wife! Cute little blonde! Blondie! Go ahead, snicker."

She couldn't help snickering. Twice in one week she'd been called Blondie. When he said it, a vision instantly beset her, a sequence of two of those frames: Aaron running through the house while pulling his clothes on, then bursting out the door and crushing the mailman. The mailman, huge bag upon his shoulders, bougainvillaea on his brow, was Cedric McAulay. It wasn't that funny, really, and her snicker had made the bartender very angry.

He decided, for some reason, that she was working for Greg, who was looking to sue him for some concocted injury. All he needed! On top of *Pub World* jerking him around.

The bartender got up; he threw his cigarette on the floor and stepped on it. Maren stayed where she was, although he obviously expected her to leave. She tossed a few questions at him. What was Greg's last name? Where could little Greg be found? But the bartender just kept moving about in a jerky, fretful fashion, picking things up and straightening. Several times he grumbled, "You know. You know."

Well, she didn't. She didn't know, and it really didn't matter. Forget this Greg. Aaron mattered, and now Maren knew, almost for a fact, that he hadn't done it, the killing in their house. Back outside, back on the sidewalk again, that was what she told herself. There wasn't time. Cedric got killed in the morning, almost certainly. Probably late morning. That was the same in both of Diane's versions. And that almost certainly didn't give Aaron time to get to the Wee Shamrock by one o'clock.

She unlocked her Bug and settled into its hard little seat.

It would have taken Aaron at least two hours to (a) walk to North Berkeley BART, (b) wait for the San Francisco train, (c) ride through the tube under the Bay to whatever station was closest to Eighteenth and Guerrero, and (d) walk to the Wee Shamrock. The time just didn't work out, as far as she could judge. She rarely rode BART, wasn't sure about how long it took; but still, she thought it extremely unlikely there would be time.

Now, as to why Aaron had gone to the Wee Shamrock, that defeated her. Who was Greg, little Greg with the funny accent? That nagged at her. Ah, forget Greg! She thrust him away as not worth thinking about, tossed him out of her mind. Aaron getting mad in the bar—this was bothersome. He'd gotten mad, in an instant, and he'd gotten physical. Raging Dagwood. Bad. But he stopped. She thought she could ask him about it; now she could. Not that it murdered.

"*Mattered*, I mean," she said out loud, as she buzzed around a pedestrian. In accordance with San Francisco pedestrian tradition, he was crossing against the light, as if no cars were in the street. She was going to State for a little more asking around, as long as she was in the city. Let's see what went on in the morning, that morning, Monday. Put an end to the whole mess, her anxiety which, she was almost sure, was silly, unfounded, and not at all typical of Maren Matthews, who always kept her head. Taught children, lived in her little house. Was not anxious.

Unerringly she cut through the city, making a lengthy urban journey which, were she to consult a map, would seem to require going north and south at the same time. No streets are straight in San Francisco, and the ones that seem straight are particularly deceptive. She knew this and didn't mind, didn't even think about the route, but simply threw herself north-south. Eventually she found something called Portola Drive, which smelled right, and followed it to the campus. One thing Maren could always count on was her sense of direction.

At least it had always worked until now. She had entered the large chunk of concrete which, she was sure, contained Aaron's office, and ascended by elevator to his floor. Now she was standing in front of his door. Taped to the crumbly wall on either side of the door were no fewer than eleven 4X6 cards indicating office hours for eleven occupants, all somehow accommodated in a space big enough for one desk and one filing cabinet, but none of the cards said "Matthews." It must be the wrong building. They all looked the same. She'd screwed up. All right. She'd only been to his office a few times. She would have to find the English Department and ask.

As she had looked at each of the eleven cards in turn, she had been amazed by the variety of composition classes. Who would have dreamed? At least eight levels of remedial English, variously targeting "native" and "non-native" speakers, were taught by part-time lecturers whose office hours ranged from six in the morning until ten p.m. A miracle that none was in there now, sitting behind an open door, welcoming students. She wondered. With all the cards plastered around its border, the door itself seemed excessively blank, as if it were hiding something. This is Aaron's office, she thought. She remembered. She touched the knob, made of greasy metal, then turned it. The door seemed to open by itself, without her pushing. Somebody told her to come in, so she had to.

Three middle-aged women sat around the single desk, which was littered with the papers they were grading.

"My hour starts in ten minutes," one of them said to her. "But since you're here, I'll see you now. I hope you brought your sentences."

"I'm sorry," Maren said. "I'm not a student. I just need…"

She didn't know what she needed, but the woman ignored her; haughtily, she addressed her colleagues: "You two! Get out! I have a student."

"You didn't go yesterday," one of them protested. "You wouldn't!"

"I! I have seniority, remember? I'm just being nice letting you work in here, grade your sentences."

Maren said she was looking for Professor Matthews, whose name meant nothing. They didn't know any of the regular faculty except the Coordinator of Composition, a Ms. Siskin. They spoke of Ms. Siskin in hushed tones. They didn't know where the English Department was. The question seemed to strike them as somewhat peculiar, a little off—as if she had burst in upon them, these three composition specialists, to demand the address of a paint store or a chiropractor. After looking at one another, they then turned blank faces toward Maren, who backed into the hall. No one was there— with all those teachers, one would expect a howling mob—and she closed the door behind her.

The building which she had thought, still thought, was or had been Aaron's seemed to contain no English Department. It was just a hive of offices. She walked around the campus for a bit, seeing almost no one. Friday afternoon, she thought. A campus cop rode by on a bicycle. Flagging him down, she got directions, as well as his services as an escort. She didn't want them, him, this beefy man in blue shirt and shorts, clunky things dangling from his middle. She was conspicuous now, and so she felt intrusive. This was Aaron's place, as Hillside School was hers. She was checking up on him, yes. But minimal fuss was best.

Now, however, here she was in the English Department office—it said so next to the door—making a fuss. In fact, she felt so thwarted and edgy that she was ready to have what they at the nursery school called a fuss-fuss, a real tizzy. That might mean throwing herself down upon the floor. It was the English office she was in, but the student, Maren assumed, who sat behind the desk seemed not to know the language.

"Mattoos?" she said. "Is who? Ours?"

"Hours! Office hours. Math-hews!"

The girl was pretty; dark and dark-eyed, she somewhat resembled Uzma, the au pair from parts unknown. She wore jeans, while Uzma floated up and down the school steps in a voluminous caftan, but her modish, assimilated appearance deceived. A very weak grasp of the language of the country, and she had the nerve to grow snappish, or at least very intense, with Maren for not knowing *her* language, whatever it was. Or languages, since her dialect seemed to change occasionally. No doubt she was a very useful person on a polyglot campus in a multicultural city, but the only word Maren consistently recognized in all she spoke was "sentences," repeated several times. Fuss-fuss loomed, but she kept herself upright, ceased to protest that she did not understand, regained control.

Finally she said, "Thanks," and then she turned to go.

"You welcome," said the girl to her back, sounding tired.

Maren was not doing a satisfactory job of investigating here. So she told herself. Apparently she blended well in bars in the Mission, Mission Deluxe anyway, but not here, in a university. Still, she didn't want to leave. Not until she found out, at least, where Aaron was supposed to be on Mondays. Such a little thing. It occurred to her then that the glass case into which she happened to be absently staring contained a long typed list of names. Yes! There they were, instructors' names, classes, office hours. Speedily she found him. No! She was looking at Mattoos, a Melinda Mattoos, who taught one section of "Feminist Po[lem]etics," along with a batch of composition.

But then she did find Matthews (the composer of the list had been rather cavalier about alphabetical order), found Aaron on the list, and observed that he had two regular freshman composition classes, each meeting on both Tuesday and Thursday, and also "Nineteenth-Century American Fiction," a title reassuringly, traditionally, bland. This he taught on Wednesday afternoon. Three classes? She thought teachers at State had four. Maybe he got one off for his show. No schedule of committee meetings was listed for Aaron, although some of his colleagues seemed to spend most of their week on committee work, and his office hours were simply a blank, not indicated. How helpful! No wonder he never got any farties.

His office was indicated: Pres 18A. What the hell was that? Everybody else had just numbers, keyed to the numbered buildings shown on a campus map. Maren waited for someone to come by whom she could ask. No one came by. No nice old professors. Maybe the whole department had Fridays off, or they were all ensconsed in their committees. She went back into the office. Be calm, be calm.

"Hello!" she said to the polyglot student. "Can you tell me: what is Pres 18A?"

"Pres? Pres is Presidio. Oh, Math-hews. Him! You are *his* student?"

"Ah, yes."

Now the student spoke many sentences in English, at which she proved not too bad, certainly better than Maren could ever have become at Urdu or similar tongues. It took a good while, just the same, before Maren thought she had understood, at which time her informant seemed considerably pleased with herself. Perhaps she was just relieved.

"You no complain bout him?" She asked this several times. Maren kept saying no, not one complaint.

"You leave now, yes?"

She left, went to her car.

What the hell had he done? And how often might he have done it? How could she ask him? She wouldn't. Such were Maren's thoughts while she drove to the Presidio, formerly an Army base, Army Deluxe, a sprawling, verdant complex situated at the San Francisco end of the Golden Gate Bridge. Getting there was no problem. In this part of the city, more north than south, probably, Nineteenth Avenue would take you anywhere. It took Maren through Golden Gate Park and then, morphing itself into Park

Presidio Boulevard, into the heart of where she wanted to be. The Presidio was a beautiful place, where the Army had maintained a large hospital, a golf course, and several cemeteries, including one for pets. It was great for hikes, and she and Aaron had hiked there a few times with Brooke, when she was little.

Aaron didn't have an office at SF State anymore. His office was here, in some old building, designated 18A. At the YMCA she eventually found, no doubt occupying the old Presidio gym, they had told her approximately where to look. She drove on, searching.

When the Army left, she remembered, no one had known just what to do with either the base's land, immensely valuable, or vintage structures, pretty but crumbling. Mayor Willy Brown probably wanted to build a palace for himself: he suffered an attack of palace-building fever every time he spied a vacant lot or even a lot that might become vacant. Developers wanted to build condos, for sale at a million dollars per, and San Francisco liberals, who usually turned out to be married to the developers, wished to erect "working-class housing," although it was generally agreed that the city no longer contained anyone who really "worked," like all day. Since these factions couldn't agree, nothing was either built or torn down, and somebody, some authority, rented out the old buildings to various parties. One of these, evidently, was San Francisco State. Or perhaps the California State University, the whole, immense, border-to-border system, had rented this block of cute, one-story brick buildings—where, they had told her at the Y, Army officers used to live with their families—to house malcontents from campuses near and far. Maren looked about her. Was she driving through CSU Devil's Island?

It must be very inconvenient for Aaron, getting out here: he never took a car to work. Well, probably there were frequent buses on Nineteenth, and he liked buses, liked not having to direct himself. Perhaps he got some pleasure from the parklike setting, perhaps not. He might enjoy having his office in a little house, in 18A, rather than an ugly office building. He might not. Aaron noticed so little. Maybe he didn't care where he was, which might help to explain his neglecting to tell her he now resided, officially, on an idyllic old military reservation. He should have told her. She didn't like not being told. He had always been so easy to understand, so comfortably devoid of mystery. He never lied. Once she had told him he was too stupid to lie. He always told her everything, she was sure of that. He used to talk all the time. That had stopped some years ago, but he would still speak freely if asked questions. If she said, "How did it go today?" he might go on for hours, griping usually. So she was careful not to ask him about much.

This was her second swing past 18A. The number and letter stood out in black, neatly printed on a white sign planted dead center in 18A's carefully trimmed lawn. Evidently, some military minds were still at work. Maren parked. Nobody was around. Were there no people in San Francisco except those in cars?

She tapped on the front door. She wondered if students ever came here to see Aaron, here in this little house. It would be like visiting someone at home, to have tea. And you, Maren asked herself, when no one came to open the door, why have *you* come here? She couldn't seem to remember. Oh, office hours. Another door, and more taped cards, here just two. One bore the name of Aaron Matthews (ENGL), who taught "SEM: C19 AM LIT" here, in the little house, on Wednesday from two to five and "COMP 24C," sections 53 and 54, on Tuesday and Thursday mornings, also in Pres 18A. His office hours were WED, 10-12, 5-6. Since SFSU students usually needed to work on days when they had no classes, Aaron wouldn't have to devote any office time to those in comp. That was a good thing. He didn't like them. Everything was good out here. He had his own digs, which he must like. He wouldn't have to see his colleagues, whom he detested even more than his composition students. Maybe he had asked to be assigned to the Presidio. Maybe he hadn't done anything.

Hadn't done anything, that is, to get himself banished to the Presidio, if banishment it was. How about the other thing, the murdering thing, Cedric? Monday. No class, so she wouldn't be able to locate a comp section of, say, twelve students ready to testify in almost as many languages that Aaron had then been telling them about the uses of the comma. No office hour. He was probably there anyway, in 18A; where else would he be? And maybe someone had seen him, but she couldn't count on it; there didn't seem to be many people here, in the Presidio. Wherever Aaron had been, he had probably acted crazy, warming up for his act at the Wee Shamrock. Yes...no! Not that crazy. Where, then? Where had he been?

As if it could tell her, Maren looked at the other card. Tammy Quint-Jones (SOC) taught four sections of "SEX PRACTICUM." His roommate. He'd mentioned this Tammy, but not that she and he were the sole occupants of a quaint cottage in the scenic Presidio. Now Maren banged on the door, which swung slightly open. She pushed it the rest of the way. This time no one waited behind it.

She stood in a large room, the living room when the military family had lived there, in which stood two square metal tables pushed together and surrounded by chairs. There was a little kitchen, visible from where she was. She could guess there was a bedroom or two, for Tammy to hold her practicums. Did Aaron have an actual office in here, where he kept stuff? Maybe he had a calendar and wrote things down on it, as he did at home, usually in the wrong squares. Maybe he had some notes jotted down someplace.

Walking about in the cottage, she discovered a small room next to the kitchen, no doubt an old pantry or storeroom. It contained a metal bookshelf, and she recognized some of Aaron's books. Not all of them were here. Probably he sold a lot or gave them away: publishers always send teachers things they haven't asked for and don't want. But one shelf held books on Edith Wharton, including at least six copies of the slim volume of critical essays Aaron had edited, *M'Lady's Glove: The Inside "Outed."* He'd wanted to call it *New Light on Edith Wharton*, but his publishers, a consortium of small university presses in the lower upper Midwest, wanted something contemporary, and insides and outsides were very fashionable in the criticism of that particular year. Unfortunately, he couldn't tell anyone what the title meant, because he himself had no idea. Then they printed it in tiny type; the book was known for this. Poor Aaron! Although she felt bad, too, she got tired of hearing him complain, until he stopped.

The shelf held also his composition books, the ones he ordered for his students. *The Five-Paragraph Essay, The Five-Sentence Paragraph, The Five-Word Sentence*. And a number of venerable-looking English and American lit anthologies. The newer ones were all desperately stuffed with examples of "emergent" literatures, a publishing trend Aaron disliked so much that he sold the books at the campus store on the same days they arrived in the mail. All in all, then, he possessed a considerable load of old and sorry stuff, into which category certainly fell the computer on his desk, with its smudgy keys and dusty screen. Therefore, Maren was quite struck by the new-looking, exceedingly slender television set which also occupied the desk, along with a VCR and several videotape cassettes. It seemed incongruous, the new amongst the old, the old books, the shades of officers and families from old wars. She couldn't imagine what the set was doing here. All Aaron ever watched was sports, which were shown mostly on weekends, when he was home. He was too cheap to buy a television anyway. Perhaps Tammy in her practicum: "All right, class! Let's run the tape and see how you did. I hope you were all sufficiently loving." Ah, wait. Tammy had a show on the campus cable station, her sex thing, as did Aaron. His kid show, Aaron the Tale Spinner.

That must be why he, or they, had the television, to critique their own performance. Maybe Charles, Aaron's friend who ran the station, had loaned it to them. Maren looked at the tapes, which were in those little containers, those boxes the video rental places use. The label on one said, Tale Spinner 10/16. She took the tape out and turned the TV on, producing a blur. It didn't seem like a regular set—for one thing, there didn't seem to be any way to change channels—but the VCR next to it was like theirs at home. She popped in the tape.

After a series of decreasing digits, the show's lead-in appeared. She'd seen this before, and it wasn't very interesting: graphics, dancing letters, A-A-R and so on through N-N-E-R, in various pastel shades. Goopy music played. A cartoon Aaron appeared holding a book. He seemed quite bestial, Maren noted with alarm, so long-snouted, and all that hair! The cartoon Aaron smiled, displaying large teeth. She didn't remember this...this character being quite that way when she had last viewed a tape, one Aaron brought home some months ago.

He looked fine when the show began. The real Aaron, in his overalls, seemed quite human and attractive, and the kids were knockouts. Juan and Rupert Sanchez were handsome and well-spoken, and Marcelline, whose last name Maren couldn't remember, was both cute and brainy. The cast talked a lot, as a regular thing. Aaron read from the books, or sometimes the kids did, but they talked them over together. In this tape, on this show, the book was called *The Dinosaurs Get Divorced*. Everybody was nice. Mr. Dino didn't drink or run around, and Mrs. Dino didn't spend all his money on clothes and manicures.

"But sometimes," ad-libbed Aaron, "things just don't work out between Mom and Dad."

"Which," added Marcelline, "has nothing to do with you."

"Exactly," Aaron said. "They still love *you*. Right, guys?"

Juan nodded enthusiastically. His big brother merely looked thoughtful.

The trouble, thought Maren, is that sometimes the parents are a lot more interested in hating each other than in loving their kid. Right, guys? For example, the Blakes. She stopped the tape and rewound it. She tried another one.

Now Aaron was reading from the book about the three little pigs, the revised version, narrated by the wolf. "Let me in, let me in," recounted the wolf, telling his story to an unseen auditor, "or I'll blow your house to pieces!" He had some devious feel-good explanation for this apparent threat, but Aaron wouldn't give him a break. He smiled toothily, causing the kids to laugh at him, but leaving no doubt that the wolf sought bloody pork chops rather than the cup of flour or sugar he claimed he wanted. Maren was impressed by his acting skill. Then Wolf-Aaron roared, "I'll have you for dinner!" With a crash, the younger Sanchez brother, pretending to be frightened, hurled himself from his hay bale to the floor. He hit hard enough to break something, and Aaron looked worried for a minute. But Juan was fine: he writhed happily in a mock fuss-fuss.

Maren stopped the tape. She should ask Aaron to bring it home. Perhaps some of the others were as good. They could show them at school, although that would mean breaking Judy's rule against videos, which the kids saw too many of at home on au pair's day off.

She tried another tape. The numbers counted down and were replaced, this time, by the image of a sturdily constructed young woman whose eyes were closed and head cocked back. "Urk urk," she grunted. "Yes. Ah, yes." She was doing something with her right arm, making a stirring motion, but her hand was down below the bottom of the screen. Maren could hear a little buzzing note, such as might be produced by flies targeting a lemonade pitcher at a picnic, or...she started to laugh. Again the pastel letters, this time dancing across the woman's chest: C-L-I-M-. Maren turned it off.

"Green Guzzle—Matthews, Aaron—Scholes & Steiner." What the hell was this? She was done looking at tapes, but somehow this one had come to her hand. Her hand had come to it. It was in a red box, while all the other boxes were blue. And on the spine was this curious combination of names, only one of which she recognized. Well, she'd heard of Green Guzzle someplace, but she didn't know what it was or meant. It could be the title of a children's book, but, if so, she didn't think the book would be very cute. Not that all books for kids were. Scholes and Steiner might be authors, or an author-illustrator team. But since the other tapes, the blue ones, just said "Tale Spinner" and the date, this was probably something else, not Aaron reading.

She popped it in. The numbers came again, but when they stopped, she saw no dancing letters of any kind. There was only Aaron, in his Tale Spinner overalls, sitting behind a desk. He looked kind of dumb. Perhaps he'd combed his hair further down over his forehead than usual. Somehow he seemed all hair, remarkably hairy, and then she realized that, as if to complement the black bush on his head and its finger-sized outposts on his brows, Aaron was wearing a false beard! In fact, the only parts of his face not virtually engulfed by hair were his nose which, because of its bareness, seemed remarkably prominent, and his mouth. This seemed very red and meaty, the way mouths do when surrounded by beards, and when he smiled, his mouth looked full of teeth. They were gray, his teeth, not white. The light in the place where he was was gray.

"Yeah," said Aaron, to someone. "Let's do it. Just keep those signs up there. What? Yes, do that, too. Tell me when I've got ten seconds."

"I was just a good old—ah shit. Pick up! Sorry."

After a moment of repose, Aaron nodded, looked expectant, then blinked and said: "I was just a good ole country boy, tendin' to my crops. They was comin' up, too, but somethin' else wasn't. Used to have a big ole thick vine growin' on my property, but then one spring it didn't sprout like usual. Oh, stop a minute. This isn't—"

Maren stopped the tape. She needed to think a bit. Was he auditioning for something, like a drama for the campus television station? Was it an ad, a commercial? It seemed somehow like that, but there was nothing there on the screen with Aaron except the nondescript desk and…and something green. There was a blurry green thing on the desk.

She rewound the tape, ran it again. She hit "pause." The green thing was a bottle, out of focus. It was about the size of a large soda bottle. Green. Green Guzzle. She hit "play."

"…sprout like usual. Oh, stop a minute. This isn't—"

Aaron stopped. He stopped talking and simultaneously disappeared from the screen, along with the desk and the Green Guzzle, to be replaced by two hyenas, large-rumped and capering. They were cartoon animals and she'd seen them before, on Paige Fuji's news show Monday night. Maren watched. On the jungle floor, the hyenas cast themselves about, laughing and crying. Fruit rained down from the trees. Maren closed her mouth. She realized she was holding her hands on her face, one hand for either cheek. Both cheeks felt hot.

The screen darkened, and then Aaron came back. He looked slightly pissed off and, so, more like himself. "Good for my career?" he said, to someone. "Thanks for your concern, Doc, but what I'm interested in is farties. Okay, it's funny, but they're raises. I mean I want a raise at my regular job, at State, for being visible and publicizing the college. But they won't give me a fartie for this."

He listened to someone whom Maren couldn't hear. Obviously this Doc. Then Aaron responded: "The overalls, yeah, they're the same as on my campus show. Oh, I look the same. The beard and the way you've plastered my hair down—they're different, but I'm recognizable. That's not the point. The point is, the college won't like it, this spot; it's bad publicity. Well, maybe. I'm not sure they think any publicity is bad. Look. *I* don't like it. Specifically, I don't like what I'm supposed to say at this point about my vine. You know, how it's no longer 'bulgin' an throbbin.' This is childish crap, to speak plainly. If you showed this script to my agent, she never said anything to me about it, about how problematic it is."

He folded his arms over his chest. After a minute or so, he nodded his great head, which resembled that of a large dog, perhaps, but not at all the head of a hyena, flat-topped, short-nosed. What was that all about? They must be reusing the tape, whoever "they" were.

"Yes," said Aaron. "Thank you. I'll be glad to wait. You told me to leave the afternoon open for Greg Farquahar, so I cancelled my Tale Spinner session. I wanted to meet him, anyway. And I *am* getting paid for this, whether you use it or not? As I thought. Okay. You write it out, let me look at it; if it's cool, I'll do it. Look, I know what Green Guzzle is. I intend to try it, and I'm hoping for results. You can be, let's say, Chaucerian. Just keep it grown-up. Chaucer was—oh, at Stanford, huh?"

Cut to Aaron looking at a yellow pad. It still isn't the real show, just someone playing with the camera. Aaron says: "Yes, I can recall an essay or two of yours. The one in *PMLA*, anyway. But I can safely say that I know quite a bit about Edith Wharton myself, and I don't think this is her style at all."

Aaron gestures at the pad, then looks up again. He says: "Yes, I did something in the field. I edited a book. Do you have a book, by the way? Mine? It's called *M'Lady's Glove*. Ah, yeah. The one with the little print. Yup. Well, it doesn't really matter whether this spot, as you've revised it, is Whartonian or not, although I'm quite sure she never wrote anything like this. But what bothers me, Doctor

Dubin, is the response of the audience to the incongruity of someone who looks like a rustic slob talking in such poetic language
about Green Guzzle. Didn't you say Greg wants to show these
commercials on wrestling programs? I mean, this is just the opposite of what it was before. Yeah? Well, okay. Let's try it."

Fade to black and then back to Aaron at the desk. On its surface now is placed not only the Green Guzzle bottle, but also a
single rose in a slender vase. Aaron lifts vase and rose to his
vulpine snout. He sniffs, then puts vase and rose back upon the
desk, looks out at the prompt cards.

AARON: This rose is beautiful now and fresh, and it stands up
proudly. Soon, of course, it will wilt. I'm a farmer, you see [pulls
at bib of overalls], and I know the cycles of all things that grow.
And when, in the course of time. I, too, began to wilt, well, I did
not repine. Repine? You know, that's not a word that everybody…pick up!

AARON: And when, in the course of time, I, too, began to wilt,
well, I just accepted it. It comes for all living things, I told myself.
Quiescence. Subsidence.

He looked dubious when he said "subsidence." Maren wondered too: the word made her think of old buildings sinking into
fields of mud.

AARON: I felt myself…er…subsiding in other aspects of life.
My hair thinned [!]. I slept less deeply. I was less creative. But
then I was apprised of Green Guzzle [lifts bottle, displays to camera, unscrews top, sniffs].

AARON: Ah! [raises bottle to lips, seems to take a swig] Whoa!
Pick up!

AARON: Ah! [drinks again, or feigns drinking] It's subtle, but
it's strong!

CLOSE-UP: the bottle in his hand. The label. Jagged letters riding upon a lightning bolt. Beneath that a handsome man's face, smiling; a pretty woman's face, smiling.

CUT to AARON: After just a few weeks, I sleep better, work harder, my hair is thick again [points finger at head], and I am very creative. And above all, well...[stands up, still holding Green Guzzle, picks up rose vase in other hand].

AARON, at maximum Aaron-depth and also with considerable elevation in volume: WELL, IT'S WILT NO MORE, M'LADY!

How nice. A plug for his book, courtesy of this Dubin, a fellow Whartonian, probably more celebrated than Aaron despite being forced into commercial video because of the tight job market in academe. As Maren thought this thought of doubtful relevance, she became aware of an odd thickening in the region of Aaron's crotch. This grew into a distinct lump, on which the camera closed. With a zzzipp noise, the denim fabric tore, and out thrust a red, oblong object, somewhat indefinite in outline, obviously electronic. Special effects wizardry. No matter how it was done, the result was apparent, and it was big and bulging and throbbing. Little lights, fireflies, flickered inside. It hummed.

"...at health food stores everywhere," said Aaron, or Aaron's voice. "Or send $19.95 by check or money order to..." He gave some box number and the nine-digit zip code for some city— Maren missed it—in Massachusetts. "Try Green Guzzle today! Why should you your instincts muzzle? Get you some of thet Green Guzzle! Should I still say 'thet'? You still want the hick thing? Okay, okay. Hope this does it. I give up. It's better than it was."

He couldn't have known about the red, oblong object. Or could he?

He said the jingle again, just the same way, with "thet." Maren rewound, removed, recased.

I'll ask Aaron, she told herself. I'll ask why he didn't tell me about this weird tape, this whole business. He has an agent?

But there was something else. Something else had happened today, here in Pres 18A, that mattered. She wasn't seeing it now, but she knew. Could she go to Aaron with that? Aaron, I saw something, heard something. It concerns you, I think. Do you know? Huh? he would say.

Someone knocked on the door of Aaron's cottage. Maren didn't move.

"Dr. Quint-Jones, are you in there? I want to discuss my last simulation."

A male voice. Was it "simulation" that it said, or "stimulation"?

Bang bang on the door. "Dr. Quint-Jones?"

"Nope," said the someone to someone else. "She's not there. I'll get her next week."

They moved off, Tammy's students.

Bang bang on the door. They wanted to come in. Let me in, let me in. Or I'll tear you or your house down or into pieces, whatever it was. I'll have you for dinner! Jimmie in the car. Mr. Guignan. Maren put the Big Bad Wolf tape back in the VCR and ran it through.

Yes. In reading the book, Aaron said what Jimmie reported Mr. Guignan as hearing, those threats that Diane had told her were just part of Derek's plot against Aaron. Aaron-Wolf had said, "I'll blow your house to pieces," and Jimmie had said, "I'll tear you into pieces." Maybe Guignan remembered it that way. There were some violent Wolf-threats on the tape that Jimmie hadn't mentioned, but she understood that he was only giving her a few examples. There was the line about dinner. That was just the same. And Aaron hadn't just said these things: he'd roared them, in the manner of an angry beast, no matter how slick when trying to talk himself out of trouble. If anyone playing that tape were to crank up the volume at those moments, it would become audible indeed, perhaps for miles, certainly enough so as to rouse old Guignan from sleep or stupor or contemplation of his past. Whatever their neighbor did when he wasn't bothering them. Someone in their house played the tape. It was obvious who.

Okay. Aaron wasn't the killer, definitely. Derek was. He killed Cedric, and then, that cold fish, he thought and he searched. Or maybe he searched first. Either way, he found the tape. He knew he wanted to pin the crime on Aaron, and he came upon their Tale Spinner tapes, of which there must be quite a few. She never viewed them. Should have. Should have! Then she could have made Jimmie see what was going on, but she could now, after talking with Aaron. She had to talk to Aaron.

She took the wolf tape out, put it back in its box, which she left on her desk. She turned off the fancy television and the VCR. Maybe, Maren thought, I should talk to Diane as well. In the story blaming Aaron, composed by Derek, Aaron makes these threats. In fact, Diane, when "repeating" them to her in Dwinelle Plaza, had made them seem quite threatening, quite real. Why had she not mentioned this trick with the tape? It was really the center of Derek's plot against Aaron, which Diane was ostensibly warning her about. But life was very complicated for Diane, poor Diane, who couldn't afford to have Derek take the rap. Now—after she told Jimmie—Aaron would be safe, at least. He didn't even know he was in trouble. Why would he? Then, she supposed, she would talk to Diane. Didn't want to.

Aaron first, tomorrow.

Chapter Seven

But tomorrow didn't work. They were together some of the time, but doing separate things, and Aaron went to bed early. The next day, though, Sunday, they went for a hike in Tilden, the big regional park that lies between Berkeley, its northern, hilly, part, and several suburban communities. When she suggested the hike that morning, he said he didn't think so. He wanted to run today, run long, and then, as usual, he had papers to grade. He needed to do those things. She didn't go away then, off to some other part of the house. So he had to tell her, yes, he'd walk. He made quite a show, however, of putting his running shorts on under his jeans, getting dressed in the living room so that she would have to see him. He would run back home, leaving her to take the car. That was the point.

Aaron ran on the Tilden trails occasionally, but they hadn't been in the park together for at least two years. She couldn't clearly remember the last time. Without their daughter, who, as a little girl, had loved Tilden, there didn't seem much reason. Brooke had loved the Tilden Little Farm most, which was perhaps the reason why they went straight there after parking. Maren was thinking about what she would say, and Aaron was probably not thinking at all, so habit took over, long-established habit from better days, before people got killed. It was perhaps a bit early for families to visit the Farm. Aaron and Maren were alone with the animals in their pens. Everything and everyone was quiet, including Frodo, a donkey who been innocently involved—employed as an extra, non-participating, in a pornographic film made by the filmmaker mom—in all the trouble they'd had a while ago. That was when people started getting killed.

"Let's walk the trail," she said.

The particular trail she meant began just beyond the farm and wound up into the hills, where deer and other nondomestic Tilden fauna roved and stalked. It was quite rocky for the first stretch; after that it was just dirt, hard dirt. Back at the farm, the donkey emitted a loud hee-haw, as if he'd finally remembered he knew them. In fact, he owed them, owed Maren, anyway, his very existence. Working through Jimmie, she had finagled him his place, room and board for life, instead of a hot shot at the humane center.

"There he goes," said Aaron. "Old Frodo."

"What is Green Guzzle?"

She surprised herself. That wasn't what she wanted to ask about, not right away.

Aaron was surprised, too. "Green Guzzle? That stuff? Oh, it's supposed to perk you up. It's supposed…why? What's it to you?"

"What's it to *you*?"

This was terrible! She was screwing everything up. Silently, Aaron stumped along. She couldn't guess what he was thinking.

They encountered two people walking five dogs, then a mountain biker slowly descending the trail.

"That's new," Aaron said. He meant the biker, not the dogs. There had always been dogs in the park. She had an idea that downrushing bikers were a menace in some places, like the trails on Mount Tamalpais in Marin County, but she didn't know anything about how they rode in Tilden. Carefully, if this one had been typical.

She was sorry she'd asked Aaron about Green Guzzle, when the wolf tape was the important thing. Unfortunately, just when she was about to start over again with that, he said, "Why did you ask me about that Green Guzzle crap?"

It was such a simple question, so she just told him. "I know about the tape you made. I went to your office in the Presidio, and I found it and played it."

"What's this? You checking up on me?"

Aaron wasn't mad. Today was one of the last of the sunny days they could expect before the drippy weather came on, and the air was cool; wearing a rather bulky jacket, Aaron looked even bigger than usual, but he wasn't mad.

"You went over there, to the Presidio? And you went in and found my audition tape?"

"Yes. Are you mad?"

"No! I'm not. But why'd you do it? What are you looking for?"

"I can't explain it now. Please."

"Oh. Oh, well. Kind of nice, isn't it, that old place? Not sure why they put me out there, but I like it, I guess."

"You might have mentioned it, but, Aaron, there was another tape. Besides the Green Guzzle one."

"Now, wait. One at a time, okay? I'm just getting this into my head. You played that crazy Green Guzzle thing? Good Lord! Hey, watch it, here come some bikers."

He pushed her to the side of the trail. The bikers came down, fast. "Slow down!" he yelled. They ignored him.

"Assholes." He just muttered it, looking at her. She didn't care about the bikers, didn't think he did either.

"Aaron." She tugged at his arm. She wanted to walk. The trail wasn't very pretty. The Russian Thistles growing on both sides had lost the brilliant purple blooms that adorned them in summer. The plants themselves, a kind of bruised black in color, had grown very high and thick.

They walked.

"Oh, tell me, will you?" he pled.

"Me tell *you*? Tell you what? I don't know anything about Green Guzzle or the video you made. Forget it, Aaron! Now I want to know about your wolf tape."

"You played that one in my office, too? Where the bad wolf's in jail and tells his story to a social worker or someone? That was one of my best shows, I thought. What about it?"

"You brought that tape home, right?"

"Yeah, I did. You'd mentioned reading the book at school, so I thought you might like to see how we did it, the kids and I. But you never showed the slightest interest."

"Well, then, I didn't see it, didn't realize—"

"You didn't *view* it. You did see it, Maren. I showed it to you. I even put it on the table on your side of the bed. Like my book you never read."

"The print!"

"All right, the print! But you could have run the tape; the tape was normal-size. It's gone now, incidentally. Glad you saw the one in my office."

"It's gone, yes. I couldn't find it yesterday."

"I noticed you poking around by the VCR and in the buffet drawers. But if you didn't know we had it, why were you looking for it? Oop! I got ya."

Maren had stepped into a small hole and for a moment had wobbled. When Aaron steadied her, she put her arms around his neck and hugged him. She hadn't known she was going to do that. He is being very nice, she thought, for Aaron.

"You definitely brought it home?" she said, into his chest.

"Yes, Maren, definitely."

Slowly he brought his arms up and gave her a return hug.

"Aaron, when did you realize the wolf tape was gone?"

"When I checked to see where everything was after the cops and Ti-Dee Crime were all over the place. Brooke's tapes, her soccer, riding horses, all that. Some basketball games I taped and other Tale Spinners we had. All there but the wolf. I checked for other stuff, too, like the notes for my article, although no one would want them. But, you know, I worry about funny things."

"Those aren't funny things."

They were standing in the middle of the path, no longer holding one another, just standing face to face.

"Beep! Beep! Hey, folks! I'm sorry, but we got to go."

Three mountain bikers, two dog walkers with three wet dogs, a park ranger leading a bunch of little kids on a nature trip. It was the ranger who had spoken, in a strong New York accent.

Apologizing, she and Aaron got out of the way. The bikers pushed hard and shot down the trail, followed by the dog walkers, who turned out to be dog joggers. The dogs yapped. The ranger ambled off with his party, braying about poison oak, much maligned but has its uses, and minah's lettuce. How could they have stood oblivious before this noisy multitude? Well, Aaron was often oblivious. That was normal for him, if not for her. Hold on. Aaron normal? How long had it been since she could say that?

She said now, "You're normal."

"Hah! I'll never be normal. You know that."

"I meant for you."

"Oh."

"Aaron, I'll settle for it, for that. I...I like it."

"Well, that's good. I feel like myself today. Somebody got killed in our house last week, but I feel, as you say, normal, normal for me. Maybe the shock did it, I don't know."

They were walking again.

"Maybe you just got over the effects of stopping Aetherion, stopping it all at once."

"Yeah, there's that. I felt weird after I quit, but not too bad. Weird, but also better. I tried that Green Guzzle, too, and possibly that messed me up in some way. There was something in the paper about it last week: your body's supposed to turn it into Ecstasy after you drink it."

She remembered glancing at the article, which said people were complaining about Green Guzzle. She didn't remember or hadn't noticed about the Ecstasy connection. That was stuff that did something extremely bad, like make your lungs shut down. She had read about that someplace else. But Aaron was thinking, obviously, about the psychological effect.

"They didn't tell me it might turn into Ecstasy," Aaron said. "I wouldn't have taken it. I think the stuff did make me feel a little funny. And I wanted sex more, I'll say that. But what really messed me up, last weekend and early in the week, was all that dried fruit."

"Your dried fruit? The mango sticks and things? But you love them!"

He had so few pleasures.

"Oh, Maren," he said. "I didn't exactly love them; I just ate them all the time, and they're ninety percent sugar. I figure I was eating about two pounds of sugar a day in there, and I must have hit some kind of absolute limit. Every time I ate one, one of the fruits, I felt dizzy, like I was standing on a very high place and about to fall off. And then I'd want to do something very energetic and not terrifically sane. So one day I just got sick of them. Don't think I could eat even a prune."

He stopped walking. He looked worried. Liable to fret if his bowels failed to move daily and freely, Aaron had long relied on prunes when nature balked. Maybe he could just eat more fresh fruit. She was going to tell him, but he began again, walking, talking.

"So I began to feel okay, really. The way I did before I got depressed. God, look at that old lady with all the dogs! She could herd them to one side of the path, at least."

They got out of the way. The lady waved as she walked by. There were only three dogs, golden retrievers, each one with a green tennis ball in his mouth. That was a kind of dog who always seemed to smile, probably could smile around a dead duck held in its teeth. Aaron, however, had never been much for smiling.

A few years ago, he had come to think he was depressed, so he started in with Schlinker the Shrink, after something went wrong between him and Jimmie in Jimmie's macho-therapy program, and then he got on Aetherion. It made him nicer, so she didn't tell him that "depression" was usually just an excuse for being drippy and lazy, and for not doing anything about it. Being Aaron, he never guessed what she thought.

Aaron said, "You didn't believe I was really depressed, of course. Yeah."

"What?"

"I said, 'You didn't—'"

"I heard you, Aaron. You and your terrible life. So sad!"

She thought he'd blow up. He didn't.

"It wasn't terrible, my life," he said. "I'm not claiming I had a right to be depressed. But there were some things that...oh, I don't know what to say. That hurt me, okay? You thought I had no reasons, that I was just being an idiot."

When she heard "idiot," Maren prepared, with some relief, to stop listening. The old you-think-I'm-an-idiot number was an Aaron standard. He wouldn't accept denials; he hated for her not to deny it. But this time, to her surprise, he simply dropped the subject of his idiocy.

"I don't think you ever realized how much I missed Brooke. I never told you. She went to college in San Diego, but then she did the summer session down there. She visits her friends all around. She really hasn't lived with us since she went away. I didn't know that was going to happen. Yeah, I miss her too."

"Oh."

"And my career wasn't worth a hill of shit. I knew that a long time ago, but it began to bother me. I go to these conferences, people say, 'Oh, you're the one with the small print.' Nothing ever happened in that area. I didn't make it, and I did try, at one point. I know it doesn't matter to you, because, you know, it isn't your world. What depresses me most, though, is money."

"Money?"

"That we don't have any. I can't even get a fartie."

"Money? We never cared about money. Aaron, you're being…money!"

She realized she was shaking her head, with vigor. And she shook it even harder, so that she thought she could feel the moist Tilden air vibrating in her ears, after he said, "Who cares about money? Well, for example, you do."

"I do not!"

"Maren, control your head. Stop that! I don't mean that you actually *want* money. Ah, you want it. You know you're never going to have it, but you wish you did, like all your parents. Whenever you talked about the school, you talked about them and all they've got. Made me tired. Made me sick, really."

"That bothered you? Oh, but it never meant a thing. Judy and I talk about the parents all the time, because they're funny! Did you really think I want all those things, like staffs?"

Some of the families, just a few, really, had what were called staffs, teams of servants. They almost all had au pairs, but the very richest ones also had cleaners, cooks, and drivers; after all, they had several homes, in Mendocino, Aspen, Maui, besides the big houses in Berkeley. And all these people, the parents, not the staffpersons, were arrogant assholes, despite the liberal principles they claimed to cherish. You had to laugh at them if you were going to work for them, taking care of their kids. Who would want to be like them? Of course, most of the parents weren't; they were fine and normal. She reminded Aaron of this. He resisted.

"I can remember meeting one guy, Adams, the airline pilot, who might be considered kind of normal. The rest...if they only have one house, in the Berkeley hills, and just one big vacation a year, in Kenya, say, it's because they don't work. They're students, their parents pay for everything. Or they 'have their own money,' you say. Whatever that means."

"I don't want that," she insisted, "anything like that. Never in my life. Where is this coming from?"

"You don't want it, you say. Well, you'd be crazy if you obsessed over it, because you can't have it, not all the stuff they have. But you wouldn't be normal if you didn't want more than we have. Our little house. One bathroom."

"In which you virtually live!"

She was sorry she said that, but Aaron didn't seem to mind.

"It's restful in there," he said. "And what better place to dream about the farties I'll never get? You know, Maren, I didn't mean to start whining. I really didn't."

He wasn't whining. She knew that, but she didn't know what to say.

Aaron said, "That's enough on that. Where were we? Green Guzzle?"

"Yes," she said, although she really couldn't remember what they had been talking about before they got off onto Aaron's depression, so-called. Maybe it had been real. Real, not what she had thought it was: typical Aaron bullshit.

"Maren! Helloo!"

Coming around a bend in the trail, striding toward them, was Irina Pownall.

"Hi, Irina," Maren said. "A parent," she told Aaron, out of the corner of her mouth.

"It is?"

What confused him, probably, wasn't that Irina was a parent—they often ran into parents, from whom Maren usually hid—but that she looked so, well, dashing. She was a sight! Suddenly the fat scientist had style, and this was more than a matter of what she was wearing, although that was quite snappy: a green cape over a sweatshirt adorned with what Maren thought to be the insignia of the U.S. Marines, a man's felt hat, leather boots rising to the knee. Somehow it all went together. And she was smiling and pink and obviously of a temper to laugh to scorn every leftist in the Berkeley Hills.

"Look, it's Maren!"

This she called back over her shoulder to Natalie/Natasha, just then slouching into sight. She wore her big jacket and a knitted cap, covering the dragon.

"Hi," Maren said, but Natalie ignored her. Perhaps she was tired, being unused to walking. As far as Maren knew, she spent most of her days lying and sitting on the sidewalk in front of businesses on Telegraph Avenue. She looked as if she wanted to flop right there, in the dirt.

"Well," said Aaron, "what exactly is this? I've never seen a dog quite like…"

And he squatted down to inspect Groucho, whom Irina, not Natalie, had on a leash, but it wasn't Groucho. It was a very strange animal about the size and color of the golden retrievers with the tennis balls, but it had a prickly ruff of hair on its neck, stripes on its body, and oddly thin legs. Its expression was incredibly disconsolate, as if life were torment. Yes. What exactly is this?

Aaron extended a hand. "Hey, boy," he said. "Is he a boy?"

"No," said Irina, tugging on the leash. "That is, no! Don't!"

"Careful, man," Natalie told him. "Don't fuck with him."

"Aaron," Maren said.

"Just, just…shit!"

The thing had growled like a lion. It was hard to believe that anything weighing less than three hundred pounds could make a noise like that. In growling, it had exposed canine teeth that seemed about four inches long. And it had suddenly expanded, not to three hundred pounds' worth, but so that it seemed to have doubled in bulk.

"Woo!" said Natalie. "I hate that stink!"

Like a skunk, a megaskunk.

Aaron sat up. He had been knocked over, out of his squat, onto his back. It was the growl that did it. She was sure the dog, whatever it was, hadn't touched him, hadn't really lunged at him. Just growled, and bared fangs like knives, and bristled hugely—the hair was smoothing down now—and made an awful smell. It sat. It looked miserable, embarrassed.

"Artie," Irina said. "Bad Artie!"

"Oh, don't," pled Natalie. "He couldn't help it."

"I'm okay," Aaron said, getting up on his feet "You could have told me he did that, but I'm okay."

Artie. This was Artie.

Maren goggled at him. This beast had been in her house, marked her hardwood floor with its paw, in human blood. And Derek Blake had kicked it. What a rotten life. She felt sad for it.

Natalie and Aaron were bickering. He was wrong to have put his hand near Artie's mouth, triggering a defensive response. Hardly defensive, Aaron opined, and he ought to know, having been around dogs all his life. This wasn't true. His mother had owned a poodle, that was all.

"Is not a dog," declared Irina, with a majestic flourish of her arm, the one not holding the leash.

Perhaps the gesture held special meaning for Natalie, who groaned and did then, indeed, lay herself down on the trail, a few feet from Artie. Artie! This was Artie.

"Well, what is it, then?" Aaron asked.

"Is aardwolf."

"That's the strangest goddamn wolf I've ever seen. By the way, I'm this lady's husband."

He made a face at Maren, who, he claimed, never introduced him to parents, because she was embarrassed by his size and noisiness and idiocy. This was an exaggeration.

"Hi, I'm Irina," Irina said. "Boris's mom. But listen, please.

Artie is not a wolf. 'Aardwolf,' like aardvark; also eats insects, termites mainly. Is not wolf. Is related to hyena."

To hyena! Hyenas were horrible. Aaron may have had the same thought. He glared at Artie.

"No, no danger. Is all right. Yes, aardwolves growl and bristle and make unpleasant odor, but all that is defensive. They just want to be alone, to find the bugs. Oh, they fight if they have to. Notice the big teeth?"

"Indeed, I did," Aaron said.

"But they won't eat meat. Unless ground well. Unless cooked. Even then, they don't like. Oh, he is so fussy-fussy."

Like a deity descending upon a favorite mortal, green-caped Irina bent over the aardwolf and chucked him under the chin. He endured it. That was all, but she beamed as if Artie had suddenly produced a ball and spun it on his nose.

"This is," Maren began. "This is—wait a second."

"Vot?" said Irina. "Is something wrong?"

Artie looked carefully about, scanning the dirt. Looking for bugs.

Maren wanted to be perfectly sure this was the same Artie, and she wanted to know where he came from. What was he doing here in Berkeley? Why was he here in the park? Because Irina was taking him for a walk, obviously. She couldn't focus well. Why did she feel that she was being watched? Hard to ask the right question. Ah, now she had it.

"Irina. Irina, did Artie ever stay with Derek Blake?"

"Deirdre's father? Yes. She is darling, but he...he is not so nice. Cold. But when Natasha's landlord was coming, we had to hide all animal companions. Artie is hard to hide. Only aardwolf not in zoo, or in that place."

Irina frowned. She didn't like that place. She would smite that place, perhaps.

"So," she concluded, "I loan him to Derek Blake. Natasha knows from animal rights work, and I know from your school. He didn't want Artie, I think, but he has reputation for rescue, squid, alligator, so he took. Was too fat when Derek returned him. Insufficient exercise! Wery bad!"

"Rescue? Was Artie rescued from someplace?"

"Yes, Maren. From my lab. I rescued him. Ultima Hyena Research Facility. Substance H! Pah!"

Substance H? Aaron had some of that for a little problem of his that came and went. No, no. Must be something else. She glanced at Aaron to see if he was taking this in. Perhaps he was, but he was stroking Artie, who was now lying in the path, apparently asleep. Perhaps Artie was nocturnal. What an odd creature! Sometimes, when she looked at him, he seemed like a dog, but then he would seem to become feline, which he was, right? Hyenas are cats, no? Of a kind.

Irina's lab. Her lab, also her husband's, was this Ultima Hyena place. Maren knew what that was. She remembered from Paige Fuji's show, the evening of the killing. It was a place that kept hyenas, to make medicines out of them. Which meant cutting them up, something Irina must have refused to do with Artie, whom she had rescued. She had gone off with the aardwolf to stay with Natalie and her friends. That must have been what had made Anthony Pownall so upset.

Maren, recalling, thinking, had been looking down at the path. Now, when she looked up at Irina, the scientist was talking to Aaron.

"My boss? George Saxon. No, I don't know this other you mention. Yes, small and dark. English maybe, but not quite. He says he report me to U.S. Marshall if I don't come back, but I say to myself, bullshit! Why he wants attention? This Substance H is no medicine! May not even exist! His brochures are full of lies."

"So, what is the stuff? I mean," asked Aaron, "what's it do?"

"What he thinks it will do is make men...ah, what do you know of *Hyaenidae*? Nobody appreciates them. Think they are silly animals who guffaw!"

"I know what that's like, believe me. But Substance H, what's it do? I mean, supposed to do."

"Be patient," Maren said.

"Shut up. I'm sorry."

"He's sorry. So listen. Aardwolf is *Proteles* genus, *Hyaenidae* family. Other *Hyaenidae* are the big hyenas, spotted and not. I know all about spotted, scientific name *Crocuta*; no one knows more. Now. Interesting thing. Females are dominant among *Crocuta*."

"All right!" exclaimed Natalie, whom Maren had thought also asleep.

"Oh, Natasha," Irina remonstrated. "I explained to you. Is not all right. Because *Crocuta* have very high levels of male hormones, so are very aggressive. Also, because of hormones, clitoris elongates into pseudo-penis."

Aaron seemed interested in this. "Is that right? A pseudo-penis, eh?"

"Through which babies are born."

"Good God!"

"So George thinks Substance H must exist. Not one of the male hormones itself, but something else that makes them work. He thinks he knows everything, but he doesn't. Business I think he knows, maybe. When he contacts me, I tell him, 'Won't work, Mr. Saxon!' Maybe he finds something, eventually, to make women more like men, but I doubt even that. And George's big idea is for other thing. Use Substance H for men, humans men, to make them more virile. Better athletes, better in bed. Stupid! Impossible!"

Perhaps Artie thought he was in bed. He certainly seemed to be very much asleep. Likewise for Natalie. No bikes came. No people with dogs. They had made a lot of noise and probably scared everyone away. The four humans and the aardwolf might have been standing and lying on a remote peak in Africa, which she presumed to be the home of aardwolves, instead of a steep but walkable trail in Tilden Park. And yet, Maren didn't feel alone, as if they were all alone. She felt watched, but it was all right. She focused on Irina.

Irina explained further.

This man George Saxon was an international entrepreneur. He did a lot of things, but most of them had something to do with science, in whose various fields and sub-fields he claimed much expertise. Pah! In search of Substance H, he had hired Irina away from her British research center, and she, by threatening not to come, had persuaded him to hire Anthony, too. In fact, it was Anthony, not even a biologist, really, but a computer guy trained to assist biologists, who pushed her into accepting the offer. Irina thought it was bad science, and she didn't like the idea of sacrificing *Crocuta* specimens for bad science. Anthony agitated. As a native of Manchester, wery cold, wery dirty, he had always wanted to live in sunny, golden California. So the Pownalls, along with other scientists and techs recruited by Saxon, had moved to Berkeley, the only place in the world where one could obtain hyenas, in bulk anyway, without having to trap them.

"And they are not easy to trap, dollink, being smart."

"I bet," Aaron said, looking grim. Perhaps he disliked being called dollink, which wasn't very nice of him.

"Besides, George wanted to come to Berkeley. He said he had taught here once. Maybe he liked the food here. Is wonderful!"

"Yeah," Aaron said. "Anything you want."

"Anthony wanted to take me to Chez Panisse, but need reservations a month in advance. Too late!"

Because she was sick of grinding up hyena glands. Four big female *Crocuta* had been delivered by truck from the University of California Hyena Project, one after another. George Saxon had dispatched each of them, messily, with a nine-millimeter pistol. Each had uttered terrible, hysterical shrieks when he took aim with this weapon. The famous hyena laugh, Irina said, was reserved for moments of mortal terror. Then she and her team looked for Substance H while Anthony stood by, nervous with nothing to do, ready to crunch the numbers. But they never could find anything from which to derive any numbers. George stomped around, blaming everyone. Despite Anthony's frantic hushings, she persisted in telling George the idea was flawed: in a decade or so, with luck, they might come up with something that would give women bigger muscles, nastier dispositions, and penises; but what George wanted no one would ever find.

"One day he brings in aardwolf, little *Proteles*. Crazy! Aardwolf is normal. Males are males, females females. I feel sorry for him, tell George, 'No, not this one!' He insists. I think, 'bullshit!' and I go away. With Artie, of course. George says I steal him, but he can't find me. Had met Natasha already, by big book store, so I go to her."

Aaron rubbed his chin, looked thoughtful. "Wow," he said.

Maren couldn't think of anything to say. This peculiar tale of hyena biology and venture capitalism meant something to Aaron, but she didn't get it, not yet.

"Hey, Irina! Can we get the fuck out of here? I don't like this dirt."

"Of course, dollink! Artie wants to run, anyway. Don't you, Artie?"

She twitched his leash. Shifting his jaws, Artie managed to let one long canine emerge and slide down beneath his lower lip. Urgh, he said, growling low. This amused Irina.

"Hah, he's angry! Up, up, you stupid boy!"

She yanked him to his feet. Natalie, arising from the soil, removed her cap and scratched the dragon across one crimson wing. Aaron looked at the dragon, but did not seem impressed.

"How nice meetink you!" Irina said. "Goodbye, sir! Goodbye, Maren!"

Aaron and Maren continued on the trail, all the way to Wildcat Peak. The last part was a bit of a scramble. They shuffled down the other side, the side less steep, to the Rotary Club Peace Grove, where they sat upon a stone bench. This had been erected, said a sign nearby, by Rotary of Orinda, to which posh suburban townlet they were probably closer now than to Berkeley. A flock of little Orinda-like kids, excessively fair and very clean of limb, ran about the grove, herded by three teachers. A field trip, even though it was Sunday. And here, in this lovely, phony setting, Aaron told his story.

"I think I know who this George Saxon is."

"You do? Who?"

"George Saxon is Greg Farquahar."

He looked at her meaningfully, but she had never heard of Greg Farquahar.

"And who is that?" she finally asked.

"Oh, yeah. That's...well, I'll tell you. But the point is that

Greg Farquahar is actually Gregor Grosz. Remember Gregor Grosz?"

"Gregor? Yes."

"Sure! We were talking about him just last week, that plagiarism spat with McAulay. Well, of course you remember him."

Of course. As undergrads they had each met Gregor in class, in separate classes. He and Aaron had taken a graduate Latin seminar together, from a famous scholar, and soon Gregor had invited Aaron over to his house to study. He lived with his parents on Grant Street in Berkeley. Maren had encountered him at about the same time, in a history course, and he had invited her over to study, too, but she hadn't gone. It was funny, really remarkable, how many different classes Gregor took. A lot of people knew him, always from class.

"Maren? Anyway, that's him. I mean, Grosz is Farquahar. That's the Green Guzzle man, I'll explain all that. And I think he's George Saxon as well. Good Lord, what names he's picked!"

"Always getting into trouble," she said. She meant the past; she meant, in part, trouble with his professors. In the seminar, he insisted on pronouncing classical Latin according to some arcane system of his own, pissing off the famous scholar, who got mad at everyone and refused to award any A's. In the history lecture—medieval something, maybe France, she thought it might have been—Gregor had once ascended to the stage when the professor was late, no uncommon thing, and sung a ballad in a language unfamiliar to her, accompanying himself on a guitar. Had she understood the words, maybe she would have known why the historian, soon after arriving, had shouted at Gregor and then called campus security.

He was little and dark, so that people often thought he was Latino until they heard his accent. Then they thought he was from India or Pakistan, but he said he was born in South Africa, that his parents had gone there from Europe after the war. When he had told her that, she hadn't been sure which war. The parents looked like him. Aaron and she had gone to a party at the house. He had sung folk songs, popular at that time.

She remembered Gregor Grosz very well.

"Tell me, Aaron. How you met him, Farquahar as he now calls himself. What is all this? I mean I just don't know. Why he, Gregor, does things with hyenas, if you're right about that."

"I think so, I think I am. As Farquahar, he's promoting Green Guzzle. That's a virility drug, supposedly, and so is this Preparation, I mean, Substance, H. Same kind of thing. And he mentioned something about hyenas to Dubin, the director who shot that Green Guzzle tape of me you saw. He also wrote a very pompous *PMLA* article about Edith Wharton, but never mind. Finally, there's this cartoon bit on that tape. You must have seen them, those stupid hyenas. Hah! Would piss off Irina, Boris's mom, whatever her name is. I guess they were saving money, taping over old stuff. I think he owns the studio, incidentally. Grosz does, I mean."

Aaron talked. She listened. He talked about money. Gregor wanted it, and so did he. That was what brought them together, as far as he knew.

Aaron wanted to enrich himself, them, via the fartie route and any other that presented itself, and his friend Charles, the campus cable station guy, had offered him advice. Take a tape, a Tale Spinner tape, and go to an agent. Charles knew of a few. Maybe Aaron could get work as a voiceover specialist. He had a great boomer of a voice. Now, if he could only learn to do a few accents, maybe he could get himself some gigs. He could make some money that way, also perhaps garner some publicity for the college and possibly win, at long, long last, a fartie. The tape did the job; Aaron became a hired voice for the mid-ranking San Francisco talent agency of Scholes and Steiner. They began giving him training, still were, and eventually sent him to several auditions. At these he waited for hours with other hopefuls, all jabbering away at one another, talking redneck, talking Irish, talking Jamaican, before getting his five-minute opportunity to shine. So far nothing had come through.

Why did he not tell her anything of this? She couldn't ask him this; he would only be embarrassed. Maybe Aaron the English professor was simply embarrassed about doing commercial voiceovers. Or he might say that he hadn't told her because he knew she didn't care and then go off, again, on the book unread, the tape unviewed. So wearisome, and, of course, this was not the time for that old stuff. But to give Aaron his due, he did not seem inclined to move in that predictable direction. He liked doing voiceovers, it seemed, or thought he would if he ever got to do one. He was limited because he had no accents yet, but everyone liked his voice. Gert Scholes was very hopeful.

"Aaron," she said, she was finally moved to say. "Why didn't you tell me about this?"

"You're kidding! I forgot?"

To that she said nothing. But she had another question.

"Is that what you were doing on the mornings when you didn't have classes, voiceover stuff? Practice and auditions?"

"Sometimes. Or I'd just sit in my place in the Presidio and work. Bullshit with Tammy."

"The sex lady."

"I have no control over office assignments."

"Fine. And on the morning when Cedric was killed, what were you doing?"

He explained that he was making a tape for the Green Guzzle spot, not a voiceover, an on-camera gig. They wanted him in the overalls he wore on the Tale Spinner tape which the agency sent around as a sample of his work. Greg Farquahar saw the tape; Gregor Grosz recognized him and asked, through Dubin, for a meeting on Monday afternoon after the morning's taping. He began to tell her about that; she hurried him, because she'd seen the tape.

"How long were you there?"

"In the studio? All morning. Ten of us auditioned. I was the last one. It went lousy. That thing is junk. I won't let them use it if they should want to, although I don't know how I could explain that to Gert. So I didn't get out of there until around noon, and then I had a Coke at a Wendy's and also ate a couple of papaya and mango sticks I had in my briefcase. After that I walked to this bar, the Wee Shamrock. I'd cancelled my Tale Spinner session, you know."

"Aaron."

"Yes?"

She confessed that she had been to the bar, had interviewed the bartender.

"What is this? Why do you have to do this? I don't understand."

"I don't understand either," she said. "Not entirely. I'm not checking up on you because I have any doubts about you, Aaron. It's all tied up with...with Diane Blake. I can't explain, not yet. Please."

"Please what?"

"Please don't ask me to explain."

"Oh. Well, I won't. Wouldn't dream of it. Anything else for you today?"

Nothing, probably, nothing important. It was clear now that Aaron had spent that Monday morning with a bunch of other people, making a goofy video. He'd been safely and provably distant from their house in Berkeley—that was the main thing. Possibly, though, if Farquahar was Saxon was Grosz, that might be also somewhat important, Artie the Aardwolf, Grosz-Saxon's lab beast, having left his mark at the scene of the crime. This connection was hard to figure out. Did it matter? Irina Pownall had boarded the little *Proteles* with Derek, who then killed Cedric. Perhaps there was no real connection with Gregor, only coincidence. His appearance, reappearance, just confused things, confused her. She was confused, for example, and bothered by the fight, if you could call it that, between him and Aaron.

"Aaron, the bartender at that Shamrock place said you attacked Gregor. He said Greg. What happened there?"

"Oh, that. Shit."

Now she had to know. She put her hand on Aaron's knee, looked around at the Orinda kids playing, looked back at him.

"You insist. Well, I'm not embarrassed, really. Anyone would have done what I did. I choked that Dubin guy for a minute or two, but I let him go. And I never got a hold on Grosz; he kept sliding under the table. Like his ass was greased. He talked about you. That's why I got pissed off. Still want to hear?"

No, she didn't, but would.

"Silence," said Aaron. "Maren the silent. Okay, I'll just go on for a while, and you stop me when you get bored. All right, I'm sitting in this place with Dubin and Gregor. Some person asked me to sing, and nobody liked it. Oh, wait. First, I make this big deal about how Greg Farquahar is really Gregor Grosz. I mean, I really was amazed, and I knew him instantly, even though he was all slicked up and not wearing glasses anymore. So we talk about how he pissed off the professor in our Latin seminar, and then we get into what we've been doing ever since. Blah blah. He's rich, he's international. He hints at these things. I wanted to ask him why he changed his name, but I didn't. After all, I want the job: I want to be Mr. Green Guzzle and do a lot of spots for them. Dubin had said that might happen, but he was also pretty unenthusiastic about my audition, so I thought I'd better ingratiate myself with Gregor, just be nice. But I don't think I'm going to be Mr. Green Guzzle. That wasn't what our meeting was about."

"It wasn't?"

"No. It was about you."

She looked at the children in the grove. One little girl had a very sticky nose, and she wanted to wipe it.

"First, yes, Gregor said I was good. He hasn't seen the tape yet, but knows that Dubin is very impressed, although Dubin doesn't look impressed. 'We'll have to try you on the other project,' Gregor says, 'the hoo hoo.' That is, he makes this stupid, whooping laugh. Somebody else in the bar then laughs in the same way. Strange place, strange people. I'm confused by the hoo hoo, Dubin's confused. 'The hyena,' Gregor says. 'The hyena product.' Then he asks me, 'Well, Aaron, how's your wife? How's little Maren?' He's two feet tall, and *you're* little? I got a bad feeling at that point, but I said, 'She's fine, got a daughter in college now.'"

"'Your daughter?' he says."

"'What? Yes, my daughter!'"

Aaron tried not to get angry, he said, but Gregor, whom he remembered as having been consistently agreeable, if crazy, kept goading him. He said that Aaron would probably make an ideal Green Guzzle customer because he had a real need for it, and that was why he might make a great corporate spokesperson:

viewers would sense his need and desperation. They would sense his happiness if the stuff worked on him, and Maren would happy, too.

"'Because, don't you see, there are only two ways to earn a woman's respect. Power! That's one way. Unfortunately, Aaron, it's not yours.'"

"'Power? Kiss my ass, Grosz!'"

Aaron began to explain how he had then summoned up a little chuckle, to make Gregor think he was jesting about kissing his ass, but one of the Orinda teachers, standing close to their bench, was glaring at him. Had he yelled? Probably. Well, not a yell for him, but quite loud by conventional standards.

"Is something wrong?" he asked the teacher.

"That's what I want to know," she said.

"He's fine," Maren told her, "just noisy. Come on."

That last was for Aaron, whose arm she tugged as she got up from the bench. It was uphill going, fairly rough, back to Wildcat Peak; they had to work their way down the other side and couldn't really talk. Maren felt tired. Aaron looked mad; possibly he was thinking of the teacher. Eventually the trail leveled out.

Then Maren asked, "What was the second way?"

"Second way what? Oh, Gregor's second way to make a woman respect you?"

She didn't say anything. Aaron said, "Well, in bed, obviously. Mastering women in bed. They're supposed to just lie there for a while, knocked out by your prowess, then hop up and fix breakfast. Old, stupid nonsense. He was serious, imparting this great secret. I forced myself not to laugh. I was thinking, who the hell could master you? You, I mean, Maren. And then Gregor said that you, Maren—"

"Yes, me."

"You especially wanted or needed…you know, I don't want to say it. It was very unpleasant the way he said it. Also incredibly juvenile. I felt about fourteen. And Dubin, who's a truly supercilious shit, was amused by it all, I believe."

"No, don't say it."

"And I needed Green fucking Guzzle if I was ever going to give it to you. So I lost it, and I yelled at him, and I tried to get him. But he slid away, under the table, as if he'd studied some martial art of bum-sliding. Greased-butt fu. Then he'd pop up again, grinning, the fucking little Nazi. Oh, Maren."

Aaron was laughing! He was laughing at how silly it must have been. Gregor Grosz popping his head up over the table in the booth at the Wee Shamrock, Aaron reaching for him, the bartender reaching for the phone. She thought she remembered the bartender saying they had beer on the table. Hard to believe Aaron hadn't knocked it all over. Probably he had and hadn't noticed. He barely noticed when Dubin hit him, he said. Felt just a tap, but he was sitting right next to Dubin and so could easily grasp his throat and give it a shake. Dubin looked frightened and made gulping noises, which caused Aaron some alarm.

"I realized that I could hurt the guy; he's an asshole, but even so. So I dropped him, and he kind of flopped down. Then I said to myself, enough. Fuck these people. Fuck Gregor Grosz, Greg Farquahar, and now, I'm convinced after what your parent said, George Saxon. I could think because he'd shut up. When I was grabbing at him and he'd slip down, every time he came back up he'd not only be grinning—he must have false teeth now, or caps—but talking: always saying your name, saying something about you.

"But now he was staying under the table. He was quiet. I told him to come up, I wasn't going to hurt him. So he did, just his head. Dubin was gone, don't know where he went. I said, 'Gregor—'"

"'Please,' he said, 'It's Greg.' Actually, he might have said 'George,' got himself mixed up. I didn't care. I kept calling him Gregor. Frankly, I liked him as Gregor. Didn't you? He was bright as hell, fun to be with. But now he's a jerk, another rich jerk. Like the parents at your school. Whoops! Don't like that, huh?"

"We've already done that today. Tell me the rest of it with you and him, Gregor."

"I said that I didn't want to work for him, something like that. I didn't want anything to do with him. And I told him to keep away from us, you too. His interest in you is pretty weird, after all those years. Maybe he liked you back then. Did he ever say anything?"

"Not really," Maren answered. "Certainly nothing I could remember. But what happened? In the bar, I mean."

"Oh, he just talked nonsense. He doesn't need you, he's done much better. Sure! I didn't say anything, I just wanted to leave. Bartender told me never to come back. Told him it broke my heart. Then, to calm down before I got back on BART and came home, I walked around in the neighborhood. Ate some dried fruit, although that was about the time I started not to like them. A Japanese tourist took a picture of me. Some little Spanish girls laughed at me. Or maybe I just imagined it."

Certainly he had. A man dressed like a farmer wandering city streets while he gnaws orange rootlike things. What's to laugh at?

"Then BART was delayed. Hey! Biker! Biker!"

He seized Maren, deposited her on the side of the trail. The biker, a chubby, older man wearing fluorescent blue shorts, smiled apologetically, bobbing head and helmet as he passed—at about three miles an hour.

"You don't weigh much."

"And you're an idiot." Bad word, that. But she was laughing, couldn't help it. She was afraid that her laughter sounded sad and that Aaron would notice, but he didn't.

"No shit, Sherlock," he said, laughing himself. A damn nice laugh, a real one.

He forgot about running back from Tilden. In the car he told her that Dubin had given him a copy of his audition tape at the studio, that he'd taken it home in his briefcase and then to his Presidio office the next day. When he looked at it there, he knew it was crap; interesting vibrating penis effect, but the rest was simply silly. Could Dubin and Grosz be serious about actually using this absurd thing? If not, why waste the time to make it, along with the seventy-five dollars they'd paid him on the spot, in cash? Were they trying to mock him, with the flower and the flowery monologue? No doubt Dubin, a fellow Whartonian unable to break into academe, envied him his tenure, but he really doubted Dubin would play such a trick without his boss's approval. Indeed, Gregor was full of insults in the Wee Shamrock, but why?

"I didn't ever injure him in some way, did I? Hurt his feelings?"

"No, you liked him."

"I know I did. Well, I just don't get it. I don't get him, in general. He sure isn't what he was. He was so damn smart, but now he's stupid. And he likes money, I guess, and must figure these dopey drugs are the way to get it. Probably right. What do I know? Look at Viagra. He's going to be in trouble with that Green Guzzle, though, if it really turns into Ecstasy after you drink it. They'll get after him for that. Maybe he knew that might happen, that it would be banned eventually, so he decided to get going on this hyena drug, which your parent says won't work. I think maybe he should have stuck with Latin."

"Or history," Maren said. "He was in my history class. He did something with Judy, too. I think it was in a Psych course. They watched people through one-way windows, but Gregor kept making odd sounds and distracting them. He had some reason. I'll ask her. Well, no, I won't."

They were home, in front of their little house. She parked the Bug, they opened the doors.

"Oh, wait," he said. "What about that other tape, the one where I read from the big bad wolf book? Did you want to know something about that?"

"No, I just liked it. I liked it when I saw it in your office. Those kids are great."

"They are. They're amazing. But the tape's gone now, the one I brought home to show you. I can bring the other one home. Want it for the school?"

"Sure. Bring it. Great!"

They went in.

Aaron went to grade papers. Maren sat on the couch for a few minutes, but it was no good. She picked up one of Aaron's *Sports Illustrateds*, but couldn't read it. Tired as she was, she got up and left the house.

She tried looking at things as she walked, but soon there came to her, unbidden, the image of Gregor Grosz as he had been long ago. Gregor asking questions in class that irked the professor and made her want to laugh. Gregor sipping coffee and talking about everything on earth. Little Gregor, with his sharp eyes and crooked, appealing smile. Gregor in bed with her, with her, Maren.

He was so little. She wanted to do something for him. Oh, she didn't know. There was something about being with a man her own size. Aaron and Jimmie, whom she was sleeping with, too—they were both so big you couldn't really hold them. She took Gregor into her bed once, hers and Aaron's; at least it was before they were married. She came to him several times, to his parents' house. The last time, when she came out of his room, she immediately encountered Mrs. Grosz, sitting on a couch or a chair. She was in a shadow and wearing gray, and she peered out of the shadow at Maren, who felt ridiculously pink and blond, like some dumb sorority girl.

That was the end with him.

Chapter Eight

Maren was hoping for a quiet Monday at school, quiet but full, engaging. In the event, the day soon went from dull to alarming, for others more than for her. She became upset about what happened later, just before she left.

Nothing is duller than a cold, and several of the kids seemed to be getting colds. Their parents should have kept them home. Now the others would soon start to snivel. The same depressing thing happened every year at about this time, when you could feel winter coming. Moby Leibling was obviously sick and spiritless; he kept wiping his nose on his whale, which became gucky in a hurry. Judy called Louise, his mom, and told her to come and take him home. Such calls, infectious kid calls, were obviously necessary, but they caused trouble by implying that a parent had been remiss in sending the kid to school. Often the particular parent confronted, not that Judy meant to confront or affront, would say that the other parent had made the faulty judgment call. Maren wondered what Louise had said this time, but Judy didn't tell her. She seemed distant. Maren took the gucky whale and rubbed it with a damp towel and then with a dry one.

Soon Louise arrived, usual dumb smile plastered on her face, although she was probably more than a little pissed off. Before falling on her listless son and cooing him into a coma, she observed the other kids, checking symptoms. If she couldn't figure out a way to stick the blame on her grad student husband, at least she could tell him, 'He got it at the school.'

"Oh, ick," said Louise. She had touched the whale.

By this time, Maren had Moby's jacket on him, having threaded his limp, clammy arms through the sleeves. Then she guided him to Louise, who was chatting with Judy, both women now wearing broad, mirthless grins. Maren moved on to her next task, assisting with the hygiene of Lark, a boy, who a moment earlier had suddenly begun to dance about and yank at his pull-ups; these actions were sure signs that he needed to visit the potty, which he feared. Feigning bright enthusiasm, Maren promised Lark a sticker, for his shirt, if he went into the bathroom and hit the bowl. The idea was for him to be a big boy. Lark didn't want to be a big boy, and he peed in his pull-ups then and there.

"Oh, Lark," Maren said. "Next time...next time, couldn't you wait, please?"

Lark smirked. He was a manipulative little rat, and all the teachers knew it.

"You still have to go into the bathroom, and you'll have to take those pull-ups off yourself. Okay? Like always."

"No. No, Maren. Nuh!"

This wasn't fear. He knew the potty couldn't get him just for taking off his wet pants. He was just lazy and wanted her to do it, and she wouldn't. He did this all the time. Why always her, with him? Where was Holly? At present she and a few of the kids were goofing with some legos, spread out on what was supposed to be the school corn meal table. The table stood by the door, through which at that moment walked Deirdre Blake and Boris Pownall. A bit late, but they were here. Maren had been worried when they hadn't shown up at the regular time. Not so much for Boris, although his parents were at odds; she trusted Irina. Irina could protect him. But who could tell about those crazy Blakes? Everybody was mixed up in the same mess, though, with Gregor at the center. No telling for anyone. But the children were here.

She had been worried, more worried than she had realized. Abandoning the sodden Lark without a word, she ran to hug the newcomers, who hugged her back. Lark then ran into the bathroom by himself, his first solo visit.

"What did you do to him?" asked Holly, marveling.

"Oh, I'm so glad to see you," she told the kids, after they had let one another go.

Boris then crashed to the ground. She should have made sure, before unhanding him, that he was absolutely square upon his feet. She and Deirdre helped him up.

"I'm cool," he said, with his accent.

"You're what?"

"You know. I'm—"

But then came a great bestial roar from outside, occasioning much concern within the room. "Shit!" shouted Judy. "What now?" Waving her arms above her head, Cloelia screamed vigorously, as did several other children. Conway threw himself at Maren's legs, almost knocking her over; he had been rushing at Boris, she judged, to bop him. "It's all right," she said, gently detaching Conway. She knew this, as did Deirdre and Boris.

"It's cool," Boris told Conway.

The bathroom door opened, revealing Lark, his pull-ups flopped upon his feet. He looked proud.

Rushing out into the yard, Maren saw there Moby and a kneeling Louise, clutching whale and child, Irina Pownall, who must have brought both Deirdre and Boris, and, of course, Artie the Aardwolf, who had also come with Irina. He was nose to nose with Lion. Somehow the great angora rabbit had escaped from his hutch. There wasn't any reason to worry: Irina had Artie safely on his leash, and Maren was sure she could handle specimens much bigger and meaner than this scrawny *Proteles*, who wasn't very mean at all. Already his fur was fluffing down, and the skunky smell he emitted when feigning aggression was rapidly fading. His mouth was safely shut; you couldn't see the big teeth. The roar had been quite loud, so much so that it seemed to Maren to be presently echoing through the Berkeley hills. Thousands of wealthy people, gardening and whatnot, were pricking up their ears. But it was nothing really. The rabbit had frightened the aardwolf, nothing more.

"What *is* it?" asked Louise, meaning Artie.

"Yes, what?" This came from Judy, who had followed Maren out the door.

"Is not to worry. Eats only little bugs."

Irina then explained a bit about aardwolves, although she said nothing in particular about the one she had with her presently, out for a breath of morning air. Perhaps she would have gone into his exciting experiences as a lab escapee, but her narration was suddenly interrupted by a terrific, bone-chilling scream. It exposed Artie's growl, which had probably been louder, for the fraud it was. Thousands of hill dwellers rushed into their houses, gardening implements left heedlessly behind. Holly opened the Big Room door and thrust out her head, on which her green Oakland A's cap sat somewhat askew.

"May I ask what all the noise is about today?"

That hat meant, "I take no sass." But this was hardly sass.

Judy waved at her to stay inside and close the door, which, grumpily, she did. Then Judy said, to those outside, "That dog, the old one. I've got to talk to those people. Maren, remind me!"

Of course there was no dog. Maren said nothing, didn't even nod.

Louise Leibling, that amiable dope, had turned white.

"That," she gasped, "that was a woman in pain. What's happening?"

"Woman?" said Irina. "Some woman."

"Maren?" Judy expected her to say something.

Maren was waiting for another cry. None came.

"There is this woman around here," she offered, "who shouts. But she's not in pain."

Judy and Louise both gaped at her. Irina, however, was staring at her own wrist, to which Artie's leash was no longer attached.

"Where is—look! In cage!"

Was not cage, strictly speaking. Was hutch. Knowing a real lion when they heard one, both rabbit and aardwolf, formidable as both could be, had jumped or scrambled in and were now huddled together as far from the hutch's open door as they could get. They formed one large heap of fur and fluff, and their little faces said the same thing: close the damn door! Irina discovered the leash hanging out of the hutch and stood holding it, uncertain whether to tug.

"I won't bring him back," she said, "when I come later for Boris and Deirdre. His growl...the other heard it."

"Are you telling me that was some kind of animal? Up here by the school? First there was that thing in there—"

"Is pet! Companion. Just makes noise. And odor, all right."

"And now something awful, shrieking! What is this? Isn't this Berkeley? We were told this was a safe community. We might as well have settled in Oakland!"

Dropping the whale, Louise picked Moby up and held him aloft, as if to demonstrate why safe communities matter. Moby yawned.

"Oh, yes," Judy soothed. "Very safe. That's not an animal or anything. It isn't that dog even. Maren knows. What was that about the woman not in pain?"

Irina was ignoring all this. She cooed at Artie, promising him "nice termites at home." Did she really have access to termites?

The door to the Big Room opened again. "Help!" Holly was badly outnumbered in there. Time for some business as usual. The cougar wasn't coming back. At least she wasn't going to scream again. Why not just say it was a cougar? Well, she couldn't. Woman not in pain? Ah.

"It's a woman who screams occasionally. She watches a show on television and then she makes that noise. It's a noise of liberation. You ever hear athletes, women athletes? Well, it's like that, Louise, a battle cry!"

"Oh," said Louise, getting interested. "Oh, I think...yes! What show?"

"That I'm not sure about. Perhaps an exercise show. Or maybe not. I just know it's on one of the cable stations, and it's got the name 'Tammy' in the title. You could research it."

"Tammy, Tammy. I will."

The Leiblings descended the steps. Judy and Maren plunged into the Big Room. Everyone needed calming down, especially their fellow teacher, who considered herself shamelessly exploited that morning. Before it had ended, in fact, Judy told Holly she could go home early. The Volvo wagons came at their appointed time. Irina came. All the kids left. No Cozy today. Judy asked Maren to come into the office.

"You have to hear this. Trish O'Bannion."

Of all their parents, this mom, to Melody O'Bannion-Bernath, left the craziest messages on their answering machine. There were three from Trish, two concerning a play date, the kind of thing that can require both complex interfamily arranging and adroit disposition of staff; the Hillside teachers functioned as a signal corps, relaying decisions and instructions. Trish's first message was simple: Melody goes home with Hannah Silverman and Dolores, Hannah's au pair, who would also take Lark. But no, change that (this in the second call): Hannah goes with Melody and Melody's au pair, Uzma. In addition, please tell Uzma to drop by Andronico's and get some Thai noodle salad and also go to Front Row for a video to show the kids. Lark to go with Ian and Ian's au pair, Rosa. Maren had noted Rosa's air of desperation when she left with the two little boys. The third message from Trish said to remind Uzma that Liz Gelman would be late because she was buying skis. Judy and Maren did-n't know what Liz Gelman was late for or even who she was; maybe she was some dad's old wife. Judy had passed all this on to Uzma.

After she listened to the messages, Maren shook her head. Oh, that Trish. But this wasn't so much. Trish had left odder, sillier messages on their machine; so had other parents.

"That Trish," Judy said. "Actually, I need to talk to you, Maren. Uh, look. I don't need to know about this Tammy show, but I'm concerned about that cougar. Hanging around all the time. What do you think?"

"All the time? How often have you seen her?"

"Oh, I haven't. But you did last week. I assume this animal lives in Tilden and comes down like the deer, after the deer. I'll call Animal Control again."

"Oh? Didn't know you called them the first time."

Maren smiled at the idea of the Animal Control people going after the cougar.

"They never attack people," she said.

"Take your word for it. Maren, there's something else. Now, don't get huffy."

Maren prepared herself to get huffy. They were sitting in Judy's office, a tiny space equipped with a card table, a two-drawer filing cabinet under the table, an adult-sized metal chair for Judy, a wooden children's chair for visitors. There Maren sat, knees almost level with her shoulders. The posture didn't bother her, for she was accustomed to diminutive furniture of all kinds. But she didn't like being tricked, as she figured she had been, with this sham of comical phone messages from Trish O'Bannion.

Perhaps Judy wanted to know where she had gone on Friday after leaving in the middle of the day, and about that she was not ready to talk. It was so shifty. At Hillside School the Volvos always came, no matter what. Things settled down. But this business with the Blakes and with Gregor—she couldn't imagine how that would end. So she didn't want to be quizzed, especially by Judy, for Judy had run off herself one day last week after getting a phone call and had not stayed for Cozy. Of course, she couldn't ask about that. Judy was the Director.

But Judy didn't ask her about Friday. Instead, she promptly volunteered that the call she had received last Wednesday, day of the dead raccoon, had come from Derek Blake, agitated as all hell. He threatened to remove Deirdre from Hillside School, because Maren was corrupting his wife.

"Me?"

"You."

"Me corrupting her? She...I...shit! What did you say?"

"I said, 'Let's talk.' He said, 'Fine! Now!' And I figured I'd better. He was, as I say, agitated as hell, and I don't want major problems with him. He pulls his kid, some other disgruntled parent does the same thing. That's bad for cash flow, morale too. All the parents talk. We've seen it before. Though with you, it's usually the women who get upset, not the men, because they think the husbands like you."

"Oh, Judy. That's happened how many times? Twice? And they were nuts. *This* is nuts!"

She said that too loudly, perhaps, and she leaned too far forward for the little chair. It started to scoot out from under her, and she quickly sat back. Judy sat facing her, behind the card table, on her adult chair. She was a big woman, anyway. Maren had to look way up at her.

"Oh, there were other complaints," Judy said, "all ridiculous, of course. I didn't need to bother you with them. But look, did anything happen with Diane? Can you think of something you did? Anything that would make Derek *think* that you were doing this, this corrupting."

"Judy! I've never corrupted anybody in my life!"

"Yeah?"

Quite a claim she'd made, Maren realized, but she answered, "Yeah!"

"Oh, I know you didn't do anything, Maren, but this could be a problem for us, for the school, because Derek is so strange. In fact, I think he's gone crazy because of this murder thing, and I'm really worried about what he might do. Whatever it is, you know it's going to have a bad effect on Deirdre. Right? Now, listen. When I met him—at Cha Am on Shattuck, that Thai place—he was very weird, going on about how Diane identified with you, worshiped you or something. So you could dominate and corrupt her. 'Curb her!' That's what I'm supposed to do to you."

"Curb me?" Maren was angry, but she kept her body still. "Judy, I think I need to know what I'm supposed to be doing to her, to this odd woman. Corrupting her how? Her life, her morals, her diet, what?"

"She's odd, Diane? Well, Derek said you had a talk with her somewhere."

"For five minutes. I bumped into her on Telegraph. We talked about the thing, the murder. All right? I didn't try to influence her in any way. What did she tell him?"

"You went to Telegraph? I thought you hated it down there."

Maren turned her gaze from Director Judy to the calendar on the office wall, a Popeye calendar. That month Olive Oyl was smashing Popeye over the head with a vase. Maren said nothing. Judy made palliative noises. Sorry, sorry.

"Ermp," Maren said. "Look, you. Explain this nonsense."

"Maren, really! It's Deirdre I'm thinking of. Didn't I say that?"

"You did, yes. But I don't think that's all you're thinking of."

"I'm also thinking of cash flow and morale. I said that. But our most pressing concern, I would say, is Deirdre. No?"

"All right. True. But I've still got nothing to tell you. Be nice if you would, as I say, explain."

"About how you're supposed to have corrupted Diane? That's what I'm asking you, I think. I don't know what Derek's thinking of, he didn't tell me. We finished the pork satay—you know, it's funny that he eats meat. Well, then he just sat there in silence. After being so excited, suddenly he was calm. No, not calm. As if something went out of him, like air. He was looking at me, but he wasn't seeing me. I had a very, very bad feeling, and I didn't know what to do. He looked at his watch then and said he was late, and he left. Stuck me with the bill. I'm gonna add it on."

"Good!"

"But I'm worried. This smells bad to me, Maren. I wanted to find out more, so I called Derek. I called on Friday, the day you left early. What was that about, anything important?"

"No, Aaron. He needed bailing out, a ride. Nothing important. Sorry."

"No problem. And I called over the weekend, but I just kept getting their machine. Talk about crazy messages! All these animal rights directives and updates. Save Buster the Sea Lion, unjustly accused of being a public nuisance at Pier 39. Trap Mayor Brown, not Buster! Meet at the pier, wear sun block. Protect the marsh rail, the upland weasel; build shelters for raccoons. Raccoons? All I said was call me, but he didn't. Today Diane picked up; I said have Derek call me, please. When she asked what about, I said I didn't know, that we were playing telephone tag. I couldn't say it was about her, and about you. And, really, I don't know: that's why I can't explain, as you keep insisting I do. You can't explain either, right? Not even a bit. You have no idea what he meant by all that stuff about corrupting?"

"No idea. I have no idea what he meant, and I think you're right about what you said before. He's nuts. He's cooked up some fantasy, based, maybe, on something Diane told him. She's none too normal either."

"She's not? You said that a minute ago, that she was odd. But I never noticed. In fact, she's always reminded me of you."

Olive Oyl's vase had flowers in it. They were flying through the air, in the freeze frame.

Judy said: "Oops. I shouldn't say that? Okay, I apologize. Maren, I'm just saying, try to remember. Is there anything Diane might have misinterpreted in some way and then told Derek—oh, hell with it! It's all so tenuous. Sorry I got you in here."

Judy's phone rang. She picked it up. She said, "Hillside School." Then she said, "Hi," and looked down at her table.

"Yes. Yes, she is. Derek wouldn't be there, would he? Oh, on a trip. You didn't say—no, you didn't. No, it doesn't. Sure."

She put the handset down on the table. "Diane Blake for you," she said.

Maren stood up to reach the handset. "Hello," she said.

"Maren, it's me! I'm so glad I've got you. Maren?"

"Just a minute."

Where she was standing, her hip was about a foot from Judy's right shoulder. Judy, sitting like a lump. Maren waited. Judy looked at the wall, no calendar, a blank wall. Slowly she got up, without a word, walked around Maren and through the door. Maren closed it after her.

"Okay, Diane. You can go ahead."

"Hi? Can I say hi?"

"Hi. What is it?"

"I need to talk to you. Not now, tomorrow. Please! It's important!"

"Okay."

"You will? Good. I want you to meet me on Telegraph, same time as last time. But at Intermezzo. Lunch, okay?"

"At three? I'll have had lunch already. I bring it in a bag. No, no food. I'll meet you at that bench in Dwinelle Plaza."

"Can't we even get coffee? It's so awkward talking on a bench. We can't really have a dialogue. But, okay. I can bring coffee, I guess, if you're really going to insist on this. Maybe it's best. Best if we're alone—I mean, without other people close. Okay. And don't tell anyone that we're getting together, especially Aaron."

"All right."

"Great! Don't tell Judy either. And, speaking of which, do you know if Derek talked to her? Some school business, about the bill or something. We're not communicating well, Derek and me."

"I don't know. I don't think he did."

Judy was standing, waiting for her, by the cubbies and coat hooks.

Maren said, "See you tomorrow."

Moby didn't come that morning, and two other kids were also out sick. Lark was healthy, but he backslid and ran shrieking from the bathroom. Irina both brought and took away Boris and Deirdre. No Artie. Maybe they had him on a treadmill back at the digs. No unusual animal noises of any kind. Holly, wearing her burgundy art hat, said, "What's wrong with you guys?" Judy and Maren were not jolly with each other. Swedish engines hummed, hauling away the children. Maren got into her Bug.

This time she tried to park on the north side of campus. Nothing. She headed south, to the same area where, last week, she had found the space guarded by the scruffy man. Today she found neither space nor man and had to settle for a lot, at five dollars per hour. This pissed Maren off, even when she remembered the ticket she had been stuck with last week that she hadn't yet told Aaron about. She hated coming here, and she had to pay, too!

Maren had loved being a student at U.C. Berkeley. There had been bad times, confusions, but they were mostly her own fault. Campus life was wonderful then. She didn't like it anymore. Everybody wanted money, whether they admitted it or not. Every new building was named after some capitalist who made clothes or computers. The kids all wanted M.B.A.'s or law degrees, or so she'd heard. There had to be some connection between this institutionalized greed and the aggressive panhandling she had to cope with, by ignoring, as she marched up Telegraph Avenue. She didn't see Natalie and her chums, but she didn't look.

Telegraph ends at Sather Gate, the southern entrance to the university, and beyond Sather Gate lies a brief expanse usually covered with tables. Students sit at them "tabling," handing out pamphlets and talking to people, as long as the people resemble themselves. Every table, Maren noticed, represented a different faction, in most cases an ethnic group: the Korean Students' Club, the Armenian Students, and so on. Berkeley was known for its factions. Everybody stuck with his or her own, which seemed a pity. At her school everyone was the same. Well, of course, nearly everyone was white, but they were all children. That was the important thing. It was what you taught your own kids, that we're all human; but at college, this one, anyway, they unlearned it. Must be the money.

Passing through the realm of tables, Maren turned into Dwinelle Plaza. She found the bench. Diane wasn't there yet, although she herself was late.

What does she want? Whatever it is, she'll probably get it. Because she doesn't care about anyone else, not even me, and because we're here, where I'm not strong.

Diane appeared. She held a cardboard coffee carrier, with four cardboard cups. "Mochas," she said, with little spirit. Jimmie Greenlee was with her, wearing a jogging outfit instead of his usual J. C. Penney detective suit. They stood before Maren. Diane said, "Mocha?" She said, "No. Thanks, no."

Jimmie looked at her, then at Diane. "It's amazing," he said. "You really don't look like each other in any specific way, and yet you're so much alike."

He looked closely at them, comparing. Their bottom halves—both were wearing jeans—seemed to interest him more than the tops.

"Sit down," Maren said. Each did, on either side of her. She looked straight ahead, at gray Dwinelle. Then she turned her head and looked at Diane.

"I didn't know about him," Diane explained. "He was just standing there at the door after my class. He must have looked it up."

"But this is convenient," Jimmie said. "I didn't know about you, Maren, but you can help. You can help me clarify things with Diane. It's good we're here together."

Neither woman spoke.

"So, cut to the chase," Jimmie said. "First, Aaron. That's

Maren's husband, Diane. Old friend. Well, he's in the clear with the McAulay case."

He looked at Maren and nodded his head. She said nothing, kept her face still.

"Okay," he said. "Okay. Now, Diane, I'm going to explain about Aaron's alibi, so you'll both understand why we have to move on to the next candidate. I think we all can guess who that is. And, you know, even if it's really awkward and causes a lot of confusion, we have to do the right and legal thing. Maren will certainly want that, and she can help you see it. We just have to."

"Oh, hold your water," Diane said.

She said this somewhat out of the corner of her mouth; she snapped it, really. Jimmie looked down at the ground, at the crumbly Plaza paving; he stroked his head reflectively, waiting for her to allow him to release his water. His posture did not connote mastery, power. Someone had been talking about power recently. Gregor had been, she remembered, to Aaron in the bar. Who had the power here? Big macho football player/cop/therapist/cop again, but look who had the power.

"All right," he finally told Diane, talking across Maren. "I can understand why you're resisting, but I'm just telling you how things are, how they have to be. Understand? Hey, if I thought there was any close bond between you and him, I'd go slower with this. But I know, I *know*, there isn't. I only want to help you, Diane, is the point."

"You're trying to push me around, is the point. You act like you have some control over me, but you don't. And you know, you *know*, you don't. Now you have to wait, Officer Greenlee. Someone else is coming, someone who's expected: by me, surprise for Maren. This is not the moment to talk about your next candidate."

Maren said, "Surprise?"

"Yeah, soon. Tell me, Maren. What's new at the school? Anything?"

"Well, Deirdre came with Boris last week. That's new. Nobody told us."

"That's right. Derek and I removed her from the house. We've got this damned tension between us. Not good for her. I...we asked the Pownalls to take her, because she's friends with Boris, and Irina said okay. She's with them, or her. I think Anthony's not around."

"Neither is Derek, is he?" Maren asked, remembering what she'd overheard Judy saying to Diane yesterday on the phone.

"Him too, right. Gone on one of his trips. You knew that." This last to Jimmie.

"Yes," Jimmie said, across Maren. "But I need to know more."

"Too bad. There isn't anything more. Maren, I know I should have told you, but everything's so screwed. Do you think it's okay for Deirdre to stay with Boris and Irina?"

"It's okay. It's fine."

Fine for Deirdre to stay with Boris and Irina and Natalie and friends and animals, at their digs? Sure. Why not? But. But...who is this?

It was Gregor Grosz.

Gregor swaggered to their bench. He didn't look like the old Gregor. So natty now, but she knew him instantly, despite his perfect, gleaming teeth and absent glasses.

"What a place to meet," he said. "There's a constant wind here." He sounded more British than he used to. There had been more in there once, another language possibly, odd traces.

He was no taller than Maren. That hadn't changed, of course, but he had grown in bulk, as if he'd been lifting weights. The old Gregor had been very slight; the flannel shirts he used to wear, always buttoned at the cuffs, had ballooned around him. That wouldn't happen now, but, in any case, he was wearing a jacket that fit him very well, a fancy thing with multiple zippers. He also wore tasseled loafers in lizard skin. Imagine Gregor Grosz in shoes like these, or lifting weights!

She said, "Hello," just that, but Gregor didn't answer, being engaged with Jimmie.

"I remember you," said the Berkeley cop, in tones of utter bafflement. "You came out for football! You demanded a tryout, although you'd never played."

"Soccer-style kicker, why not? That coffee for me? Ah, thanks, Diane."

"But you couldn't get it up!"

"I couldn't…just what is it that you mean?" The question was uttered in the coldest of tones. Maren was amazed. He had been warm in the old days, endearing, never glacial.

Jimmie seemed as shocked as she was, shocked into silence. Diane had to explain. "He means the ball, Garrett. When you kicked it, it didn't go high enough."

Garrett?

"The coach was a very limited man. I decided not to play for him. I was glad when he moved on. Contributed my little bit to that. Oh, and Jimmie—it's Jimmie, isn't it?—wasn't there something else? Some class?"

"Yes, I remember. Philosophy. We did Schopenhauer. You helped me one day, but the instructor—"

"He's gone, too. But I want to talk to Maren. Little Maren."

Give me a break, she thought. But his eyes held her. They were so keen and bright, as she remembered them, as they had been. He smiled at her, his crooked smile.

"You still don't talk," he said. "Speak, Maren, speak! Ha-ha."

She didn't remember this. He had not been like this.

He looked at Jimmie, wanting him to join in the ha-ha. Did he know about Jimmie, the old affair? No, not possible. Jimmie didn't laugh. He put his cop face on, which bothered Gregor not one bit. Gregor Grosz, or Greg Farquahar, or if Aaron had things figured right, George Saxon, or Garrett someone.

"Are you," she said, "George Saxon?"

"Yes. Diane tell you? Or that hideous Russian woman?"

"I know about Greg Farquahar. Who's this Garrett? Well, I know it's you."

"Garrett St. John, right. When I was just getting into biotech, I was Garrett. Marine stuff at that time."

Maren must have looked blank. She felt blank.

"Fish," Gregor said. "The biotechnology resources offered by fish."

"Oh."

"Not much there, it turned out. Now I'm on to the next thing.

Very, very promising. But when doing the former thing, the marine bio, I met my young friend here. Back East, this was."

Young friend here was Diane. He had gestured toward her, but she didn't gesture back. Not much coming from young friend, usually so brisk, so lively, and so eager yesterday to speak with Maren today, which she seemed not even to be trying to do. Why are these men here?

"Diane's a lot like you," Gregor continued. "Did you know that? Younger, of course. Like you as you once were, back then. That's what I mean. It's really quite striking. You have the same...I don't know what to call it, dammit."

Now he wasn't smiling. Not knowing what to call it, this inexplicable sameness, seemed to bother Gregor. Finally, he sat down on the bench, next to Diane.

Maren glanced at Jimmie. He was still making his cop face, but not at anyone in particular. Maybe the expression, so bluntly dumb, only signified dumbness, helpless confusion.

"How's old Aaron?" asked Gregor, but he didn't let her answer, yacking on without a break. "I know about his book. Does he ever look it up on Amazon-dot-com? I did. It takes six weeks to get and is about one millionth in sales. And the print! How could he have ever have permitted that? But Aaron was always careless. Understand he teaches a lot of composition these days. That must be exciting. And he can't get a fartie. Dubin told me, one of my people. Man can't get a fartie."

"At least he's the same man," she said. Why this interest in Aaron? This contemptuous interest.

"I'm the same man, too, the one you used to know quite well. But better, stronger. Do you mean the names? That's just business. A fartie! Ha-ha."

Nobody said anything for a while. Maren was about to say something; she didn't know what it would be, but she was angry, and not just because of Aaron. But the Campanile bonged four times. Afternoon classes let out. Hundreds of students rushed down the Dwinelle steps. To her horror, they all resembled Gregor! A pack of Gregors, male and female, all alike. They weren't, really; she could see that, but what she saw and what she felt weren't the same. Oh, many of the students were Asian, dark and dark-haired, like Gregor, and often quite short, so there was a broad physical resemblance. Not important. Somehow the big black and white ones resembled Gregor just as much. The new Gregor.

"Little Maren," he said again.

"What is this shit?" The question came from Jimmie, who asked it of Diane. He sounded queasy and repulsed. Diane shrugged.

"One day little Maren just wasn't there anymore."

Now Jimmie was looking at her, no cop face, and she turned away.

"Not pleasant," Gregor commented. "Not nice. I learned something from it, however. Never take anything freely given. Negotiate, negotiate, negotiate. So they get something too, even if they don't want it. Then they can't pull away from you. Disappear. Poof."

The afternoon light was an unpleasant dirty gray. Anything touching bleak Dwinelle Hall turned gray, she knew that, but today this effect somehow conveyed an aura of ill health; it was like the light in Aaron's video for Green Guzzle. For a moment she saw the four of them, framed, sitting on their bench, all in a row, Gregor, Diane, Maren, Jimmie—awkward, much swiveling required. Hard for big-shouldered Jimmie, who didn't have much of a neck and so couldn't see what Gregor had just begun to do, to rub his little hand in a circle on the inside of Diane's left leg, by her crotch. Whir whir.

Diane's face. Could Jimmie see that? Maren was almost sorry she could. It was absolutely still and closed, the face of a hunting animal. Gregor, fool, take away your hand.

"So," Gregor said. "Little Maren. Help me out, huh? I need my aardwolf back, the *Proteles*."

He continued to rub. He knew she could see.

"Is this a negotiation?" Maren asked. "What do I get?"

"Oh," Gregor said. "You're funny. I don't remember that. Maren's funny. Isn't she, Diane?"

Diane expressed no opinion. Diane was being very silent. Gregor removed his hand from her leg.

"What, then, what do you get? Unfortunately for you, that animal isn't terribly valuable, and so I must begin the negotiation with something small. Aaron. I mean, a little job for Aaron, a wage supplement, since he can't get a fartie. Send him around to the lab! I'm serious. He can carry the buckets. We have lots of buckets. Well, that's the offer. Ah, Maren? You're a negotiator, remember? So you have to respond. Oh, right. You don't talk."

He drank some of his mocha and made a face. It must have been cold. No one else had drunk any mocha, Maren thought. Gregor resumed.

"But maybe it's a ploy." Gregor smiled. "Never thought of that. Could that be what you do? I've seen it since. These silent people, making you guess what they want. I never...I didn't know about that then. So if you wanted something, I didn't know what it was. And then, poof! Why didn't you just tell me? Maren, could this be true?"

He was not smiling. He thought it might be so. Maren touched her own face, which she had felt tensing, becoming a mask. I'm trying not to laugh at him, she told herself. She turned to glance at Diane, but Diane was looking away, back toward Sather Gate. Gregor started talking again.

"What do you want now? A job for yourself? Sorry, baby! You still look good. Yes, dammit! But I don't need a receptionist. We do science, with commercial applications, of course. I wouldn't ask you to haul buckets of hyena dung around, and I can't imagine any other possibilities. If you had done something with your life besides work in a day-care center, but...well, you like children. Fine! Someone must. Oh, no! My God, is *that* what you wanted?"

Jimmie said: "That?"

Diane said: "Shut up."

Maren said: "Nursery school. Not day-care. And I didn't want anything, and I don't now. Can't help you with the aardwolf."

"You're amused? Something is tickling you?"

Evidently, her mask had cracked a bit, which relieved her. Babies with Gregor! Tiny, tiny babies!

"I want my aardwolf back!" he huffed. "It's my property, and you have it, or you know where it is."

Maren said, "Nope."

"I need it!" Gregor didn't care for 'nope.'

Leaning across Diane, he seemed ready to place his little brown head in Maren's lap. Then he poked his head in the direction of her stomach. She felt he might bite.

"My scientists," he exclaimed, "*they* need it! The whole project's coming to a standstill. You can't!"

The whole project! A few hyenas ground up for nothing, according to Irina, the head scientist, who had taken Artie and split for Natalie's commune.

"I have no idea," Maren said, "where that animal is. Can't help you, Garrett. George. Greg. You can straighten up now, please. Sit up straight!"

She wanted to grab his head and flip it away. He did sit up, but only somewhat. Now he seemed to be squeezing his little shoulder into Diane, forcing her to sit sideways.

"And," he said, "you're corrupting them, my scientists. That Russian sow."

Maren felt angry, but said nothing.

Jimmie said, "What's this about scientists? Aard*what?* Is this important?"

These weren't cop-like questions; no one bothered to answer them. Jimmie wasn't thinking like a cop, and Maren knew why. Stupid, she thought.

Diane decided she was sick of Gregor leaning on her. She snapped, "Stop pushing into me! Get off me!"

He didn't move. Diane sprang up, twisting her hips, and took a few steps away from the bench. Gregor slid into her space, next to Maren; without thinking, she turned to face him, and a scary thing happened. He looked now as he had when he was young. He had been a boy when she knew him. He was a boy now, to her. She must not let him know this.

His eyes were black and birdlike, crowlike: much like Aaron's, really, although he and Aaron were dissimilar in every other way. Maybe Aaron's parents, his grandparents, that is, came from

Gregor's place in Europe, some squalid district in the east. Saxon! St. John! England never bred a pair of eyes like these. She was okay now, having thought of Aaron, having put Gregor in his place. But she seemed condemned to think of eyes. Diane had dark eyes too, but big and sad, not beady and sharp. Maren raised her head and looked at Diane, standing before her, facing her. Yes, big and sad. Something else, too: they were luminous, full of light, but the light was cold. Maren felt drawn in, as if into a large room with a cement floor and hard, bare tables, and that light, coming from some fancy equipment that was up to no good.

For no clear reason, Diane said, "Still green."

She meant Maren, Maren's eyes.

"Yes," Gregor said. "So what? Diane, I think it's time for us to leave."

He stood up. Maren didn't look at him, the new Gregor.

"The animal," he told her. "I'll get it back without you. It's a matter of finding Pownall, the sow. Obviously they're together. When you see her, Maren, tell her to get in touch before I come looking. Tell her she can come back to the lab on a trial basis, at reduced pay. Ha-ha! With her I can negotiate."

No you can't. Not with Irina.

"Even if I can't with you. Well, what have you got that I want? Nothing, really. But can you do me a favor? A little one?"

"What?" she said.

"I want you to tell Aaron something," Gregor said. "His book is not so bad. The worst essay in it, and I'm afraid it's his, is better than the best thing Cedric McAulay ever did, ever did himself. He shouldn't be dead, of course, but...well, things happen. Don't they? I'm going now. We're going. Maren, it's been a long time. You've changed. Kid in college now, Aaron said. Yes?"

Maren nodded.

"But you haven't changed a lot. All right, Diane. Let's go."

He put his hand on Diane's elbow. Diane seemed to like that, for she smiled at Gregor and looked decidedly non-chilly for the first time that afternoon. She said, "In a minute, Garrett. I need to talk to Maren, just for a minute. About Deirdre. Okay?"

Gregor sat back down on the bench, next to Jimmie.

"Whatever became of you?" he asked. "I take it you never made it to the pros?"

"I played seven years," Jimmie said. "NFL. Packers and Bears."

"Oh? Are they good?"

"Maren," Diane said, to draw her away.

Rising from the bench, she followed Diane up the broad stone steps leading to Dwinelle Hall. They sat down on a low wall, just before the entrance.

Diane said, "Jimmie screwed things up. I didn't know about him. I knew about Gregor. He was with me when I called you yesterday. He wanted to come late, make an entrance. That was the plan, his plan. So, before he came, I was going to tell you what's really going on. Couldn't, can't now. But it's cool. Don't worry."

"What, Diane? What's going on?"

"Asshole! Here he comes."

Gregor walking up the steps, chest puffed out. He looked like a pigeon, one of the flock that always strutted about in the Plaza.

"Tell you soon. Promise. Don't worry. Whatever happens, we'll be fine."

"We!"

"Diane, come!"

"Asshole," she whispered. Then she went to Gregor's side.

Maren watched them go, then walked down into the Plaza again. Jimmie was watching a young man sitting on a bench and smoking a joint. He didn't resemble Gregor and must not have been a student; he resembled an idiot. Maren heard him giggle to himself. He had blond dreadlocks.

"Let's go," Jimmie said. "Let's walk. Okay?"

They walked in a northerly direction, away from Sather Gate and Telegraph, circling around the Doe Library, which had recently moved most of its millions of books into vaults underground. The shelves were all jammed together, and you had to turn huge wheels to separate them so that you could get at the books. She'd heard this, hadn't gone in to see. Beyond the library, a wide trail wound through a bit of hilly territory to the campus's northern end. This terminus was marked by a large and ugly gate, gift of the class of nineteen-fifty-something, constructed at about the same time the vaults were excavated for the library. Jimmie must have his car over there, beyond the gate, on some quiet northside street. Not his cop car, his own. She was sure his department didn't know he was hanging around Diane's classroom. He was troubled; he was in trouble.

They stopped at the university's northern border, at Euclid and Hearst, to wait for the light. Jimmie said, "That was Gregor Grosz. Gregor Grosz is also other guys, right? Including Greg Farquahar. Right?"

"Yes, right."

They crossed Hearst, were now passing before a large brown apartment house. She had been living there with two roommates when she had met Aaron, who had simply begun to talk to her one day on the street. He'd noticed her before that, and she had seen him, bumbling around. Interesting-looking guy, but had a hard time avoiding collisions with other pedestrians. She already knew Jimmie at the time. He had visited her in the apartment. That was long years ago. He wasn't thinking about that now, if he ever did.

"Aaron's in the clear," he told her. "I said that, but I didn't say why. You didn't ask. On that Monday morning he was making a film, a videotape for Farquahar. He was with a lot of people. Why do I think you know this? Farquahar wasn't there at the time, but he owns the studio. Gregor Grosz does, I mean. That's a striking coincidence. Or is it something else? Do you know? Do you know more about this than I do?"

Maren was sure she did, but she decided to lie. He was too embroiled.

"No, Jimmie. I don't. I knew about the video Aaron made in the studio, but that's all."

"Okay. Well, Aaron's safe. Those threats your neighbor heard, the old guy—you know what those were?"

"No," she said, although, of course, she did.

They stood together on the street, in front of a little market, while he explained about the other video, Aaron as wolf.

"Ah," she said, when he was done.

"My car," he said, pointing at a large gray vehicle hunkered at the curb. The parking meter next to it had expired, but he didn't have a ticket. Maybe the parking cops knew all their colleagues' civilian cars.

"What'll I do?" Jimmie asked.

She put her hand on the door handle.

"My car's southside in a lot. Run me back, okay?"

"Oh, Christ. Yes, of course. Don't know what I'm doing, this walking."

To get back to southside, Jimmie had to drive around the entire university, taking either a westerly or an easterly approach. He chose west, which meant first forcing his big car to labor over Holy Hill, seat of the Pacific School of Religion.

"Maren, what'll I do?"

"Talk to Derek Blake? I don't know. Hey!"

He had suddenly flung the car into a small parking lot reserved for high-ranking potentates of the Pacific School. There was only one space left in the lot, next to a sanctifed SUV the size of a tank, and he took it.

They sat in the car.

"I don't know where Derek is," Jimmie told her. "That's one damn problem. Diane may know. That's part of why I came to campus, to get it out of her. But you—"

Maybe he was going to say, "But you screwed it up." Well, if so, he thought better of it, and she didn't care.

He rubbed his head again, the way he had in Dwinelle Plaza when Diane had snapped at him to hold his water. Then he laughed, "Huh-huh-huh." Quietly, so that he seemed to be sighing.

She said, quietly, "Are you even looking for Derek?"

"Where, Maren? There are several places he might be. Not places. Regions. He goes on these trips, you know, the woods, beaches, the Sierra. He meets with these groups all over the place. That's what he told Diane he was going to do, go meet with some animal activists. On Friday, this was. But they were so pissed off at each other then that he didn't tell her where, and she didn't ask. This was before we found out about Aaron's video session. What was that, anyway?"

"A promotional thing, an ad. He's trying to make extra money. But he might just be running away, right? Derek, I mean. Aren't there things you do for fleeing suspects? Roadblocks, checking at airports, all that."

"Diane said not to do that: he'll get in touch with her. He always calls after a few days to check on the kid. If we start looking for him and he finds out, he might take off where we couldn't follow him. With his wilderness experience, the fucking guy can just disappear and live off the land. But what if he doesn't call?"

Maren doubted Derek's competence as a survivalist. She had seen this eco-warrior in action, vanquished by old Camilla Faucett and her hose.

"Okay, then," she said. "You're waiting for him to call Diane and tell her where he is, and then she'll tell you."

"Yes, but I don't feel real confident about Diane. She keeps changing. She was really enthusiastic, you know, really happy to be working with me on this. Then suddenly she's unreachable; I finally get her on the phone, and nothing. So I came today, and she was hostile as hell. You saw. And now this Grosz guy. So, right now I'm not sure what I should do."

"Well—" She was going to say that she didn't see that he could do anything right then and that maybe they should drive away, as a very fancy car was now making a majestic entrance into the lot. Jimmie didn't see it, didn't let her finish.

"Because I have no damn idea what Diane is going to do or has done. I'm really concerned about this. She's got me kind of in deep shit, Maren. Deep shit. I don't know how I let her—"

Bawwwp! The fancy car, a Jaguar, made its displeasure known.

"Out of there, now!" demanded its driver.

White-haired man with a big, red face. She couldn't tell if he was wearing priestly vestments. Puffing with vexation, he backed the Jag into the street, giving Jimmie room to get out. He got. They proceeded to drive around the campus.

At Hearst and Oxford they stopped for a light.

"Maren, I got involved with her."

"Well, duh," she said.

"Don't tell me she told you."

"Didn't have to. It's obvious. You wasted no time."

"She pushed it. Didn't give me time to think. But I was crazy. She's a factor in a major case. I'm in deep shit, Maren."

The light changed. He turned left.

Deep shit. He had an obsession with this concept, which was not at all imaginative. Nonetheless, she saw him sinking, waving his arms above the muck. She wondered what might happen to him. He could lose his job, or maybe worse, for screwing a factor. She thought of Diane's eyes and felt a little chill.

"I wouldn't have done it if she hadn't been you."

"She isn't me."

"Like you, I meant. And she is. Like you."

"Here's the lot. Let me out!"

"What'll I do? Maren, come on, help me!"

But he had stopped, and she got out. She marched to her car. Paid the man his money.

'What'll I do?' She was in charge of children, not adults, but these ridiculous adults wanted things from her. Diane, Jimmie, Gregor. I have nothing for you, she thought.

Chapter Nine

Whon she got home, the sky was still a cruddy gray. Back from his Tuesday comp classes in Pres 18A, Aaron was getting ready to go jogging, changing from cords and sweater into shorts and a T-shirt. Before he went out the door, he kissed her on the cheek. She went for a walk, over to King, home of female soccer warriors. None were there. Maybe the soccer season was finished. Some college kids, or college-age kids, were throwing a Frisbie around. Maren had never been able to throw a Frisbie half decently, but she had always thought she would have made an excellent soccer player, had girls played the game when she was young. She could kick and had been good at running. Now she walked around the track. That's what most people did at King, walk. She knew she wouldn't see Aaron, who didn't like tracks.

She went home. Aaron then returned, all asweat. At least he'd kept his shirt on. When he didn't, the sweat rolled freely down his chest and dampened unto sogginess the front of his skimpy nylon shorts.

"I did three pull-ups," he said. He didn't seem proud of himself. It was just a fact he was reporting. He got down on the living room rug, sweating into it, but it was old and dirty beyond Hoovering, and did some sit-ups. In the bathroom, after his shower, he talked to himself. That wasn't unusual. He pretended to be other people, Aaron had once explained, who talked to him or, occasionally, to still other people; in that case, he wouldn't be in the scene at all. It was an old pastime. He might pretend to be an appliance salesman or a stockbroker and then a customer. Sometimes, though, he said angry things, and she suspected that then he was being himself talking to someone else. Tonight he sounded mad. She couldn't quite hear the words he mumbled.

She fed him. He cleaned the kitchen. They watched the news. Paige Fuji.

Stainless Paige had the latest dope on crime, the statistics. In the Bay Area, all the violent crimes had gone down for a fourth straight year, mirroring the national trend. That was good, of course, but Paige then went on to announce the latest Bay Area murder, in Hayward, that place with the wetlands. Somebody had strangled his wife down there, not in the wetlands, but in a Hayward neighborhood called Mt. Eden. Nearer to Berkeley, in Richmond, finally getting gentrified after years of being famously scary, a man had lived up to civic tradition by sticking a kitchen knife into his child's fifth-grade teacher. He thought the teacher was plotting with the federal government against the child. The father had not been taking his medication, according to his wife. "Why should I take that stuff?" he asked. "I'm not crazy." No reaction from Aaron.

Less crime, but these awful things still happen. Awfulness remains high. No commentary from Paige on this discrepancy, if that's what it was.

At eleven Aaron went to bed. Maren waited. She knew something would happen. The phone rang.

"Yes," she said.

The caller said nothing. Finally Maren hung up.

In the bedroom, Aaron said her name. She was surprised that he was awake. He asked, "Who was that?"

"Nobody."

Wednesday. Maren endured school. Lost the rabbit again. Judy looked at her hard, worried, probably. She smiled at Judy. Moby didn't come. Lark did. Backslid. She got out of there as soon as she could and went to Monterey Market for fresh fruit. This was a good time to shop; not many people came in then, in early afternoon.

Aaron was home by four.

"Don't you have a class?" she said. She knew he did, she remembered from the card: C19 AM LIT, 2-5.

"It's down to seven people," Aaron said. "And two of them didn't come today. So I just killed it after half an hour. There's only one kid who knows how to read."

He changed and took a short run. Into the shower, and out. Angry dialogue in the bathroom. She got up close. Through the door, she heard, "Your ass. Kick your little ass."

At eleven Aaron went to bed. She waited. She knew something would happen. The phone rang.

"Yes," she said.

She knew it would be Diane, but it wasn't. At first Maren didn't recognize the voice at all. She had to help, the voice said; she had to come. It was a foreign voice.

"Who...Gregor?"

"Of course it's Gregor!"

He didn't sound British. The British style doesn't work with panic, so evidently afflicting him.

"I need you!"

"But you have Diane now," she said.

"What? *She's* the problem. I can't believe what she's done. She's coming back, I think. I hope! I don't know what to do. What'll I do?"

Oh, why?

"You have influence over her," pled Gregor, when she said nothing. "Please come! We can work something out, with you. Don't bring Aaron! That fool! Or the football player, whatever his name is. The stupid detective. Help me!"

Notorious for her silences, Maren usually knew what she was expected to say, but sometimes preferred not to say it, preferred not to say anything. Now she was simply stumped. She hadn't been expecting this.

"I'll give you whatever you want," said Gregor. "Do you want anything?"

It happened again: he got young. It was the kind of question one young person might ask another.

"Well, of course you do. I've seen your house, your car. You have a daughter in college. Tree! Think of Tree!"

"What? Oh, you mean Brooke."

"I'll...I'll sponsor her in the corporate world! I'll *mentor* her. Better than working in a day-care center, right? Right?"

You're not young, she thought.

"Just help me now. You went away before. You left me, Maren, and you never said why. What that did to my confidence! You owe me. I became distraught. I became upset with that fat fool McAulay in the English Department. I need you, now! Come, Maren, now! You have to!"

McAulay. There was a McAulay connection. Gregor had mentioned him Monday in the Plaza. There was this old story about Gregor accusing Cedric of plagiarism. Aaron had told her about that a long time ago, before everything went nuts.

Gregor was chattering away. She said, "Where are you?"

"Just told you! The lab. Ultima Hyena. It's on northside, Leroy and LeConte. There's a big truck in the driveway. Oh, in the seventies it used to be the Cryogenics Institute. You remember them?"

"The people with the head?"

"Yes, the head. I threw it out. Do you remember seeing their building, though, with their sign?"

"Yes."

Just like him to get rid of the head, she thought. Cryogenics had been in the business of freezing people after they died, so that they could be thawed after a cure had been found for whatever they died of; no one ever gave them a body to freeze, however, just a head. There had been speculation about reviving the head some day and attaching it to a new body or to a machine. No more. No reviving.

Gregor continued to implore, and she waited for him to run down. When he finally stopped, she asked, "And Diane's involved in this problem you have?"

"She caused it."

"All right. I'll come."

"Good!" he said. "Hurry, can't you? I want you here before she shows up, so we can plan how to handle her. And, remember, no Aaron!"

She went into the bedroom, expecting to find Aaron asleep, but he was awake, with the light on, no book.

"What is it?" he asked. "Who was that?"

"That was Gregor Grosz."

"I knew it, little prick! I told him not to bother us, bother you, but I knew he would. Not the first time, is it?"

"The first call. I saw him yesterday, though. It was a surprise."

"Well?"

"He's like you said. Really changed. Not nice."

"Slimeball. Shithead."

Aaron sat briskly up in the bed, evidently intent on going somewhere, probably the bathroom.

"He's at his hyena place," she told him. "You were right about that. He's Saxon, the hyena man. But there's some awful emergency, something caused by Diane Blake. He wants me to come over to help him with it. He said not to take you."

"You say Grosz knows Diane? Ah, man. All this wild shit. All this wild shit—McAulay in our kitchen, Diane, and Grosz. Now Diane knows Grosz. That animal, that aardvark. Something had to happen. I knew!"

"Aardwolf."

"What I meant."

Aaron rolled out of bed. Maren was mildly astonished to see that he was wearing a pair of boxer shorts. Usually he wore nothing.

"Where we going? Where the hell is he, Gregor?"

"His lab, where the old Cryogenics Institute used to be. Northside."

"Don't remember that."

He said this while rushing out of the room. Now he rushed back in, briefcase in hand.

"There was a head," she explained. "They froze it. Anyway, I know where the place is, I remember. Uh, Aaron, what's with the…?"

She plucked at her sweatshirt. Why had Aaron yanked his Tale Spinner overalls out of his case? Why was he presently stepping into them?

"I can't explain," he said, adjusting the straps. "I just feel more physical in these. I'm myself in these."

Accoutered exactly as he had been in the Green Guzzle commercial, except for the beard, he loomed before her, the very image of a brutish bumpkin. Involuntarily, Maren eyed his crotch, but nothing there burst forth.

"You know," Maren said, "I don't think it's necessary to come in disguise."

"Disguise? This is me! This is me, and I'm going his kick his little ass. He's been playing with me, and with you, and now it stops. Stops dead."

"Hold on, Aaron! The object here is to find out what's going on, to..."

To what? Well, to find out, as she had just said: unriddle these mysteries and then, maybe, she could do something. Not for Gregor. Gregor wasn't Gregor anymore. Children were involved, Deirdre and probably little Boris, too. They had to be helped. They were her responsibility, and she would see to it. There was Diane. There was Diane Blake, at the bottom of everything, and somehow Maren had a responsibility toward her, too. Not of the same kind, Diane being no child. Not really. She was too smart for her own good; that was obvious, and what she needed was to have someone make her see that. Derek wouldn't, wouldn't help her in any way. And Jimmie was hopeless: sprung on Diane, blubbering on about how he knew not what to do. Idiot Jimmie blaming her, her likeness to Diane. She was better off with Aaron.

Aaron, she observed, was chomping on a large, orange, rootlike object. A dried mango stick.

"What are you doing with that thing? You told me they make you crazy."

"Wanna be crazy. I saved it."

"You calm down, or you can't go! And take it out of your mouth right now."

"Oh, all right."

She didn't tell him to change clothes. He shouldn't be insane, but a little brutish is good. Might be. As long as he was coming.

Aaron stomped out into the living room and lay down on the

couch. She didn't see him lie down, but she assumed that. When they were going someplace, the movies or out to dinner, he always got ready before she did and then would do this collapse, waiting for her to finish dressing. She was almost ready now, having never undressed for bed. She was, however, in need of shoes, although she didn't remember taking them off. Her little blue tennis shoes. Presumably they were out there by the Aaron-occupied couch.

Getting cold at night now. Winter was coming. Winter never came to San Diego. Maren went into Brooke's room. Tree! Had she ever met a man with a brain? She got Brooke's Doc Martens out of her closet and put them on her own feet. They were a little loose, but she could wear them.

She walked quietly into the living room, despite the heavy shoes. She considered Aaron, who was gazing at the ceiling. Indeed, he had no brain, but she really didn't want to go away without him. He...he would feel bad.

"Let's go," she said.

"Finally! I'm looking forward to this."

He heaved himself up.

In zoos? Had she ever seen one before? They used to take Brooke to the Oakland and San Francisco zoos. She couldn't remember.

This particular *Crocuta*, a female named Munchie, was chunky in build and about the size of a very large dog. She was sandy-colored with dark spots; her face was long and narrow. She had bat ears and a thick tuft of hair sticking up from the top of her head. Was Munchie a good specimen? She had a potbelly. Maybe that was normal for hyenas, but she also appeared to be blind in one eye. It just seemed dead. Munchie's upper and lower jaws didn't meet squarely, the lower angling off to the right, exposing a mess of teeth. Each one seemed twice as long as little Artie's longest fang. All crammed together, they looked like a bunch of hypodermic needles.

Through the bars of her cage, Munchie was giving Maren the "eh?" look that a cat will assume when some silly human is making much moan over a slain bird. That ridiculous tuft, as if she were sitting at the breakfast table before sprucing up for work. Do mass murderers present the same expression, bland and goonish, to those they appall? Do serial killers? Squatting on her thick haunches, the hyena made Maren think of awful men, although Munchie wasn't male, who sneak into people's houses and do unspeakable things. Oh, Maren remembered. Maleness, female-ness—that's all different with hyenas. The females are the real guys.

Aaron lay on the floor before the cage. She should have stead-ied him when she saw him begin to sway. Now he was stirring, groaning. Then she realized he was barfing little bits of mango.

"I told you not to bring him," Gregor complained, probably referring to the mess.

He was being silly. This place, his grayly lit specimen room, was dirty and stinky. Someone should hose it down. There were three cages, but Munchie was the only beast in residence. Presumably, Ultima had a lab, to vivisect and brew, and a big computer some-place for Anthony Pownall; Gregor hadn't offered her a tour. But she hadn't been at all impressed by what she had seen: a dark hall, some rooms haphazardly furnished with plastic chairs and metal desks, and then the animal in the cage. It was hard to believe that anyone actually did anything in here, in this shabby place, let alone cutting-edge mammalian biology. Of course, once it had been the Cryogenics Institute, but that operation had never amounted to much.

Just the head, the frozen head which Gregor had thrown out. Well, it had been replaced by another.

There it was in the corner of the cage, the head of Derek Blake.

The flat eyes were unmistakable, although they didn't seem blue anymore. No color, now. No hat, of course, so that his brow rose and rose, as if he were astonished beyond all reckoning. His lips were tightly clamped together, which seemed odd and lent a grumpy air. There it lay in the corner, remarkably round. Munchie seemed not to have sampled this object, Derek's head. More meat on the legs, which, severed, lay in front of her. All his parts seemed to be there. As Maren watched, the hyena bent, sniffed, bit. She brought her jaws together and ground them, producing a crunching sound.

"What?" asked Munchie, with her face.

Aaron was getting up. She grabbed his elbow and tried to help, but he seemed to weigh a ton. Slowly he made it. He stood, looking first at Munchie, then, abruptly turning his face away from the hyena, at Gregor. Finally, he looked at Maren. He seemed amazed. He wanted her to answer all his questions, but couldn't even ask them.

Maren could think now, as had not been the case when she had first seen this. That was after they had followed Gregor, quacking frantically—not very British, she had noted to herself—running through the house, looking over his shoulder. "Quickly, quickly! Before she comes back!" He threw one disgusted glance at Aaron, then ignored him. Suddenly he said, "Specimen room! Right here." He threw open the door, and they saw. "Oh, my," said Aaron, in the mildest of voices, and down he spun. Dizziness took her, too, but she resisted. It got worse when she closed her eyes, so she opened them and stared at Munchie and the remains of Derek. She had to, couldn't not. But now she could think. No animal, she thought, would ever divide its prey into pieces before eating, would neatly hack off the head. Well, not neatly. She'd seen something like this before. She remembered.

"You see? You see! What'll I...ah, you've thought of something."

Gregor was standing in front of her. Maren realized she was nodding her own head, nodding and nodding, and made herself stop. He grabbed her by the wrist, and she pulled away. Wearing blue coveralls, lab garb, he looked like a diminutive farmer from Thailand or some other land of small, dark farmers.

"Call the cops," grunted Aaron, large farmer. He was pawing at a phone mounted on the wall, near the door.

"That," snapped Gregor, "is not a real phone. It's an intercom. Maren, tell him we're not calling the cops or anyone else. You're going to talk to Diane. You, not him. He has no purpose. Dammit! He's just another damned problem."

"Oh?" said Aaron, returning the intercom to its hook. "Well, please tell *him* that I'm calling the police right now, as soon as I find a real phone. Where is one?"

"You can shut up, big fool!"

"What makes—whoop!"

In turning to face Gregor, Aaron had inadvertently caught a glimpse of Munchie, bent over Derek's legs.

"God!" he fervently exclaimed. "That churns my guts. Fucking mango stick! Never again."

In the cage, Munchie bit down. They all heard the crunch.

This ghastly sound appeared to bring good cheer to Gregor Grosz, whose black eyes grew less wild. He was wearing glasses, Maren realized, as he had when she used to know him. He even smiled a crooked little smile and said, "They can bite through anything. They can digest bone. This may work."

"Want us to leave?" Maren asked.

"I want you to wait." Gregor meant just her. But would he let Aaron go, if Aaron tried to go? Probably not. Of course not. Aaron would get the cops.

"I need you for Diane. Diane did this. She's coming, I hope. I have no idea what she wants; she was a terrific mistake. I don't know how I let myself. If only she hadn't looked like you!"

Aaron entered the discussion. "Fuck you!" he remarked. "She's my wife. Got nothing to do with you, little asshole."

Gregor looked at the hyena, waiting for her to chew up some more bone. "It'll take forever," he said. "In the wilderness, the Serengeti, there's always a lot of them, always the clan. Eat, eat. Alone, I don't know. And this one never seemed terribly hungry."

"Maren!" Aaron called. "We're going, now! Okay?"

"You amaze me," Gregor said, addressing her. "I'll never understand you. Why did you bring him? Don't you know why you're here? You can help me with Diane. She feels that you're her older sister or her mother, I don't know what. But can I rely on you? I don't know now."

crunch

For a moment, Maren felt that Aaron was about to say, "I'll never understand her either."

But he said nothing. He squared his shoulders, then strode

towards them, intent, she thought, on grabbing her, not Gregor, and hauling her out to the Bug. She felt her own shoulders grow tight. Gregor scuttled away.

The little man opened a drawer in a metal desk. He took out a large pistol and pointed it at Aaron, who stopped short.

"This is what I use for killing hyenas," he told Aaron. "I think you probably weigh as much as two hyenas, but I don't think I'll need two bullets for you."

He said this without a trace of accent, British or other, in cold, hard American.

Now Aaron moved away from her, slowly backward, toward the door, but she doubted he was trying to escape. He just didn't want her to get shot if he tried something heroic, as Maren feared he would. During their many years together, he had performed several heroic actions, perhaps three; but the trouble was that he was good for only one such action at a single time. If he rushed at Gregor and knocked away the gun, Aaron might just stand there frozen while gathering his nerve for the next step. Gregor could pick the big gun up and shoot him dead.

"Aaron," she said. She was going to add "Be careful!" or, simply, "No!" But she thought better of it. That might be the push he needed—or didn't need—to act brave.

The men ignored her, talking man talk.

"Don't go out that door! Or do you want to die?"

"You don't have the—"

crunch

"Shit!" said Aaron. "Does that thing never stop eating?"

"Come over here, now, and lie down, there." Gregor gestured at the floor with his pistol, which he then pointed back again at Aaron.

Aaron stomped to the designated spot, where he sat, scowling. He didn't lie down, but Gregor appeared satisfied. For some reason, Aaron was scowling at her. She would never understand him.

"Maren," Gregor said. "Little Maren. Do you see the open drawer, where this came from?"

He waved the gun, so black, so obviously weighty. A wonder his tiny hand could control it.

"Well, in it there's a large ring with keys on it. Get it. Bring it. There's a good girl."

The British was back. A good sign? A bad sign?

She got him the keys and he set about putting Aaron into a cage. The process proved awkward. The keys were heavy: getting the right key into the lock was really a job for two hands, and when Gregor tried he kept screwing up. First he put the gun on the floor for a moment; Aaron's shoulders jerked in a disconcerting way. Snatching it up, Gregor made as if to thrust it into his belt, but the coveralls had no belt. He tried to dangle the pistol from one thumb. As he fumbled, Aaron regarded him beadily. She was relieved when Gregor finally said, "Maren," and handed her the keys. Gregor marched him in.

His next-door neighbor, Munchie, padded over and stuck one of her paws between the bars of her own cage. It almost reached the bars of Aaron's. She grunted. The sound was not unfriendly. Rather than grunting back, Aaron merely retreated a bit. There he stood, forlorn, a captive of Gregor Grosz.

To whom he said, "Don't hurt my wife. Just don't do that."

"I have no such intention."

To her Aaron said, "Nothing matters but that."

After a few moments, he said, "I have to go to the bathroom."

Gregor merely smirked. Maren didn't know what to say to either of them about Aaron's need, possibly feigned, or any other matter. The little—what was he, anyway?—venture capitalist put both gun and keys back into the drawer.

"I presume she's coming," he said. "She left a note. 'I'll be back, and don't bother to feed Munchie.' Of course, I had already noticed what Munchie was doing. I had had no idea what Diane was capable of. My God!"

He gave her, his little Maren, a furiously indignant look, as if she might also feed her husband to a spotted hyena. Little Maren began to consider doing something heroic upon the body of Gregor Grosz. A few swift steps and a boot in the balls! He was no bigger than she, and he no longer held the gun. Aaron warned her.

"He's a mean little fucker," he said.

For once he had read her mind.

Nor was she confident about her own ability to be heroic more than once. She had never booted anyone in the balls. Had only, could only remember, at any rate, kneeing Cedric McAulay in them, and that was by accident.

"You bait me," Gregor said, to Aaron. "You always did. You all did. You taunted me at that bar in San Francisco. Such are your pleasures. At least I got to—"

He paused. Maren stopped breathing.

"—to get somewhere in the world. And trust me: I will do to you only what I have to do, no more, no less. To this little fucker you mean nothing, big boy, absolutely zero. Your Wharton criticism—now, that bothers me. At least you haven't published much. Can't say the same about old McAulay. A lot of his stuff, and all ridiculously bad, except for...hah...the one good thing. Do you know about that? Do you remember?"

"Oh, that. That old story."

"It's no story. Don't think you can annoy me. But look, Matthews, you know his work. You must read something besides all those remedial essays. Twenty years worth of formalist rubbish from old Cedric and one glowing piece of real criticism, and it was Marxist. How interesting! When else did Cedric do Marx?"

"That was Marx? I know that essay, the one you said he took from you. Nobody ever said it had any Marxism in it. What? A study of paragraph length in *The Age of Innocence*? That isn't formalism?"

"No! Obviously not. That's what Dubin said, too, and he regretted it. All he lost was his job."

"Well, it might be some now-obsolete kind of structuralism, but Marx?"

"Marx is misunderstood in this country. The secret to Marx is cabala, the cabala on paragraphs! It's not really a secret, just unacknowledged. People won't see it! I don't know why. I tried to explain all this, several times, but the academy resisted, as always. Nobody ever listened to me here in Berkeley, which is supposed to be so forward-looking. What a sham this place is!"

"I don't recall Marx being even mentioned in that piece. Not a footnote, not a—"

"All right! If you must! But it was implied, unmistakably implied. How dare you judge me! Your criticism makes people laugh! And you! Standing in there and picking away at me. You...you took my girl!"

Is that how he looked at it? One more incarnation for Gregor, as lonely teen-age broncin' buck, teasing plaintive chords out of an old guitar.

"Girl? Who? Her?"

"Yes," Gregor said, or barked, upset with Aaron's slowness. "She was. She came to me in my—"

"Gregor, please," Maren said, but she was talking to Aaron, too. "It was nothing."

They were distracted by an odd, tumbling sound. Evidently Munchie had batted Derek's head, so that it had rolled across the floor of her cage. It was in a different corner now, tilted up upon its nose.

"Nothing?"

She wasn't sure which of them said it. It didn't matter.

crunch

Not the head. That would go *pop*, she thought.

Now Gregor sat in silence on top of his own desk, it must be, the one with the gun and the keys. Maren sat behind another, in a plastic chair. In his cage, Aaron paced. He bristled and wiggled his eyebrows at her. At first she thought he was angry because she had brought him here or because he'd begun to understand about her little episode with Gregor, that bit of ancient foolishness. But Aaron, she decided, wasn't really angry; he was trying to signal something to her, maybe just reassurance. He was mad at Gregor, though; that was obvious. Upon Munchie he gazed with seeming calm, except when the hyena crunched once again.

Diane Blake entered the door to the specimen room and strode briskly in. She was carrying a large shoulder bag, quite like the one Maren usually hauled around. She looked good.

"Hi, Maren," she said, briskly. "Recognized your car. Old man's in the cage, huh?"

Maren thought, Your old man's in the cage, too.

Gregor said, "Diane?"

Diane looked at Munchie, who looked away. The hyena ceased eating.

"Takes time," said Deirdre's mom. "Takes time, I see. I thought they just *gobbled*."

"Diane?"

"Garrett! Little Garrett Grosz. Yes, Garrett?"

"Why? Why did you do this? Someone could have come in, one of the staff."

"Has anyone been coming in? I thought you closed down when the Russian left. I guessed that no one had been feeding her"— she tossed snaggle-toothed Munchie a breezy wave—"so she'd finish up with Derek pretty fast. We'll have to help her out, though, it looks like. You'll have instruments. I used Derek's bush knife at home."

Diane slid a hip onto Gregor's metal desk, held her bag in her lap, presented her face to Maren.

"You took the other one, didn't you? The one I put in that can in your garage with the little rocks? I went back and checked. Thanks, I guess. Did you hide it because I made you think Aaron used it? Or did you know who really did?"

Maren said nothing.

"You can tell me later. Also, I'd like the knife back. It means something to me, and it might come in handy, although I doubt it, not where I'm going. With...I'll explain it later. Anyway, we'll be fine, I promise."

Going? Going where? What was this "We'll be fine"? Diane had said that in the Plaza. Aaron must have been wondering about these things too, for he was giving Diane a quizzical look. So was Munchie. Only Gregor, perching on the desk top next to the Hillside mom, seemed not to care. Something else interested him.

To Maren he said, "You hid her knife? You hid her knife, Maren? Well, then, you're implicated. You're an accessory to the first incident. We'll all have to work together, it would seem. You understand I'm in no real danger, like you, both of you. But I have concerns about reputation, my clients, people who look to me for various services, and so on."

"I didn't hide the knife for her," Maren pointed out. "I did it for him." She waved at Aaron, in his cage.

"But you hid it," Gregor observed.

The women ignored him.

Diane wanted Maren to understand something. "Implicating Aaron, that was a dumb plan. Derek thought it up. It was stupid. Aaron must have been doing something that morning, even if it was only riding BART. People would see him, and who could forget him in that outfit? By the way, why is he wearing it now?"

"I don't know, Diane. He just likes it."

Diane glanced at Gregor in his blue lab garb. "Makes them look like a father and son team. That's cute. Well, then it came out that Aaron was making that Green Guzzle tape, for him." Another glance toward Gregor. "With about sixteen people in attendance."

"Let's cut to the chase," said Gregor. She took no notice.

"Now, playing the Big Bad Wolf tape, playing those threats—that was my idea. Confuse the law a little, buy some time. We have a lot of friends in Marin County, animal activists. It's like here that way, lots of dipshits. Their kids watch Aaron's show, but they resent it, because the animals in the stories are anthromorp...anthropomorph...ah, I can never say it. But we heard quite a bit about that particular tape. Wolf people are real sensitive. I remembered, and I found it. I played it, and then I took it away."

"Diane!"

Gregor had climbed down from the desk. Standing in front of Diane, he grasped her wrist, which she jerked down to her side, breaking his grip.

"What? What is it, Grosz?"

"Why did you kill him?"

"McAulay? Oh, you want to know? All right. Because he was an asshole, and he was going to get me in trouble and seriously affect my career plans. And I know why you're asking. Because you're pretending not to be involved. But, Maren, it was all part of the plan. Payback for Cedric, from Garrett. Gregor. Whatever. He wanted revenge, and he used me."

"I didn't want him dead! The plan was to hurt his reputation, his status. Now we've got complications up the ass."

He pronounced it "ahs."

"No, we don't. I fixed it. Derek did it, we'll say, and Derek's gone, we'll say. Gone into the animal activists' underground. In the jungle someplace, the mountains. With his wilderness experience, Derek can just disappear. In reality, he always got lost, but who knows that?"

"You told this to Jimmie," Maren said. "This story about Derek disappearing. You set Jimmie up with it."

"Yeah, I did. I thought he was nice until he showed up outside my class without telling me. You know, it's nice that these men who had a thing for you all get that way about me: Jimmie, Cedric, the little guy here. But that big dumb guy in there, Bozo in the cage, I couldn't get a rise out of him. I tried, at this Wharton tea."

From the cage: "What? You did?"

Aaron grasped his bars. Munchie came forward, too. Munchie belched. She closed her good eye when she did it. Molecules of Derek Blake flooded the specimen room.

"All right, Diane. What's done is done. But what now?" Gregor was coming on reasonable, overcoming the resentment he must feel at being called "the little guy here" and being generally disrespected, so Maren judged, by Diane.

Diane seemed about to speak, but Gregor wasn't done.

"We must make a plan," he said, "or do you have a plan? I was afraid you didn't, that perhaps you had become simply irrational, so I asked Maren to come here. To help. But perhaps you do."

"Have a plan? Well, I did. Munchie eats Derek. Then you reopen the lab, and your technicians dissect Munchie and grind her up."

"Hoo-hoo," laughed the *Crocuta*. Not a happy laugh.

"But," Diane continued, "problem is that Munchie is going kind of slow. So we do it. We cut him up, put the now smaller pieces into your vat in the lab, and then dump it all at the disposal and recycling place in El Cerrito, like you always do after finishing up a vivisection. Not pleasant, but it'll work. Complications? I don't see any."

Maren sometimes went to that recycling center to rescue old *National Geographics*. The kids liked the animal pictures. For a moment, she thought, she dreamed, of children, and then she put her brain to work. The others talked.

"The head," Diane said. "I just wish she'd eat that, get rid of it."

"Not likely," Gregor told her. "They don't like heads. And El Cerrito is awfully close by; we may go elsewhere. Fremont, maybe. But we can do it. We'll have to. And after that? I suppose nothing has to change, really."

Maren couldn't guess what was to happen "after that"; whatever it was, he seemed less than confident about it. Obviously it involved further dealings with Diane, in whom he must have lost some faith. She wasn't supposed to murder, but she did.

"Nothing?" echoed Diane. "Oh, some things, I think, Garrett. Some changes, Greg. George. Gregor. You know, maybe I ought to get a new name now. I guess I'll do D's, huh?"

"It helps," Gregor said.

Then he got out the keys again. He unlocked the third cage and tossed the keys on top of the desk, where Diane picked them up.

"All right," he said. "So we know what to do with Derek, but what do we do with Maren and Aaron? I suppose we should...look, I'm sorry, Maren, but would you mind stepping into the third cage? Diane and I need to go into another room for a while, to discuss, and I want to be sure where you are."

Diane laughed.

"What?" Gregor asked her. "What now?"

"You ask me what to do with Maren and Aaron? Gregor, the question is, what'll we do with Aaron and *you?* I like Maren. I don't like you."

"All right, you've made that obvious. I have to say that I don't care much for you, as you've become, so completely me-oriented. I'll decide about them for myself, then, if that's how you want it."

"Here's what I want, Gregor. You get in the cage."

"Ha-ha," he said, in a rather weary tone. Diane slid off his desk. Holding the big shoulder bag, into which she slid the keys, she walked slowly across the room and stood next to the chair where Maren was sitting. Maren wanted to get up, but she didn't.

Gregor put his hand on the desk, in the area where Diane had been. "Try to be serious," he told her. "Try, Diane, try. Money is involved, remember? Money, money."

"Where's your money? Do you have any left? The Pure Food and Drug people are going after Green Guzzle. And I don't like it, anyway. It induces rapes. And Substance H is a myth. The Russian told me it won't work except to make women develop pseudo-penises, like cutie pie in there."

Maren hadn't noticed. Now she looked. Yes, there it was, furry, normal-looking. Munchie might give birth through it one day, if she didn't wind up in El Cerrito.

"Deal's off, Gregor."

Gregor went for the drawer, where his gun was. Diane dipped into her bag. She pulled out and pointed a small pistol of her own. He froze.

"Go ahead," she said. "Get your cannon. I'll let you. When I came in here with Derek, I got it out and emptied the clip. I fired the round in the chamber into the wall behind the cage. Nobody can hear anything that goes on in here. Munchie screamed when she saw your gun, might have been bad for her appetite. Go ahead, check it out. Or don't. Just don't take all night."

Slowly, Gregor took the big gun out of the drawer, pressed something; the clip popped out, and he held it for a second. Empty, obviously. Gregor tossed it on the floor, but still held the gun. What was he going to do, throw it?

"What are you going to do, Garrett, throw it?"

He put it back in the drawer.

Diane turned to Maren. "You know, I really don't know what to do with these two guys. Didn't plan this far. I trust my instincts, too much maybe. That's how Cedric bought it. Any ideas? I have absolutely no interest in killing anyone, I'll tell you that. We need to talk. We really should."

"Diane," Maren said. "let's get out of here. Let's go someplace. I can't think in here, with *that*."

She glanced at the head, then at Munchie, who bent her head to eat.

"Oh, I can't believe it." Diane seemed exasperated. "Now you want to go someplace. But we can't, because if we do and there are other people around, you might decide to yell 'help.' So that's a no-go. Sorry, Maren. Uh, Garrett, please sit down on the floor. Yep, there."

Maren resumed. "I meant, let's go where it's quiet, where no one is. Then you won't worry, and we can really talk. Tilden. Let's go up to Tilden Park."

"Tilden! Derek hated that place. He hated all the eucalyptus trees because they were foreign, even though they've been there for eighty years. He also got poison oak on his balls up there, and when he tried to resolve the dispute between the red fox people and the feral cat supporters, he just got both sides more pissed off. I think he'd rather be in that cage than up in Tilden Park. Sure, great idea! Let's go. Hey, Gregor, which cage you wanna be in, his or hers?"

Both Aaron and the hyena looked interested. Gregor was testily unbelieving. But they locked him up, in the third cage, after making sure that the bars were too narrowly spaced to let the little guy slip through. Maren remembered Aaron's tale of Gregor's greased-butt fu in the Wee Shamrock.

The two women took Maren's car. They left Diane's bag in the lab. There was a blanket in the Bug's back seat, and this Diane, settling in the front, spread upon her lap, where reposed her little gun. Maren, driving, assumed it was pointed at her.

"Go straight to Tilden," Diane said. "Go straight north, and get there fast. I believe that you intend to treat me right and really listen for a change. All I want. But I'm always concerned about other people's sudden impulses, having a lot of them myself. Which doesn't mean I can't make everything come out all right. Always do, in fact. Go! Put your little foot into it."

After a moment, she asked, "By the way, are you the impulsive type?"

"No."

"No. Well, you can change. And I don't think you're telling the truth, anyway."

They were driving up Spruce Street and would reach the entrance to Tilden in a few minutes. This would make two Tilden visits for Maren in a matter of days, after not having gone up there in years. She thought she liked the place, felt strong up there, had a connection. That was why she had suggested Tilden Park. She hoped the connection wouldn't aid Diane in some fashion. She hoped that a ranger wouldn't see them and chase them and make Diane do something nuts. You weren't supposed to be in Tilden at night, after ten, she believed, and the hour was well past that.

Diane said: "Well, Mom, tell me what I did and how I did it, and why. Have you got me figured out?"

"Why do you say I'm your mother?"

"Oh. Well, to begin with, you're a mom for everyone at Hillside School. We're moms, you're The Mom. You're the little green-eyed Mom of Hillside School. We have a special relationship, though, you and I, everyone remarks on it; so I thought maybe you would understand me in a special way. If you do, then one thing you already know is that after I dropped Derek off at Ultima Hyena, I expected Garrett to call you. I'd been telling him how much I loved and respected you, valued your advice, all that. She understands me, I told him. And it's all true; but you should care about me in the same way, and it seems to me that you don't, not yet. But let's test you. Come on, Maren, what did I do? How? Why?"

Maren veered a bit, turning into the street that swept downhill into the park. She didn't know where she would go once inside and didn't want to just keep driving and risk attracting the attention of the rangers in their little green cars and trucks. She had to think, but Diane wanted her to talk, too. She talked.

"You killed Cedric McAulay in our house. You did it with that knife, which you brought in with you. You had a backpack, I remember. So you probably intended to kill him, but there was some arrangement with Gregor, who wanted you to hurt Cedric in some way, not kill him. But you did."

"Pretty good. Except I didn't intend to, in the sense of being sure in my mind, until just before I did it. You're a smart little lady anyway. Still got your legs, too. They all said it: you've got her legs. Not Cedric. I don't imagine you boned Cedric?"

"No! God, no."

"No picnic. Hard work! Okay, so, Ced's dead. And? Incidentally, where are we?"

Maren was pulling them off the road behind some trees, near the Little Farm.

Chapter Ten

"There's a trail here," Maren said. "We can walk. We can get to some place and sit, or we can just keep walking. But we've got to get into the bush a bit, so the rangers won't find us. There's a curfew."

"Fine. Just don't run away on me. I'm sure you won't, but I don't know what I'd do if you did."

Inside the Little Farm, otherwise darkly silent, a large animal snorted or farted. Diane and Maren found the beginning of the trail, walked along it for a few minutes. The sky was clear, and there was most of a moon. They saw a clearing off to their right, a little place Maren didn't remember from her hike with Aaron.

"Oh, that looks nice," Diane said.

Several logs lay in the clearing, and each woman sat on one. They faced each other, a few yards apart. Diane had brought the car blanket with her, and now it was back on her lap and, beneath that dirty old thing, the gun. Maren decided to go on with her reconstruction. Hadn't she done this before, making up variations, different versions of what had happened? Now she knew the truth, she had the real version. But hadn't she always known?

"Okay," Maren said. "He's dead. So you call Derek, who comes over. He brought the aardwolf, Artie; I can't imagine why, but he wouldn't have if you had told him what happened, or even that Cedric was dead. You told him something that didn't upset him much. He comes over, sees what's in the kitchen. He panics, I imagine."

"Not really. He wasn't embarrassed. That's what panics him. Did."

"You do this thing with the wolf tape, which was smart, but blaming Aaron wouldn't get you far. You realized that, if Derek didn't."

"Sure, but I told him it would work. He needed a story, something he could say, so that he wouldn't blurt out the truth to the first cop he saw. Then I sent him to that place where those wetlands are. For a while there was this mystery about Aaron. Does he have a class or what? So Derek and I have this little plot going. Then I get hold of you."

"You got hold of me and told me that Derek did it, so I'd be ready to support your story when you changed it. I could say later, to the police, that Derek was forcing you to lie to them, but that you told me the truth. Only problem—"

"Was that when Jimmie and Gregor both told me that a ton of people knew where Aaron was that morning, Derek naturally didn't want to say that he'd killed Cedric. Of course not. I made a suggestion: that he turn himself in and say he was guilty, but keep this story up for only for a week, while I disappeared. Then he could say it was me. He didn't like this at all."

Diane laughed, a little yip. "Just to piss him off, I told him it was your idea. He didn't like you, anyway, because of the time you took Deirdre and didn't go right to your house, made him wait."

"I remember. But would you have done that? Gone someplace and hid?"

"Certainly not! Me? Even if I didn't have plans, wonderful plans, I wouldn't do that. So, for things to work out right, when Derek recanted and said he wasn't the one and that I was, everyone would have to think he's lying: he's *still* the one who killed Cedric. I thought that just maybe, since Derek did animal escapes, he'd be interested in doing one for me. But he wasn't. He got very cranky, kept insisting that I turn myself in. He was going to rat me out, in fact. I'm sure he was. So I did what I thought I had to do. Okay, Mom? Best thing, obviously. He gets blamed for Cedric, and he's gone, out of my life."

"You cut him up?"

"After he was dead, and he died easier than Cedric. Look, Mom. I did what I had to do. Everybody does what they have to do. You don't understand? Time you got out of that nursery school and entered the real world."

Maren heard a light clacking noise behind her. She turned around and saw two big deer trotting down the trail. One had antlers like an elk's. These beasts seemed fit for huge northern forests, not Tilden Park, but she assumed they were leaving that animal haven to embark on a garden raid through the streets of Berkeley. When she saw them, she started. Even when you hear them before you look, deer are always suddenly *there*. Diane didn't even blink. Maren looked into her eyes. They didn't look sad, they looked blank. Maybe everyone's eyes look that way by moonlight.

"It's quiet here," Diane said then. "This was a good idea. I think I can explain something to you. I want to explain myself. Not everything, not the past, my roots or whatever. That was all unhappiness and disorder. Forget all that. What matters is this: Maren, I'm twenty-six years old, I'm still young, and now I'm ready to live. I know what I want to do and how I can be happy. I do have to go back in the past a little, to explain, so...so I'll talk. And you'll listen, please. When I'm done, I'll make you a proposition. Remember Gregor in Dwinelle Plaza? Negotiate, negotiate. We'll negotiate."

Diane shifted her weight. "Ouch, this log! It has knots!"

She put her hand under the blanket and adjusted the gun.

"I married Derek because I was going to have Deirdre and because there's a lot of money in fish sticks, his father's business. So we're a little family, living off Dad while Derek works for harp seals and swordfish and blowfish and also some birds. Garrett St. John appears, promoting an opportunity in biotech. He has a hot plan to cure skin cancer with something made from pollack scales. Pollack is the main fish for fish sticks, okay? It's a type of cod. Dad turns Garrett over to Derek, I meet him. The project flops, Dad loses a little money, but somehow Gregor makes money. He's good at the financials and manages to go bankrupt at just the right time. I think that was it.

"Well, I'm impressed, and I've perceived that Garrett has a thing for me. That's okay. He's cute, you notice? Oh, well, of course you did. Okay, he's much cuter than Derek, who comes from the bottom of the sea. I should have arranged to have him eaten by a shark. Ha-ha! So we go to bed a few times, and then he starts going on about how I remind him of you. You're imprinted on him in some weird way. And somehow, although he's always raving about how you clasped him between your magnificent thighs and boned his brains out and made him happy, for a little while, he seems to associate you with his mother."

The lady who sat in the shadow. Maren remembered.

Diane kept on.

"It didn't piss me off that he liked me because of you. I thought I'd like to meet you, that's all. Then it turns out that Garrett wants to go to Berkeley, because that's where hyenas are, his latest project. And also it's a good place to promote Green Guzzle, which is already in production, Californians being adventurous and eager to try these stupid virility things. He has a media connection there, too, that studio. He has you there, finally. I should say that although he has these wonderful memories of you and your—"

Hopping off her log, Diane bent forward and slapped Maren playfully on her magnificent right thigh. Maren made herself sit there, just sit there. Diane returned to her place, readjusted blanket and gun.

"Despite all that, he's very pissed off at you for disappearing, as he says; besides, he hates his mother. So it's pretty obvious that he wants revenge on you and on Aaron, the big, mean dude who stole his girl. I think he thinks that you were his only chance to become a regular person. That might be it. Now, he doesn't want you back after all this time, that would be pathetic. Besides, he works out and is youthful while you're old and, for some reason, gray. He imagined you gray, but you're not, and you didn't look old to him when he saw you in the Plaza. Really saw you, that is. Sometimes he drove by your house or the school. You notice anything?"

"Somebody was out there. I only saw the car."

"That red thing? He rented it. I bet he stiffs them on the bill. Anyway, you still look good. This upsets him; it means his revenge trick doesn't work too well. That's me, of course: the new you, the young you. So he's rubbing my leg there in the Plaza, too dumb to know that he means nothing to me by this time. They're all dumb. Aaron's so dumb he didn't realize that the Green Guzzle taping was meant to humiliate him. Garrett even found a Wharton scholar, that Dubin, to help out at the shoot and make fun of Aaron's tiny print. Where am I? What am I supposed to be talking about?"

"I think," Maren said carefully, "about why you and Gregor came out here. To Berkeley."

"Oh, Berkeley. He makes me a proposition. Why don't I leave Derek and come to Berkeley with him? Well, he knows I can't do that, and I know he doesn't want me to; Derek has access to money, and Garrett has plans for that money. So we talk money. I tell him I'll try to facilitate the cash inflow for his projects in exchange for payout at the end. Fine. We understand each other. And I'm delighted to go to Berkeley, being sick of the Northeast and Derek's anal parents and family. Graduate school! I really enjoyed my courses as an undergrad, so, being in Berkeley, why not? My grades weren't so good, okay, and I kind of bombed my GREs, but next year U.C.'s gonna start work on the Blake Cod Products Ichthyology Center, unless old Blake backs out. Which I now don't care if he does."

She shut up for a moment, then said, thoughtfully, "I'll get to that, why I don't care now. But I did then, and I got in. No problem. And Derek, he was crazy to get out to Berkeley, where activism was born. Yeah, sure! Eat, eat. That's all people do out here. So, we came west. Understand so far?"

Maren did, yes, so far. She did not, however, understand why Diane had killed Cedric McAulay in her kitchen, and that was something she really wanted to know.

"So we're in Berkeley," Diane resumed. "We're going to work together on hyena stuff and the Green Guzzle thing. I had some faith in him then, thought he was smart. He might become a biotech Bill Gates; then I could be Mrs. Gates. I speak metaphorically: I wouldn't marry him, but you know what I mean. Having money, even just *more* money, I would be less dependent on Derek, who I'm getting very sick of being nice to. Also, I'm still slightly fascinated by this little fucker Garrett. He told me all his names, I liked that."

Silence. Thinking about liking Gregor, his trickiness. Diane continued.

"After we both get out here last spring, though, I begin to see that he has some serious limitations. For one thing, he seems to know nothing, zero, about biology, whereas Gates probably knows a little about software; and second, he keeps getting distracted, it seems to me. He's thinking too much about the past, personal things. Meanwhile, Derek's becoming a bigger pain in the ass than ever; I'm still pretending to like him, but it's getting harder. Then something funny happens."

What, to this young woman, is funny? Maren got up from her log, flexed her knees, looked behind her before reseating herself. No deer. She would have heard them, probably. No anything.

"What?" Maren said. "What happened?"

"I got serious about something, is what happened. You know, I always loved literature. Derrida, Lyotard, Cixous, Fish—all those people. I'd never read much of the other stuff, the novels and whatnot, but I'd liked what I'd seen of it. Well, what happened was that I took two summer courses and decided, at age twenty-six, on what I really wanted to do in my life: to teach English at a major university. You do what you want! You hardly have to work! You go to exciting places for conferences! I can't really go into business on my own; you know, business business. I'd have to be Mrs. Gates, as I said. But I can be an English professor, no problem. It's good to be a woman now. We're the ones with the balls, right?"

"Was one of the summer courses from Cedric?"

"Oh yeah, Wharton: "Elegant Edith: Her Life/ Her Work." With him, McAulay, you had to pretend he had the balls. That's what everyone told me. They sent him nasty e-mails, but they kissed up in class and laughed at his sexist jokes. Me too. Now, I had a special mission with McAulay: Garrett wanted me to do something to him. He hated him! It seems there were *two* terrible events in—ah, fuck Garrett! I'm talking about the deep past now, I'm going to call him Gregor."

"Okay, that's good. A 'special mission'?"

"Yes, Maren. Cause there were two bad things in Berkeley, way back. You disappeared. Poof! That's one. The other was that old McAulay took a paper Gregor wrote in a seminar—something about the paragraphs in a Wharton novel—and plagiarized from it. Gregor read his own words in some journal, in an article under McAulay's name, and went to confront him. And then—"

"Cedric laughed."

"Yes, he did. You knew?"

"About this? Something, not much."

"Well, he didn't keep laughing, because Gregor was very insistent. He had no real proof, because he had no copy of the paper. Computers weren't in use then, you know. He'd presented an early draft in the seminar, but none of the other students would help him; they didn't want to piss off McAulay. Oh, Gregor said he went to Aaron, who wasn't in the seminar but did Wharton, and asked him to testify that he'd read the paper and that McAulay's published article was just like it, but Aaron wouldn't. He said Aaron laughed, too."

"He might not have understood what Gregor wanted."

"Whatever," Diane said. "Anyway, Gregor didn't let this discourage him. He went to see McAulay every day. He'd go to his home and hammer on the door. Once Cedric's wife came out and said she didn't want any lawn furniture. Apparently, East Indians used to do this in Berkeley, make wooden chairs and things for outside and peddle them, and I guess Gregor looked foreign then. Now he doesn't look like anything, or maybe he just looks like everybody. So that really rankled his ass, on top of everything else. He threatened to go public, letters to the *Daily Cal* and like that, unless McAulay wrote a "confession" and sent it to the Wharton journal, which would have to publish it and give Gregor his full due. This could all be made up, you know, a fantasy. I mean, I believe he caused all this trouble, knowing him, but the original paper...that could be a fantasy.

"Here's the end of the story, until now: McAulay got him kicked out of the university. He was just an undergraduate, although he had hundreds of units, a lot in graduate courses. He never finished up anything, any single program. He got kicked out of town, too, he told me. More work by McAulay, his major enemy, who went to the police and claimed harassment. No reason to stay, anyway. No classes to take, no little Maren. Embarrassed as hell, all-resenting, he leaves for the East. But Gregor didn't forget."

"So he's finally back," Maren prompted, "with you. And you said you had a 'special mission' with Cedric. Gregor wanted you to do something. What?"

"It wasn't much. I could have done better, if I'd wanted to plan a revenge on somebody."

I bet, Maren thought.

"He knew McAulay hit on the women in his classes, so if he hits on me, me acting cute so that he would, I threaten to claim harassment—unless he finally writes that confession. By this time Gregor wanted it published in both *The Chronicle of Higher Education* and *The American Scholar*, and he kept talking about releasing it to the major wire services. Why they should care, I don't know. Also, he wanted me to tell Cedric I'd lead a feminist protest against him, which he would have laughed at, I'm sure. So that's the great plan: either the old asshole confesses or I cause him a world of hurt. I considered it. It seemed interesting. I didn't like it that he hit on women all the time.

"But soon I realized that I was, well, destined to be an English professor, and I thought I'd better put that interest first and not cause any disruptions. Besides, the class was all right, really. I liked talking about Edith, good as anything else. The other seminar, though, that was what made up my mind. Intro to Theory. Theory...theory doesn't matter! Literature...it doesn't exist! Theory *talk* is all there is. The more you talk, especially if you talk people into things, the better you do. I'm a born postmodernist, Professor Tugbenyoh said, and he didn't even want to screw me, being queer. His word, okay? But Cedric did want to, and can you guess why?"

"Oh, no."

"You got it. On the first day, he actually thought I *was* you, with my hair dyed. 'Why'd you do it?' he asked me, in front of everyone. 'It was so tasteful. Karen, why?' He kept calling me Karen, and then you Karen, after he figured out I wasn't you, so for weeks I didn't know what the hell he was talking about. Then I did, but I didn't tell Gregor. It's all amazing. You, me. We wind up putting Deirdre in Hillside School. There you are. It's you, me.

"Cedric. Cedric hit on me, hard. It really was harassment. If I bone him, I get an A, a comp section to teach, and his influence on publications and jobs; no boning, and I'm just like everybody else. So I did bone him, but, you know, not like an idiot. I played with him a little after the first time, jerked him around. Wouldn't when he wanted to, made him when he didn't. One of each. Ha-ha."

Maren also produced a chortle, sensing it was required. Huh-huh.

"We had a short paper due at midterm time. I didn't have anything ready. Deirdre was sick, and Derek refused to let us have an au pair. I say, fine, you sit with her and clean up her vomit, but he's off to save some alligators. Asshole! So, there's the net."

For a moment Maren thought she was talking about how to bag a gator in the wild. But Diane continued: "McAulay knows nothing of the internet; he can't even do his own e-mail. He's proud he's a techno-moron, always bragging about it. And it's common knowledge that he reads absolutely no Wharton criticism published after 1967 except his own. Why did Aaron ever believe Cedric would put his essay in a book? I was in his office when he threw it away.

"Okay. Paper's due, and here I am, stuck with a sick kid I have to bathe in the kitchen sink, cause Albert's in one tub and fucking Alberta's in the other, dying! I download a Wharton paper from the net, screw around with it, shorten it. I really change it, significantly. It's post-postmodern feminist, but I turn it around so that my paper's more or less *anti*-post-postmodern feminist. I have to quote a lot, to make everything clear, and I don't know where the quotation marks went, some of them. That's a convention I don't always choose to adhere to. McAulay loves the paper, thinks it's wonderful. Fine, but now I've got to write another one for his class, a big term paper. It won't come together. There's nothing quite right on the net. I bone him more. Our house. Derek's gone a lot. God, I hate to write! We did hypertext when I was at St. Olaf's. What I do, I convince Cedric the paper's a major project that needs more time to finish, and he gives me an IP, In Progress, which eventually has to be replaced by a regular letter grade. In the other class Tugbenyoh allows hypertext, so I do fine there. What are you getting up for? Am I making you nervous?"

"This log is too low. Kills my knees."

"Oh, yeah. Good idea."

Diane stood up, too. Something squawked in the forest behind her, a squawk of mortal fear, abruptly terminated. Diane didn't seem to notice. Clouds moved across the sky, visitors from beyond the Golden Gate in the west. The moon went dim. Diane didn't notice. Her hands were down by her sides. Maren couldn't quite see if she was holding the gun.

"Okay." One of them said it, and both sat down again on the logs. Diane pulled the blanket back over her knees.

"Fall semester starts. I'm supposed to be learning German and am doing a seminar on clocks and feminine subjection in the early novel, but the instructor hardly ever comes. No reason not to go to Vegas. I hope, from what I've heard about the place, that there I'll finally find out what 'postmodern' means. Do you know? God, who does? I didn't find out, and it's generally horrible. Everybody's old, from the sixties. I worry about Cedric. He bones me only one time, in a hot tub full of other people's cum. Someone took a picture of us, after we got out. He looks normal in it, really thick, but he's not. Something's up with him. Doesn't say much. I mention my project, and he says it's great. But he hasn't read it. I know, because I haven't written it. I'm not sure whether he's just being stupid or, as I begin to suspect, sarcastic. We leave Vegas and go to your house. I thought maybe he wanted to do a Gregor and show you the new you. But he didn't seem all that interested in you, not then. I liked it when you kneed him in the nuts. Aaron was all upset. I felt sorry for you. Don't know why Aaron said we could come if it was so terrible having us."

"Aaron was having a chemical problem at the time."

"Sure sounds like it. I gather he had a funny week, going wild in that bar with Gregor."

"Funny week for everyone, Diane. What happened? What happened after we left?"

"Suddenly McAulay says, 'You're a plagiarist, and I'm going to give you an F in Elegant Edith.' At that moment, I'm cutting up a grapefruit. 'I advise you to accept this without further discussion, unless you want an even harsher penalty.' Prick! Fat old prick! I say, 'Well, may I at least have an explanation, Professor?' And I play around with the knife, one of your little silver knives, but sharp, twirling it in my fingers. Oh, he wants to explain, he's enjoying it, getting me dead to rights. His story is that he showed the paper to a friend, a 'female colleague' who's a 'great gal.' Bullshit! He has no female friends except harassed students like me. The great gal recognizes it, tells him who wrote it, most of it, ninety percent of it—but just the words! I provided a whole new...um...horizon, but it doesn't matter. He's embarrassed to death, and I'm a terrible disgrace to him, to Whartonians everywhere, to the profession of English.

"Now, what I think really happened is that he took my essay and said he'd written it, so that's why he's so embarrassed. And I tell him that, fuck him! He doesn't like it, but fuck him!"

"'*Me* claim someone else's work as my own?'" he says. 'Me?'"

"I say, 'Yes, Professor, you. I know! Do you remember a guy named Garrett St. John?'"

"Well, of course he says no. I say, 'I mean Gregor Grosz.'"

"'Grosz!'"

"I didn't know he could get that mad, but I guess Gregor really had a talent for pissing people off. Ced's all red, raging, when I wanted him cringing. It's not working out. He's gonna flunk me, and then I'll get kicked out of the program. Wondering what the hell I'm going to do, I listen to his pompous drivel."

Diane then began to alternate roles, as herself and as Cedric, in a mono-dialogue eerily akin to Aaron's performances in the bathroom.

"Grosz couldn't prove that then," she said as Cedric, "and he can't now! He...you know him! And you never told me! Oh, you're in big trouble, Mrs. Blake! You want to be a professor, like me? You...*you* would be a Whartonian? You get out of here, right now!"

"It's not your house."

"They're my friends! Out!"

"Wait. Wait, asshole!"

"What did you call me?"

"Listen, Professor. We just got back from Vegas. So you must have talked to this 'female colleague' before we went there and you fucked me in that dirty tub."

"Yes, yes. I knew, all right. Thought I'd give you a little treat before I lowered the boom."

"And he—"

"Laughed."

"That's right, Maren. Haw-haw-haw. So I put your little knife down, got up, went to the bedroom, where my pack was, got the bush knife, my knife. Came back, holding it down by my leg. I don't know if he saw it. He turned away from me in his chair. Might have been laughing, I can't remember. I came up behind him, hacked him in the neck. Once didn't do it. It was hard. It took some time. Then...you know what I did then?"

"Yes, I do. You called Derek, and then you did everything else. Derek, Jimmie, Gregor. Told us things. Me."

"You. Oh, yes. Next subject. Let's talk about you, Maren. Remember that proposition I was going to make? Negotiate, negotiate? Well, here it is, and we'll negotiate, but only about the peripherals, like what airline. The main thing, I now realize, is not negotiable. Just being honest."

"Okay. What is it?"

"It's gonna happen, because I really want to do it. I'm leaving, with you. You and me. I don't imagine you're surprised. You know I can't stay here. The people in the department at Berkeley—the old farts, anyway—they won't like me because of the scandal; you know, grad student's husband kills prof. I don't want to learn fucking German, anyway. Maren, we're going to

England! I want to go to the Open University and do cultural studies. Tuggie told me about that. There won't be as much money, old Blake won't give me as much. But I'll be a professor eventually. That's what I want. I won't need a whole lot of money. I'll have my work, and I'll have you. Oh? Getting up again? Bum knees again? You're getting old, Mom. Need someone to take care of you."

Maren walked back and forth before her log, hands on hips. "What about them?"

She pointed vaguely south. Diane understood.

"The guys? Probably they'll be fine with this. Gregor won't talk. With all the shit he's pulled? Not a chance! Aaron? You take care of Aaron, okay? You don't want me to. Stay still, Maren! You're making me crazy."

Maren stopped pacing, but she didn't sit. "What do I have to do?" she asked. "What do you want from me?"

"Want? Nothing! Share my life. I just found it, and you're in it. Don't do anything for me. I'll do everything for us. I can always find a way. Never got into any trouble I couldn't get out of. Hey, are you looking sad? I can't really see. Are you?"

Maren sat down on the log again. She said, "I have a job. I teach."

"You can teach. Little kids, you mean? Sure. There's always a day-care center around. Wait, don't say it. Your family."

Maren didn't say it. She said nothing.

"Your daughter, she has a name like something in nature. I can't remember."

"Brooke."

"That's pretty. But she's in San Diego or someplace, right? They go, Maren. You went, I went. She's gone."

Maren felt pain, right in her heart. She swayed a bit, on the log. She was weak, although up here she had hoped to be strong. Now she was very unsure.

"And there's Aaron. By family, you're including him, yes? Okay. He's a genuinely nice guy, unlike these mean-hearted pricks I keep running into. He's somewhat crazy, but I like that. But, Maren, you know he's a flop. That stupid book, *M'Lady's*

Glove, that everyone laughs at. Composition courses. Ugh! Your little house on that dumpy street in the flats. How can you live in the Bay Area and not have a view of the Bay? It's all so stupid! It's wrong! Want to live better? You know you do. Guess what, Mom. You can."

Maren didn't do or say anything, so Diane went on.

"Oh, boy. I wasn't counting on this. You talk to the guy much?"

"No."

"But you love him? I'll bet the answer's yes."

"Yes."

"The way you love the kids. He's a big kid, which is fine. But you don't love him as a man. I know. He gives you nothing, and he's only interesting to the degree that he's crazy—and you don't like him being crazy. This is all obvious, so obvious. So, one more time. Love. Do you love him as a man? What? Getting up again? I'm really upsetting you, huh? Sorry, but the truth can do that."

Maren took a step, stood now above Diane. "Yes," she said. "I love him as a man." She thought, I think.

"Well," Diane answered, "I don't accept that. I trust myself on this one. But even if it were true, it wouldn't make any difference. I'm not asking you, Maren. I want this. You don't understand. You don't even understand the other parents. We've talked about it. *We* want things. And I want you. What the fuck."

She was moving her hands around under the blanket.

Maren stepped toward her, one step. She had a question, one last question: "Deirdre? What about her?"

"Oh!" Diane relaxed and stopped fumbling. "Oh, she's such a sweet kid! But right now, no. No, we can't take her. To England? She can live with Derek's parents. Or if you think that's too much moving around, I'll give her to that Russian pig and her little creep of a kid. You're sweet, Maren, but don't worry about Deirdre. She'll be fine. Kids are resilient."

Maren took another step. Then she kicked Diane in the face, knocked her off and behind the log. The blanket and gun went with her. As Maren was doing it, swinging up the heavy shoe, she knew it wasn't enough. Diane screamed, "You! You!" She scrabbled on the ground, found the blanket, shook it, threw it to the side.

On her knees behind the log, Diane had the little gun. Maren looked at her face, then at the gun. It was shaking. Then it flashed and made a bang, a pop, really, and there was a pocking noise behind her. The gun dipped down, and Maren saw Diane framed, not moving, down low. Her own foot came into the frame, something pushing it. Thanks, she thought. Oh, thank you. There was a tremendous thunk. Then she felt it, and she knew she had kicked Diane under the chin as hard as she could kick.

She realized she was standing on the log.

Diane was down, flopped, out. Maren hoped her neck wasn't broken, but if it was, it was. She found the gun, which warmed her hand, and stuck it into her jacket pocket. She ran down the trail.

She came back up again in the Bug, driving too fast, bumping over the ruts in the dirt. Now it would be good if the park people came, but they didn't. Maren half-expected that Diane would be gone, vanished into the woods. In that case, she would have to be found. But she hadn't moved, and Maren dragged her from the clearing to the trail, where she opened the trunk of her car. It was way too small to hold Diane, she saw, but it contained many bungees, as well as a rope. Trussed well, wreathed 'round with the elastic straps, packaged, Diane fit into the front seat quite neatly, although it took much pushing and puffing before Maren could lodge her there. Then she went back to the clearing, the logs, and stared into the forest. She listened. Everything quiet.

She drove out of the park, through the city, to the police station downtown. There was a chain across the entrance to the police lot, but Maren unhooked it and rolled in, finding a place among a flock of tan and blue official vehicles. Now Diane came awake, woozy, moaning. She didn't seem to grasp that she was all strapped up and kept trying to move her arms. A tank-shaped female officer came out of the building and yelled at Maren to park on the street.

"Please come here," Maren said. She opened the door and got out.

The cop made a wary approach. Peering into the Bug, she said, "What's that?"

"It's a citizen's arrest. Is Jimmie Greenlee here? Officer Greenlee?"

"Him? No."

"Well, you might want to call him. It's his case. She is."

"Are those bungees? Why, you've got a woman all tied up with bungees! Hey in there."

The cop rapped on the window. Diane looked dopily out at her.

"I think," the lady said to Maren, "that you need to explain."

"Yes, all right. I arrested her. She's dangerous."

"Doesn't look—"

"She is. She tried to shoot me. Just take her, will you? I know some men in cages who will tell you what she is. They're in this place north of campus."

"Cages. And your abductee who's all tied up. I think maybe you need somebody else, not the police."

"People are dead, dammit!"

The cop didn't seem to hear. "Desire takes many forms," she said. "In this community we understand that. Put that down! Oh, please! Put it down."

Maren had taken Diane's pistol out of her pocket. "I'm not pointing it at you," she said. "Go on, take it. It's hers. She killed a guy. He's in a cage, too. And McAulay, the dead English prof? You must know...well, she killed him, too. Here, take the gun."

Maren marched into the building and, after some convincing, came out again with three fat old cops, lazy males. She explained and explained. They took Diane away. Later Maren learned that they delivered her, unwound from the bungees, but cuffed, to Alta Bates Hospital. She was diagnosed as having a broken jaw, but no other fractured parts, and spent the night under observation for concussion. From the hospital, the forces of law went on to Ultima Hyena, having asked Maren where it was, and released Gregor and Aaron. They summoned Animal Control for Munchie, who was eventually transported back to the U.C. Hyena Project. Gregor fed the cops some story that induced them to let him go home; they took his address, but when they went there later, the house proved to be the residence of another person, one who had never heard of Gregor Grosz, George Saxon, etc.

Aaron, however, provoked their suspicion, was driven to the station in a howling patrol car, and interrogated until six in the morning. They talked to Maren again, too, but finished long before then, so she just sat and waited. It was all right. Jimmie showed up just before dawn. He asked if Diane could talk, having heard about her jaw. Maren said maybe, maybe not. She knew what he was worried about.

Jimmie had a problem all right, an adult problem. It was no one's concern but his. Deirdre was a child, so her case was very different. It was a mistake to say, as Diane had, that children were resilient. That old, dumb line! Many people said it, and it meant, precisely, don't worry and do nothing and blame everyone else when trouble comes. Oh, children survive. They can survive bad parents, but they need good ones. Now Deirdre had no parents, her father being dead and her mother likely to spend many years in a cage of her own. Was she better off without them? Maybe. Was a home with Irina and Boris the best thing for her? It might well be. If there was a better solution, she, Maren would discover it. Deirdre Blake would be happy, Maren would see to that.

Aaron came out. He was eating a doughnut and not mad at anybody. They went home. They showered. He went to bed. She came to him.

Epilogue

People told Maren she needed to obtain closure, which she thought usually meant, in the case of violent crimes, that somebody was executed or at least put in jail for life. But how was she to obtain closure? Neither of those things happened to Diane Blake.

She was charged with two counts of Murder One. The jury, which met for several weeks in Oakland, Alameda County Superior Court, acquitted her on both. Cedric McAulay was dead, yes, and she killed him, yes, but in self-defense. The story was cobbled together out of Diane's testimony and the police report. She had a smart lawyer. The smart lawyer, a lovely woman, celebrated for her expensive clothes, also had a story for Derek. Poor Derek! That awful night, distraught, at odds with his wife (yes, that must be admitted) but also confounded by the thought of her going off to prison and leaving him and little Deirdre, Derek shot himself in the heart.

His torso in Munchie's cage, that piece, was all a bloody mess. But the *Crocuta* hadn't eaten the heart, preferring harder things that crunched, and there was a bullet inside it from one of Derek's guns. He had four guns, it turned out, poor brute.

Could any of this be true? Maren was sure that none of it was. Diane had said nothing to her of any physical struggle between herself and Cedric. They'd argued, and then she got her knife and hacked him in the back of the neck. That's where the wound was, suggesting a sudden assault rather than a fight. The prosecuting attorney talked about that, but it didn't make much of an impression. He was a big guy, a former Cal football player who knew Jimmie. Perhaps the jury thought he was a bully. And Derek's supposed suicide? Sitting upon her log in Tilden Park, Diane had uttered not a word suggesting that. Although she may not have precisely said she killed him, certainly she had, with his own gun. Maren couldn't clearly remember everything she had heard that night, but it didn't matter. Neither of the lawyers ever asked her. In fact, they required very little testimony from her about anything. She could understand why the fashionable lady would want to keep her off the stand, but why the other?

Later Maren thought it might have had something to do with her having hidden the knife in the little park, within the rock, where it would remain, no doubt, forever. When she told the big lawyer about that—because she thought she should—he thanked her, but then broke off the interview and didn't speak with her again. She supposed he worried that the jury would doubt everything she said if they found out about the knife, to which any of several lines of questioning might lead. The lawyer's connection with Jimmie, a guys' connection, might also have inclined him to limit her testimony. Probably he knew that she knew Jimmie had slept with Diane.

She and Aaron were asked questions only about that Monday morning, early, when Cedric and Diane showed up from Vegas. Nothing else. This made Aaron mad. He wanted Diane to get some real punishment. Called her a "cunt," though not when testifying.

"That cunt belongs in jail," he told Maren, at home. And then he said, "Ah, sorry."

Diane looked great all during the trial, small, cute, vulnerable. Aaron said that when she, Maren, testified, the jurors and many in the audience kept looking back and forth between witness and defendant. Diane smiled at her constantly on that occasion, in a melancholy way, and made her eyes especially sad. Maren didn't feel sorry for her, not one bit, but she could tell the jury did. Nonetheless, although Diane beat the murder rap, the jurors decided after much discussion that she was guilty of other infractions.

Diane had obstructed justice, a misdemeanor, at least in this case. That was because she hadn't told Jimmie she'd killed Cedric. For dismembering her husband, that sorry suicide, and feeding him to a hyena, she was convicted of "improperly disposing of the remains of a deceased human being." The big lawyer worked hard on this, bringing up a recent case in Vallejo, a squalid town twenty miles to the north, where a bunch of lowlifes had burned up a dead body abandoned in their street. They claimed sanitation, but it didn't fly.

"I was terrified that I would be blamed for this death, too," squeaked Diane.

Didn't fly.

"Improperly disposing" is also a misdemeanor. For the two offences, she received a sentence of 1000 hours of community service and was allowed to perform them in her home town, which turned out to be Minneapolis. She still had family there.

Jimmie quit the Berkeley P.D. He started doing therapy again, relocating, in fact, to Vallejo. A good many ex-cons and parolees lived there; maybe the prison system paid Jimmie to keep this population calm. Aaron and Maren didn't know. They didn't see him.

Gregor Grosz disappeared. Occasionally, reading the *Chron*, Maren would notice a G-name in connection with something both biological and shady, such as a diet pill that clogged heart valves with deadly goop. Nothing had quite Gregor's touch, she thought. Aaron never said anything about him and her; he didn't understand, probably.

Irina was snapped up, swiftly hired, by the U.C. Berkeley Hyena Project. They found something for Anthony to do. The Pownalls were back together again, with Natalie/Natasha in permanent residence. Her friends often visited. Groucho and Artie had the run of the place, one by day, the other by night.

Deirdre became the ward of Irina Pownall. She kept going to Hillside School, seemed generally happy. Not giddily so. She was sad sometimes. That was all right, a sign of real adjustment.

Maren did not obtain closure, if death, or life, was what that took. She had what she had before, was what she was before. Can't that count as closure? Yes, she thought. And if Diane came back and caused any trouble, she would kick her ass back to Minnesota.

They had a very wet winter. It lasted until April, with few sunny periods of more than two days. Mud was everywhere. April was quite nice, however. It was a good month for Aaron, who learned that his college had granted him two farties for getting his name in the papers during the Blake trial. He also did the voiceover for a cartoon turtle who praised, in Aaron's rumbling tones, a new brand of depilatory.

Also in that month, Boris had a birthday. Acting on Maren's advice, Irina had as many kids at the party, which took place on a Sunday afternoon, as there were years in his new age. Five years and five kids: Conway, Moby, Cloelia, Cloelia's nerdish friend, Crystal, and, of course, Deirdre. A piñata, also Maren's suggestion, and ice cream and cake. After they sang "Happy Birthday," Deirdre kissed Boris on the cheek, causing him to run and hide under the piano. In doing this, he knocked his head, but he didn't cry. Conway and Moby approved.

Groucho didn't want any cake. Neither did Artie, who rather resented Conway's waking him up to see. He growled, faintly, and briefly exposed a fang.

Natasha/Natalie was there, with Groucho and a placid youth from the digs named Beagle. Maren and Aaron were also guests. This was unusual. When she first began to teach at Hillside School, Maren had accepted invitations to children's parties, but soon she realized that the parents expected her to babysit the kids while they kicked back with the other adults. She stopped accepting, but this party, she knew, would be different. Most of the time, the kids and adults kicked back together. There wasn't much babysitting to be done, therefore, and Anthony Pownall did it. He and Aaron, who read the children a story.

When the party ended, Aaron stood in the street—first on one foot, then on the other—and removed his trousers, which he handed to Maren. He was wearing his running shorts. Giving her a peck on the cheek, he galloped off, homeward bound. She drove to the school, a short distance, to check on Lion.

He was fine. She rubbed him between his ears. She let him run about for a few minutes, then plucked him up and returned him to his hutch. When she turned around, after closing the bolt, the cougar was there. Broad daylight, like the first time, only now she was in the back. Look big! She didn't bother.

The cougar crooned, didn't scream. She sat on her haunches after that. Maren saw that her eyes were green. Then the animal stood up. She walked to the back fence, beyond which lay a raw hillside. One last look at Maren, and she leapt.

Jake Fuchs has published short fiction and reviews of fiction, written extensively on eighteenth-century British satiric literature, and worked as a writer and performer in the video and voice-over businesses. He is the author of *Death of a Dad*, also published by Creative Arts. He and his wife Freya live in Berkeley, California.